Also by Sarah Price

The Amish of Lancaster Series
#1 Fields of Corn
#2 Hills of Wheat
#3 Pastures of Faith
#4 Valley of Hope

The Amish of Ephrata Series
#1 The Tomato Patch
#2 The Quilting Bee

The Adventures of a Family Dog Series
#1 A Small Dog Named Peek-a-boo
#2 Peek-a-boo Runs Away
#3 Peek-a-boo's New Friends
#4 Peek-a-boo and Daisy Doodle

Other Books
Gypsy in Black

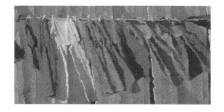

Find Sarah Price on Facebook and Goodreads!
Learn about upcoming books, sequels, series, and contests!

Fields of Corn:

The Amish of Lancaster Series

By
Sarah Price

Published by Price Publishing, LLC.
Morristown, NJ
Revised 2012

The Pennsylvania Dutch used in this manuscript is taken from the Pennsylvania Dutch Revised Dictionary (1991) by C. Richard Beam, Brookshire Publications, Inc. in Lancaster, PA.

Contact the author on Facebook at http://www.facebook.com/fansofsarahprice or visit her website at http://www.sarahpriceauthor.com

Price Publishing, LLC.
Morristown, NJ
http://www.pricepublishing.org

Chapter One

The horse, a brown Morgan with a thick black mane, trotted down Musser School Lane, effortlessly pulling the black, box-like buggy. The wheels of the buggy rattled against the macadam, creating a soft metallic humming. The horse jerked its head twice as though wishing the man in the buggy would release the reins, letting it race down the flat road. But, for the moment, the cracked leather reins remained taut and the horse, its mane dancing in the wind with each prance, continued its even pace. The horse's hooves pounded against the road in rhythm like the soothing ticking of a grandfather's clock in a quiet house on a Sunday afternoon.

Inside the closed buggy, the driver pulled in the reins, allowing a passing car to speed by. But, even as the car continued down the road, the driver continued his tight hold, urging the horse to the side of the road. The horse reluctantly obeyed the command, gradually slowing down until, at the top of the hill, surrounded by grassy knolls of long, waving brown hay, the buggy stopped with a final, noisy jolt. The man held the reins in one hand, leaning forward and peering out of the small window to take in the majestic scene before him.

The sun illuminated the farm, nestled comfortably in the crescent at the bottom of the hill, in a glorious glow of warmth. Along the hillside, neat and even rows of green corn rippled in harmony like a freshly washed sheet fluttering in a gentle breeze on washing day. The leaves brushed against each other, the music a rustling whisper of a song in the man's ears. Oblivious to nature's silent symphony, a scattered herd of cows grazed in the thinning grass around the muddy river that cut through their pasture.

"Thank you, God," the man murmured softly. Although his prayer lingered in the air, as though unfinished, he continued to pray to his God, expressing his gratitude for the beauty of setting suns, the wealth of ripening corn, and the warmth of coming home.

Shana raised her hand to shield her eyes from the mid-day sun. Her dark eyes traveled down the dusty driveway leading to the large, white farmhouse as she opened her car door and, hesitantly, swung her legs to the ground. A summer breeze, carrying the strong odor of manure, rustled her long brown hair as she got out of the car. For a second, she stretched her back, reaching up with one hand to rub the back of her neck as her dark eyes looked around.

Field equipment, most of it aged and rusty, lay scattered around the outskirts of the driveway. From the pastures, a cow bellowed. The noise broke the silence that engulfed the farm. Two cats lounged in the shade of the large white barn, which desperately needed a fresh coat of paint. The smaller of the cats stretched in the sun before it stood up lazily and began to lick its paw. The other cat lifted its head, noticed the woman standing by the car, and, jumping to its feet, raced alongside the barn before disappearing through the open doorway into the shadows within.

Shana scanned the hillside, the rustle among the cornfield captivating her eyes and ears. The sound, its crisp whistle of tranquility, faintly came and went as the breeze waved back and forth across the field. Leaning against the open car door, she shut her eyes and breathed in the pungent odor of manure. Wrinkling her nose, she kept her eyes shut and listened to the gentle lulling of the cows as they wandered in the fenced-in field between the barn and the corn.

"Hello," a voice called from inside the barn.

Glancing over her shoulder, Shana squinted and peered in the direction of the voice. A short man, a battered straw hat tilted forward on his head and a mustache-less beard covering his chin, emerged from the depths of the barn's darkness. His dirty brown pants, held up by loose suspenders, had a slight tear at the knee. He walked toward her, a friendly smile lighting up his golden brown face. "What can I do for you?"

Drawn out of her momentary lapse, Shana glanced down at the piece of white paper in her hand. "Is this 317 Musser School Lane?"

"317, ja." The man gave her another smile as he shifted his weight and jammed his hands into his pant's pockets. "You the Englischer looking for a place to stay, then?"

Shana glanced around the farm again. She noticed a small boy wearing similar pants and a bright purple shirt peering at her from behind the open barn door. When he saw her staring back, he dashed back into the shadows. Redirecting her attention to the man, she returned his smile. "If you have a place to offer, I'd like to see it."

The formalities over, he wasted no more time with idle chatter. "I'll get my daughter to show the room to you then." The man disappeared into the barn, leaving Shana standing by her car. As she stared after him, her eyes noticed another cat, this one striped and fat, as it scurried out of the barn and across part of the driveway. It leapt into the air as it reached the edge of the grass and tumbled onto its back. Shana smiled at she watched it playing.

A moment later, a young girl, wearing a plain olive green dress with a long black apron covering the front, ran around the side of the barn toward Shana. She was barefoot and her feet were dirty. Her hair was parted in the middle, pulled back, and twisted into a tight bun at the nape of her neck. Yet, her expression was softened by the smoothness of her skin and the glow in her dark brown eyes. She held a single, rusty key in her hand. "You want to look at the room?" she asked, her voice hidden beneath her downcast eyes and thick German accent. The girl led Shana behind the barn and toward a smaller building. "It's a nice apartment. How long you want to stay?"

Shana waited for the girl to unlock the door. Behind the building was a large cow pen. Beside that was another paddock. Both were empty. "A month or two." She stepped into the apartment and immediately held her breath. The air was stale, thick of manure. The young girl hurried over to the two windows and, pushing back the simple lace curtains, threw them open.

A small metal table stood in the center of the room and a faded orange sofa sat against the far wall. The walls, painted a dark peach with sporadic red clusters of flowers, added to the emptiness emanating from the rest of the room. Along the walls were several hooks, each painted a clumsy imitation of the dark peach. A small gas stove and refrigerator stood next to the stained sink with two separate faucets, one for cold water and one for hot. A neatly handwritten sign hung over the sink: "No Alcoholic Beverages. No Indoor Smoking. No Pets. Thank you. Katie and Jonas."

The girl walked quietly across the floor and opened a door. "Upstairs," she murmured, her eyes darting away from Shana's.

Holding onto the railing, Shana followed the girl up the tall, narrow staircase, most of the wooden steps creaking under their feet. From the landing, Shana noticed that there were two bedrooms. The one bedroom had carpet but both had the same dark peach painted walls. The bathroom was small and cramped but livable. While there were no closets, each bedroom had a large armoire. And, if each room had one thing in common, they were remarkably clean.

"Who lived here before?" Shana asked as they descended down the staircase.

"Another Amish family. Had so many children they were forced to move."

Shana stood in the middle of the kitchen and, for a split second, while the girl's words sank in, she stared at her. Amish. That explained the plain decor and thick German accent, she thought. Then, when the girl looked back, Shana moved toward the windows, pushed back the curtains, and stared at the green land that stared back. The countryside was untainted by telephone poles or electric wires. The roads lacked racing automobiles or noisy motorcycles. On top of the hill, she could barely make out the outline of a stopped black buggy, so characteristic of the Amish. Letting the curtain fall back, her fingertips lingered on the light fabric before she turned around and followed the girl out of the house. They returned to the barn, Shana walking a pace behind the slender Amish girl. Neither spoke. Nearby, a dog barked until someone called out for it to quiet. Obediently, the dog's bark dwindled to a low whine until Shana no longer heard it.

The man stood just inside the barn, shoveling manure out of the open cow stalls, the metal from the blade scraping systematically against the damp cement. He set the shovel against the wheelbarrow and wiped his hands on his pants when he heard them approaching. "Sylvia show you the house, then?"

Shana nodded as she looked out the barn doors toward the road. "How far is Lancaster from here?"

"Driving? Vell, let's see." He pondered her question for a moment, his thumbs hooked around the bottom of his suspenders, before answering slowly, "Guess fifteen miles or so. Depends on what part you looking to travel. How long you planning on staying?"

"No more than two months," she answered as she met his gaze.

"That long?"

"Is that a problem?"

The man leaned against the railing by the cow paddock. The tranquil cheerfulness of his expression struck Shana. "Most Englische come and go. You work in the area?"

Shana glanced around the barn as she answered. "I work in a restaurant." She looked back at the man, who, curiously, seemed genuinely interested. "They just promoted me to a managerial position in the Lancaster branch for a couple months," she added softly.

The man scratched his beard, as if contemplating what she had just told him before he said, "*Ach vell*, rate's usually fifteen dollars a night. But folks mostly come and go, staying for only a night here and there. Since you staying for so long, how's $250 a month?"

"$250 a month?"

The man held up his hand, as if stopping her from continuing. "If it's too expensive, let me know and we'll lower it."

"That's just fine," she heard herself say. For a two bedroom house so close to Lancaster, she had expected the rent to be at least twice that. She found herself taking the key from Sylvia as Jonas returned to his work. No handshake, no papers to sign. Just a verbal "ok" after a quick character analysis.

Shana smiled to herself as she left the barn. Tucking the house key in her back pocket, she opened the trunk to her car and began unloading her two large suitcases. Living on a farm after leaving the hustle and bustle of the noisy, polluted New York suburbs with their quick tempered people and congested roads would be a welcome, if not interesting, change; even if for only a couple of months.

During the course of the early afternoon, as she unpacked her few belongings, the rattle of a buggy driving along the road whispered in through the open windows. The first time she heard it, Shana hurried to the nearest window and, pushing the curtains back, looked out, too late to catch anything more than a glimpse of the black boxed buggy and the majestic horse pulling it over the hill. The second time, having missed the buggy, she noticed a lone man walking behind a mule-operated machine in the fields.

The machine moved across the field of corn, a narrow path dropping behind as the corn stalks collapsed to the power of the plow. While she watched, the young man's straw hat, worn and tattered, blew off his head, revealing a tousled set of brunette curls, and fluttered to the ground. Quickly, the man pulled back on the mule's reins. When the mule stopped, the man walked over to pick up his hat. For a second, he held the hat in his hand, glancing over the field of waving corn. Then, his hesitation over, he slid the hat back onto his head, returned to the mule, slapped the reins on its back, and continued harvesting the corn.

Shana spent the rest of the afternoon driving along the winding roads, acquainting herself with her new surroundings, more from relaxed boredom than from pure interest. The massive farms impressed her. Each was very similar: Large white buildings with pastures where Holstein cows were grazing. Yet, at the same time, very individualistic: From the pretty flowers that surrounded the mailboxes and the dogs lounging on the front porches to the clotheslines flapping in the wind, most adorned with brightly colored clothing, all spoke of the different personalities living within each dwelling.

In town, Shana parked her car along the main street. Horses pulling the black Amish buggies trudged along the streets amidst the hundreds of tourists, bending their necks to get a quick glance at the people inside. Shana fought her way across the street and into a small bookstore. She nosed through several books and, after much deliberation, she stood in line to purchase the latest edition of a book about Amish society.

She wandered through the small town, pausing at an antique furniture restoration store to admire the tall, cherry oak armoire in the window. A loud car horn blasted behind her and, startled, she turned in time to see a battered, green pick-up speed past a buggy. The driver in the pick-up shook his clenched fist out the window and his passenger tossed a burning cigarette at the horse. Then, the truck was gone and the frightened horse, quickly steadied under the calm hand of its driver, continued patiently down the road.

Her last stop before returning to the Lapp's farm was the local grocery store. Although she would spend most of her time in the restaurant, she knew she'd want a small supply of food in the house for her days off. The store reminded her of an old general store. Everything from hats and shoes to flour and sugar lined the aisles. In the back, dried herbs hung over the glass cases filled with fresh smoked Pennsylvania Dutch ham and sausages. And, at the register, as she waited in line behind an older woman in a floral polyester dress, she noticed that the cashier greeted most of the people with a personal hello and a warm smile.

When she returned to the farm, the cows stood noisily in

the barn and in the outside paddock near her new home. Shana stood by her car, staring across the paddock at the luscious corn fields, rich and green in color. The air, while ripe from the manure, was not necessarily unpleasant. She shifted the grocery bag in her arms, glancing around at the now quiet barn. She could see a bright light burning in what she imagined was the kitchen window of the farm. But she saw no activity from within.

Behind her small house in a shed-like barn, a muffled neigh caught her attention. Squinting, she could vaguely see several large mules eating out of the troughs. In the background, two mules nipped at each other and jumped in a semi-playful manner. Curious, Shana walked toward them. The closest mule lifted its massive head and stared at her, its rabbit-like ears twitching nervously. Shana smiled as she dared to reach out and scratch the mule's forehead. "You're a big fella, aren't you?" she murmured.

"You like the animals then?" a low voice said from the shadows behind her.

Startled, Shana whirled around, dropping the grocery bag. The carton of eggs fell out, spilling onto the dirt floor, several of them breaking. Shana knelt to examine the damage. The young man set his pitch fork aside and quickly bent down to assist in the assessment. Shana glanced at him and smiled. "Only three."

He tilted back the straw hat perched atop his forehead as he met her gaze. "Sorry about frightening you like that."

They both stood, each quickly surveying the other. Shana wondered if the man before her, with thick curly brown hair and sparkling blue eyes, had been the same man she had watched briefly in the field. His face reminded her of a child, soft and innocent, although the twinkle in his eyes whispered otherwise. His voice, soft and even-toned, had a slight German accent, spoken in the same dialectical slang as Jonas Lapp. She knew at once that he was certainly Jonas' son.

"I hadn't seen you standing there," she said apologetically. While he was short like Jonas, he still towered over her. She couldn't tell how old he was, possibly eighteen, maybe older.

He plucked a piece of hay from a nearby hay bale and stuck it in his mouth. "You the Englischer that's moving in?"

The Englischer, she repeated to herself. Then, with a smile, she replied, "My name's Shana." She held out her hand.

He hesitated then shook her hand. "Emanuel. My daed said you'd be here for several months."

"I work in the area," she quickly explained.

"What kind of work?" He spoke with a gentleness that Shana found soothing.

"I manage a restaurant in Lancaster. Actually, I've just been temporarily transferred from my hometown in Connecticut."

His face lit up. "Connecticut? Why, you must've been driving all day!"

Shifting the bag in her arms again, Shana smiled, amused at his sudden enthusiasm. Certainly, not familiar with the speed of automobile travel, Connecticut might have been another continent to Emanuel. "If I hadn't gotten lost, it wouldn't have taken me so long."

Emanuel laughed, his crystal blue eyes crinkling into half moons and his mouth twisting into a lopsided friendly grin. "Ay, you got lost." Then, he quickly sobered and lowered his eyes. "Maybe I shouldn't laugh. It isn't funny, getting lost, is it?"

"I didn't mind. The country is so beautiful."

"Emanuel!" They both jerked their heads in the direction of

the female voice calling for Emanuel.

"That's my mamm." Emanuel lowered his head as he excused himself. "*Ach vell*, I must finish my chores 'fore the evening meal." He started to walk away then, hesitating, he turned back. "It will be nice to spend some time with you, Shana." He gave her a final friendly smile before hurrying off to the barn.

The dog barked from the other side of the barn and one of the mules snorted loudly. Shana returned her attention to them, long enough to run her hand down the closest one's nose. Its velvet flesh warmed her touch. From the other barn, a cow bellowed and Shana quickly glanced over her shoulder at the barn, quiet from noise yet busy with activity. Then, giving the mule one more friendly rub, she whispered, "Good night, big girl," before she left the mule stable and walked to her house.

It was shortly after eight o'clock, the sun fading rapidly behind the hill, when someone knocked softly at her door. Shana shut the book she had been reading and walked toward the open door. Sylvia stood outside, a bulking towel in her hand. She shuffled her feet, her large eyes peering eagerly inside the house, curious about the few knick-knacks Shana had set about the kitchen. When Shana opened the screen door, the girl handed her the towel then retreated toward the large farmhouse.

For a moment, Shana stared after her. Her two encounters with the young Amish girl gave Shana the impression that Sylvia was equally curious about the non-Amish woman now living on her father's farm. Shutting the door, Shana peered inside the towel to find three large eggs, nestled in the scratchy, yet clean, cloth.

She smiled to herself and leaned against the door for a minute, listening to the sounds of the farm. The cows wandered noisily from the paddock into the fields. The dog barked twice then quieted down, as though bidding the farm goodnight. Sighing, Shana turned the brass lock. It clicked shut. Amish, Shana thought as she turned off the lights and headed upstairs, tired from moving, anxious about her landlords, and excited about starting work the next day.

Chapter Two

Driving down Musser School Lane, Shana suddenly felt overwhelmed that, after twelve long days working at the restaurant, she needed the long weekend that her Regional Manager had insisted she'd take. Her former manager, Robert, had promised her a challenge in Lancaster and he certainly had followed through. Since her move to Lancaster, she had spent every day at work, often until two o'clock in the morning, trying to balance the books and supervise the too-often lazy wait staff. The restaurant, though small, needed a lot of work in order to match Shana's standards.

Four days to myself, she thought as she parked her car outside of her small house. She hadn't spent much time familiarizing herself with the Lapp farm. Most days, the farm seemed distant and surreal to her. She rarely even thought about her Amish landlords. Now, as she leaned against her car and looked around, she saw the farm in a fresh, bright light.

The plain white kitchen curtains fluttered through the open window and the plant she had purchased one day as she drove to work hung from the rafters of her front porch. A gentle breeze blew through the laundry Katie had left drying on a clothesline stretched from the corner of the farmhouse porch to the side of the barn. Yes, she thought, after twelve long days, she found herself relieved to be away from the restaurant and even more relieved to be able to spend a couple of days around the peace and tranquility of the Lapp farm.

She had tried to capture some of that serenity. Most nights, even though she arrived home so late, she usually sat outside on the porch, listening to the crickets chirping in the cornfields and the cows fussing in the paddock. Some nights, the stars would illuminate the sky around an almost full moon. Slowly, Shana found herself absorbing the tranquility that surrounded her. After stressful days, she often caught herself daydreaming and yearning for her special time at night on the porch. It relaxed her, helped her unwind. She'd shut her eyes, lean back in her old rickety chair, and hear the sounds of the sleeping farm.

Now, the cows stood impatiently in the paddock as two of Katie's sons spread hay into their troughs. Shana returned their eager waves as she walked from her car to her house. While she hadn't spent much time on the farm since her arrival, she had met Jonas' wife, Katie, on her second day. Usually before Shana left for work, she bumped into Katie walking back from the mailbox with the previous day's mail. Katie's hair, always neatly parted in the middle and rolled back into a bun, hid under her white prayer cap. She walked around barefoot in the yard as she weeded the garden, hung out the laundry, or swept the long driveway. Fortunately, the mother of ten children, she had plenty of help.

"Home early today, ja?"

Startled, Shana dropped the house key as she whirled around. When she recognized Emanuel, she smiled as she bent down to pick up her key. "I think you like sneaking up on me," she teased.

"Don't mean to," he quickly apologized. He leaned against the porch, his hands thrust deep into the pockets of his faded black trousers as he followed her with his eyes.

Several flies swarmed past her head as she opened the door and she waved her hand at them. "I suppose I'll get used to it, eventually."

"Getting used to the cows at night, are you?"

While it was true that the cows had kept her awake during those first few nights, their soft mooing and clambering around the paddock had become quite relaxing and peaceful. "They don't bother me. I get home so late some nights that I fall right asleep, never even noticing the noise."

"You work hard at your new job, then, if you come home so late," he observed, more to himself than to her.

"I suppose I do, yes," she admitted. "But that's what they pay me for, isn't it?" she added with another smile as she met his curious gaze.

For a brief moment, they stood there, staring at each other, neither one certain of what to say. Shana hadn't spoken to Emanuel since their first encounter, although, one day, she had seen him along the edge of his father's field. At first, in his dirty work clothes, she hadn't recognized him, thinking the man must have been an older son with those muscular arms and intense seriousness as he followed patiently behind the team of four mules and heavy machinery. But, when the man in the field took off his hat and waved at her, she recognized the curly brown hair and cheerful smile. Shana had rolled down her car's window and returned the gesture and, to her surprise, her thoughts had lingered on him and the Amish for the rest of her ride to work.

Emanuel broke the silence. "Just bought a new horse today," he said, his eyes never leaving hers.

"Really?" When he didn't say anything else, Shana quickly added, "I'd like to see it."

She set her purse inside the door and, quietly followed Emanuel around the barn and toward the stables. The young dog tied to its doghouse perked up when he saw Shana. Barking loudly, the dog lurched forward. Emanuel walked over and untied it. The dog quickly ran toward Shana, sniffing at her legs and finally, jumping up on her. Shana took a step back, steadying herself, as she rubbed the dog's head.

"You're a frisky one, aren't you?" she asked, laughing as the dog started chewing at her hand and licking her arm.

"Down boy," Emanuel softly ordered and the dog ran off toward the cow paddock. "He likes to chase the cows sometimes," Emanuel explained.

Inside the stable, Shana let her eyes adjust to the dim light. There were several buggies in the wide aisle between the six stalls. Each buggy had a bright orange reflector triangle screwed onto the back, one with a Great Adventure Amusement Park bumper sticker neatly stuck onto it. The horses, five in all, stood patiently in their individual stalls, waiting for their evening meal.

"Which one is yours?"

Emanuel pointed toward the one in the center. "The fat little one." He opened the stall door and stood next to the horse. "Name's Lucky Monday." He rubbed the horse's neck and tugged gently at its ear. "She came in from Iowa."

"She's beautiful. You should be very proud." Shana watched Emanuel as he ran his strong hands down the horse's neck. While his religion might have frowned on pride, the glow in his eyes could not hide his pleasure with the animal. Feeling more comfortable as she watched him stroke the horse's neck, Shana reached out and ran her hand down the horse's muzzle as she teased, "Do you think she likes it here?"

Emanuel shrugged his shoulders and smiled, his crystal blue eyes crinkling into half-moons. "*Vell*, no reason she shouldn't learn," he replied modestly as he patted the horse's shoulder affectionately and met her gaze again. "Went riding today with her.

You ride?"

"I haven't in a while," she replied. "I used to ride when I was little. I'd go to summer camp for horseback riding. Out in Connecticut. But, when I got older, my parents didn't have time to keep it up." She remembered now how disappointed she had been, crying about not being able to visit Lollypop, the small gray pony that she had adopted at the children's equestrian center. But, before long, she had forgotten about horses, especially when she got a part-time job after school.

"There's always time to ride horses on a farm, " Emanuel said softly, his eyes downcast and the tone of his voice sounding almost sympathetic. For a fleeting second, Shana almost felt sorrow, too, at the aspect of her childhood that she had missed once her parents hadn't let her continue attending summer camp not to mention the friend she had lost in Lollypop. Emanuel interrupted her thoughts as he smiled again, staring at her with his dancing eyes. "Maybe we can go riding then, ja?"

Shana met his gaze for a moment, wondering what he thought of her. Their worlds were separated by a large three hundred year gap. The society that embraced him continued to prosper by stressing the family unit and their close-knit community. Hers prospered by forcing independence and self-sufficiency. Every man for himself, she thought. So, she asked herself, if his religion frowns upon unnecessary relations with the non-Amish world, why do his eyes light up when he talks to me?

"I'd like that, Emanuel," she heard herself respond.

"I don't believe I remember your name," he asked quietly.

"Shana."

"Shana," he repeated as though engraving it in his memory. "I haven't heard that name before," he said. "Who were you named after?"

Shana laughed. "Myself."

He frowned. "It isn't a family name then?" When he saw her confused look, he explained. "Amish children are usually named after aunts or uncles or some other relation. Keeps the family names going. Although," he admitted, lowering his voice, "it can get confusing. I have five cousins named Linda Lapp."

Shana smiled at his sincerity. "I imagine it can be confusing."

Another wave of uneasy silence struck them, although Shana realized that she was the one uncomfortable with the silence. She was so used to being surrounded by noise and people talking that she hadn't learned the joy of nothing. She watched as Emanuel rubbed his hands over Lucky Monday's neck, his body leaning against the horse's side. Despite his silence, he was communicating with his new horse just by touching it. The mare responded with a gentle snort and a lift of her head.

Emanuel took a step back and began to withdraw his hand when Shana noticed that most of his pointer finger was missing. He looked up and, as though reading her mind, explained with a simple, "Farming accident last year."

"I didn't mean to stare," she apologized quickly, a blush covering her cheeks. She looked away, embarrassed at herself.

"It was strange at first, trying to get used to not having it. Sometimes in the field I have problems with the reins. They slip through my other fingers. But, I just pick them back up and steer the mules back on track. It is easy to adjust when one has no choice." He laughed at the startled expression that clouded her face as he wiggled his fingers and said, "That's why God gave me nine others."

It dawned on her that Emanuel's calm, gentle character came not just from within but also from the culture that surrounded him. Unlike her world of aggression and occasional self-pity, Emanuel had grown up always looking for the positive aspects, even in the most hurtful situations. Unlike me, she thought. For weeks before her move, she had felt sorry for herself, being torn away from friends and family to move so far away. Yet, here was Emanuel, cheerful and teasing about an accident that had caused him to be physically maimed.

Emanuel, sensing her discomfort, quickly changed the subject as he moved away from the horse and leaned against the side of the stall. Resting his arm on the ledge of the open door, he stared at her curiously and asked, "Aren't you lonely living by yourself?"

"Lonely?" she repeated. Was that the word for what she had been feeling? "I hadn't given it much thought, Emanuel," she answered truthfully. In the past few days, she hadn't time to feel lonely. Her work occupied most of her days and, when she was away from the restaurant, she relished the quiet. "And I sure do know that I'm looking forward to some time alone, away from work," she quickly added.

"What kind of work is that again?"

"I manage a restaurant." Last year in college, she had started waitressing for the chain restaurant where her enthusiasm quickly found her promoted to a part-time assistant manager. Then, after her graduation several months earlier, they had promoted her to a full-time manager, offering to transfer her to a slightly more challenging restaurant with the promise that, if she fared well, she'd be transferred again with another nice promotion. While hesitant about moving away from home, she had finally agreed, knowing that the benefit of accepting certainly outweighed the disadvantages of turning down their offer.

"I get tired of the people sometimes," she found herself confiding in Emanuel as she leaned against the hard, wooden stall. "They can be so demanding. Yet, even though the problems that come with working in a restaurant get bothersome, all in all, I guess I like it."

"There's a bar, then?"

The mischievous gleam in his eyes almost made her laugh. So, she thought, Emanuel Lapp is a rebellious youth, eager to learn about the outside world. But she held back her own smile for fear of insulting his curiosity. "That's a problem in itself," she admitted before changing the subject. "But I have a few days off, now. And I'm certainly looking forward to that." She reached out and gently rubbed Lucky Monday's nose. A silence ensued and Shana reached for something to talk about. "Is this your first horse?"

"Other one's over there," he said as he motioned toward the other side of the barn. A tall, brown stallion reared his head as though he knew Emanuel was talking about him. "Probably give him to my daed now."

"He's a beauty, too."

"Not as fast as cars though," Emanuel commented with another mischievous gleam, confirming Shana's earlier suspicion.

"Certainly much nicer to deal with."

"I had a car when I was younger," he admitted quietly, refusing to meet Shana's eyes. "Kept it at my uncle's apartment. Brown Dodge with fat wheels on the back. Drove all over the place. Even went down to Philadelphia." He grinned, his eyes crinkling again. "Fast car, that one. Took me less than two hours to get down there. You can drive anywhere in just a few minutes and time becomes just another thing we take advantage of, never appreciating each moment that passes as a blessing from God. So, I sold it. Too worldly, ja? And I was getting too old for such things. Besides, my parents weren't too happy about the car and if I want to join the church..."

While the Amish fought so hard to shelter their youth from the modern culture surrounding their farms, it didn't surprise her that a few managed to find it anyway, its inevitability always lingering on the outskirts of their community. Shana suspected that the Amish youth rebellion was mostly male-oriented, a type of male-bonding and perhaps a form of soul-searching before they joined the church, settled down with their girlfriends, and started their own farms and families.

"How old are you?" she heard herself ask.

"Twenty-six," he replied solemnly.

"I hadn't thought you to be that old," she murmured, suddenly feeling very foolish. His youthful glow and small stature had, indeed, misled her.

"Ja, old *buwe*," he said teasingly, although Shana didn't understand the Deitsch word he spoke. She frowned and looked at him but he didn't bother explaining. Instead, he quickly added, "Don't know if I'm ready to settle down yet. How about you?"

"Part of me is, part of me isn't," she replied softly, again feeling uncomfortable discussing such personal thoughts with Emanuel. Yet, when she looked up and glanced into his face, she saw that genuine sincerity that reminded her of his father and made her realize that his curiosity wasn't meant as prying.

"Some kids get married too young out here," Emanuel told her. "Nineteen, twenty. That's too young. Don't know if I'll ever marry."

Shana laughed at his announcement, raising her hand to

push a stray hair away from her face and over her shoulder. She noticed him watching her movement, staring at her loose, brown hair. He shifted his weight and diverted his eyes as though suddenly uncomfortable with speaking to her. Shana guessed his discomfort came because he was used to speaking with the plain Amish women with their tightly plaited hair and balding parts down the middle of their scalp. And here he stands, she thought, speaking to a young Englischer woman with long, wavy hair and wearing makeup.

"You say that now, Emanuel. We all say that at some time or another. You'll marry. Wait and see. I'm too young right now, but I plan on marrying someday after I have had time to focus on my career."

It was Emanuel's turn to look startled. "Too young? Why, I'd guess you to be twenty-six or so!"

Lucky Monday nuzzled at Shana's hair. Another laugh escaped her lips and she turned around to stroke the horse's neck. "Emanuel, you'd have me an old maid before my time," she teased. Then, sobering, she said, "I turned twenty-two last April."

A frown crossed his face for a split second but, as quickly as it was there, it vanished and he stared at her, his eyes large and approving as though seeing her in a new light. "What a big girl to venture out here on your own!"

She'd been called many things in her lifetime but never a "big girl." The approval in his eyes and the awe written across his face made her suddenly feel very young and alive. The color rose to her cheeks and she had to look away, ashamed at her pleasant embarrassment. "Hadn't thought of it that way before," she heard herself whisper in response, almost too overtaken by the feeling inside her chest to speak at all.

An awkward silence fell between them again. Shana focused her attention on Lucky Monday but her mind raced. How odd we must look to an outsider, she thought. The young Amish man in his dowdy work clothes and the young Englische woman in her business attire. Whatever could they have in common, an observer might have commented, to share such innocent intimacy? But Shana knew otherwise, that even though Emanuel's offering of friendship was rather racy and bold, the one thing they had in common was curiosity about the other's world.

But despite the fact that Shana felt certain that Emanuel was considered a rebellious Amish man by his church, his curiosity about her world was so innocent that she knew his loyalty remained faithfully planted within his religion. She found herself feeling sorry for him, mostly for being ignorant of all the things he didn't even know he had missed. How controlled their lives were, she thought as she scratched Lucky Monday's nose again. From the straw hat tilted back on his head to the people he associated with, everything he said and did had to follow the Ordnung, the rules of the Amish church. Yet, she couldn't help realizing as she watched Emanuel for a moment, he seemed happy enough.

"*Ach vell*, I must finish my chores," he finally announced softly, breaking the peaceful silence. He lowered his eyes away from hers and, for a second, Shana wondered if he had read her thoughts. Emanuel shuffled his feet as he reached out to tug at Lucky Monday's ear again. For a moment, he hesitated as though considering something. "Perhaps tomorrow when I ride into town you would like to come along." He glanced at her. "Have you ever ridden in a buggy before?"

Slowly, they walked out of the barn. "Can't say that I have," she smiled, almost regretting his departure. While the thought of having the next few days off from work pleased her, she suddenly realized that, unless she accepted his invitation, she would be spending her long weekend completely alone.

He smiled as he started to walk toward the cow barn. "Perhaps in the early evening, then?"

The setting sun cast orange shadows across the driveway as they parted. Slowly, Shana walked back toward her house, watching Emanuel disappear into the barn, straightening the straw hat on his head. At the doorway, he glanced over his shoulder and spared her a final smile. She responded with a good-bye wave and continued walking up the driveway.

Several kittens scurried under the tool shed at the edge of the yard in front of the farmhouse. As Shana passed it, she noticed Katie kneeling in her garden. In the past, Katie had always greeted Shana with a warm smile. Now, when Katie looked up, a dark frown crossed her face and she merely nodded at the Englische woman. The apparent interest her son had taken with the pretty Englische woman obviously displeased her. Certainly Katie had overheard the end of their conversation. While Shana knew that it was against the Ordnung for an Amish man to be so friendly with an Englische woman, she wasn't about to worry about it if Emanuel wasn't.

Chapter Three

When the gray-topped buggy stopped in front of her house, Shana pushed back the curtain and, steadying herself against the upstairs window sill, stared at it for a long moment. She watched as Emanuel slid back the buggy door and quickly emerged. He straightened his straw hat and brushed some dirt off of his black pants. Before he walked toward her front door, he paused long enough to give Lucky Monday a reassuring rub on the nose. Then, he quickly disappeared under the window and she heard him walking across her small porch.

All morning, Shana had lounged around her house, cleaning and organizing the few things she had brought with her. She had enjoyed the tranquility of doing nothing for a while. But, as she grew restless, later in the afternoon, she had ventured out of her house and began to explore the farm.

First, she wandered over to Katie's large garden, admiring the neat and organized rows of bushy lettuce, overgrown zucchini, and luscious red tomato plants. Most of the corn stalks were already stripped, although Shana was certain that, with such a large field of corn, the family never wanted for any. Then, she had wandered up the hill, breathing in the sweet smell of the recently cut hay as she watched the activity in the fields. Far in the distance, several silhouettes, hurrying behind a mule driven wagon, lifted large bales of hay up to another figure riding on the back. As she watched, she could occasionally hear the wagon driver shouting out a command, but to whom, the mules or the men, she could not tell.

On her way back from her walk, Shana noticed Sylvia lugging a large bucket of milk to the calves. When the young girl stumbled, milk spilling over the edge of the dented, metal bucket and splashing her plain brown dress, Shana quickened her pace to come to Sylvia's aid.

Together, quietly, they carried the bucket to the far side of the mule shed where, in little wooden lean-to's, the weaning calves hungrily awaited the milk. Shana held the bucket to one calf's face while Sylvia's took care of the second calf. Shana laughed as the calf hungrily drank the milk, wearing most of it on its face.

"Messy eater," Shana said, mostly to herself, but, out of the corner of her eye, she saw Sylvia smile.

And, when the calf stepped on Shana's foot and refused to move, the two girls shared a laugh together. It was Sylvia who finally pushed the calf off of Shana's foot before they finished feeding the rest of the calves. During all of this, Shana hadn't thought much about the buggy ride Emanuel had promised to take her on later that evening.

But now, as she heard Emanuel knocking twice at her door, her stomach tightened into a knot. She let the curtain fall back into place and took a deep breath before leaving the bedroom to hurry down the narrow staircase. She shut the doorway to the staircase and glanced around the house.

She had meticulously cleaned that afternoon, making certain everything was put away and organized. She didn't know why. It isn't as though I must impress him, she had reprimanded herself. Now, as she saw him standing patiently behind the open screen door, she was glad she had made the extra effort.

Emanuel smiled when he saw her. He wore the same outfit she had seen him wearing the previous day except now his shirt appeared freshly washed. "Enjoying your day off?"

"So far," she replied, swinging open the door, uncertain

whether she should invite him inside. She waited, hoping to take some direction from him, but he continued standing outside. She propped the door open with her foot and said, "It's a beautiful day again, isn't it?"

"Ja," he replied cheerfully. Silence.

The horse neighed softly, shaking its head. The rest of the farm was quiet. He stood before her, his hands thrust deep into his pockets. Shana fought the urge to smile, pleasantly surprised at the formality of his fetching her to ride into town. Emanuel shuffled his feet as he glanced over his shoulder at the horse and buggy then looked back at her.

Finally, he broke the silence and, his eyes meeting hers, he asked, "Would you care to go into town? I have to stop at Zimmerman's for some things."

"I'd love to." She heard herself say before she retreated inside for her purse, taking an extra second to glance in the mirror at her face, flushed with excitement. Running her fingers through her hair, she gave herself an encouraging smile. "Your first buggy ride," she whispered to herself. The excitement she saw in her face suddenly made her feel ridiculous and like a young schoolgirl. It would be no different than if you gave him a ride in your car, she scolded herself as she turned off the light and hurried outside.

As she started to open the door again, she noticed Emanuel staring at the closed book situated on the corner of the kitchen counter. Her cheeks reddened and she found herself explaining, "I thought I might as well get to know the people I'm living with." Somehow, the words sounded dry and flat, only an echo of the truth. She wished she had thought to take the book upstairs to hide her curiosity about his way of life from his wandering eyes.

A frown clouded his face. He didn't reply as he walked

toward the buggy and waited for Shana to lock the door to her house. Then, he helped her step inside before climbing next to her and shutting the door to the buggy. He didn't speak as he slapped the reins on the horse's back. The buggy lurched forward and Shana grabbed awkwardly for the side, laughing uneasily as she tried to decide whether she liked the loud rumbling of the metal wheels against the macadam. But Emanuel didn't laugh with her. Instead, his face remained solemn for the ride into town.

Trying to lighten his somber mood with carefree chatter, Shana commented on the beautiful fields of ripe corn and the different herds of Holstein cows grazing in the brilliant green pastures along the road. Still, Emanuel refused to say anything as he drove the horse along the narrow roads. Taking his silence in stride, Shana finally sat back and tried to enjoy the ride.

The store was crowded with people, mostly tourists, the women with oversized battered purses and the men with cheap straw derbies shading their heads from the sun. Several dared to take pictures of Emanuel as he pulled up to the hitching post. Shana glanced at him, noticing the crease in his brow deepen. She wondered why he didn't say anything to the people. But, not questioning his silence, she quietly climbed out of the buggy without his assistance and followed him past the staring tourists into the general store.

For a short while, she browsed through the aisles, hardly noticing anything but her own turmoil of thoughts. The day before, he had seemed so young and innocent, his curiosity about the non-Amish world amusing her. Now, the way he quietly shuffled pass the gaping tourists, his mind oblivious to their curiosity, caused her heart to flutter. He seemed much older, much more in control, and much stronger than he had appeared the day before. Occasionally, Shana found her eyes seeking Emanuel, watching as he nodded to an elderly Amish couple, addressing them by name, or stopping to say hello to the young store clerk as she restocked the shelves. Then, afraid Emanuel might catch her, Shana would avert her gaze and wander further down the aisle away from him.

"Shana," Emanuel softly called out when he stood at the cash register.

The way he looked at her with his large blue eyes sent a wonderful chill down her spine. There was a softness in his expression and a hint of pride in her acknowledgement of his presence. She nodded her head and hurried to his side to wait for him to pay the clerk. She was in his world now, she realized, and needed to fall under his gentle protection.

After Emanuel had paid, she followed him outside. He held the door open with one arm, his other clutching the large grocery bag. He started to smile at her as Shana walked past him when a man abruptly shoved her aside. She stumbled into the doorframe, steadying herself against the side of a Coca-Cola machine. She spun around in time to see the tourist waving his camera as though to take Emanuel's photograph.

Aware of Emanuel's discomfort and feeling a sudden surge of anger at the tourist for having spoiled the moment, Shana quickly stepped between the two men and, pointing her finger in the tourist's face, snapped, "Shame on you!"

Startled, the man held his camera motionless. Seizing the opportunity for an escape, Emanuel grabbed her arm and quickly lead her back toward the hitching post. More than a few people had witnessed the scene and stood watching the Amish man with the Englische woman, surprised to see them both disappear inside the Amish buggy.

He had barely slid the door shut before he turned to face

her. Immediately, his silence lifted. His soft, gentle eyes searched hers as though seeking some explanation for her outburst. "There are some things we get used to in our life. Many burdens we must carry while seeking our salvation, Shana," he said. "Tourists are one of them. But how can you chastise that man when you are no different?"

"I don't understand," she whispered, horrified at the solemnity of his words.

Emanuel shook his head. "You are living with my family, ja? If you want to learn about the Amish, you have only to ask. Buying those books only feeds the fire, Shana. And most of the books don't tell the truth, anyway. What do those books say about how we feel? How we think as individuals? If the tourists knew anything about those things, they wouldn't come here in the first place."

This time, it was Shana who sat in silence, her eyes downcast and her heart heavy. She realized that he was right. She was no better than the thousands of tourists who plowed through Lancaster County, each trying to learn as much as they could about the Amish from the wrong sources. They always left satisfied but just as ignorant as when they came. It was as if they thought they could bottle up the tranquility felt by the Amish and take it home. If only they could, she thought wistfully, her own sympathy falling with those tourists that sincerely wanted to learn but didn't know how because the tranquility of the Amish could not be learned in one day.

"Teach me," she whispered.

"Excuse me?"

Shana looked at Emanuel's surprised face. "Teach me about the Amish way of life."

The tension gone, Emanuel smiled at the seriousness of her

request. "It isn't something you learn, Shana. It is something you believe. We are a people of faith."

"I have two months."

"Two months, ja?" Then, mockingly, he added, "*Ach vell,* where shall I begin?" But he lessened the blow of his teasing words with a smile.

For the next two hours, they drove back toward the farm along different, out-of-the-way roads. Emanuel, recognizing her desire to learn, spent his time showing her the tangible aspects of his life. He slowed down by the one-room schoolhouse he had attended until he was fourteen. She noticed the large outhouse behind the building and the rusty water pump in the play-yard. But it was summertime now and the dusty yard was overgrown with thin patches of grass.

"Amish children go to school up to the eighth grade," he explained. "Then, we have a year of vocational school. That takes place three hours a week and the rest of the time, we have to keep a journal of what we've learned on the farm. Sylvia, my sister, will finish school this spring and attend vocational school next fall."

"Why only eighth grade?"

Emanuel shrugged, slowing down as he gazed at the schoolhouse with its dark windows and closed front door. The children would not return to the schoolyard for another couple of months. "We learn what we must know to survive. English, reading, writing, a little geography, and mathematics. But our families need us on the farms. So, the government agreed that after eighth grade, Amish children are exempt from further education."

"Don't you ever feel cheated? I mean...well, there's so much out there. So much to see and do and learn."

If Shana had thought her question might have offended him,

she was pleasantly surprised when he merely raised his eyebrows, a hint of a smile lighting up his eyes. "Don't you ever feel cheated? We take care of each other here, help our family and friends. We have time to watch God bless the earth every season, with new plants and new cows. We have time to ride the horses, play with the kittens, enjoy our families. No one has to move far away to make a living. No one is ever alone." he paused, as if searching for the right words. "We live our lives, loved by our families and our community, Shana. We know exactly what we are going to do tomorrow because it's the same thing that we did today. But each night we pray that we do it better the next day. There is no pressure to perform, to succeed, because we already have. If your family and community accepts you, who else must you impress?" He waited for her response and when none came, he smiled. "Just yourself and God, ja?"

In truth, she was starting to feel cheated. Here in Amish country, everyone knew where they belonged. There was no doubt about the present or future. The work was rewarding, the rewards satisfying, and the satisfaction endless. "Aren't you ever curious?"

"*Ja vell,* maybe when I was younger," he admitted, his eyes still sparkling at her. "Now, I'm content."

They drove on, Emanuel telling her about the few years of his youth when his teacher lived on his father's farm. "Her family was from another district, too far for her to travel everyday. So, throughout the year, she lived with us. I was so glad when she got married and they hired another teacher, one of our neighbor's daughters. It's hard to have any fun with your teacher always nearby."

He paused the horse at the bottom of a hill. In the pastures nearby, a foal pranced eagerly around its mother. Two small Amish girls, obviously sisters for they looked identical even from the road, sat a safe distance away, watching the beautiful scene. One of the children, the smaller of the two, held a fistful of daisies in her hand. The other girl, dressed in a plain pink dress with a patterned apron covering the front, plucked another flower that grew near to where she sat and handed it to her younger sister to add to her collection.

"It's so peaceful," Shana declared, seeing the land in a different shade of bright. "There are no problems out here."

Emanuel glanced at her. She stared out of the side window, her dark eyes glowing. "We do our work and follow the church rules," he replied, still watching her. "But we are people first, Shana. Everyone has some problems."

"If only we had your problems," she said softly, her eyes momentarily glazing over causing him to wonder what she was thinking. Then, her inner spell lifted, she looked over her shoulder at him and smiled, "If only the rest of the world was at peace with itself the way the Amish are."

As they approached the farm, they both fell silent again. The sun was setting over the neighbor's cornfields, casting beautiful red rays over the quilted land. The neighbor, just returning to his farm from a day in the fields, waved from behind six mules. Emanuel and Shana waved back. "That's Jacob Hostetler. He comes over every once in a while to visit. After the spring planting, anyway. And during harvest, he often helps my daed since his fields are not as large."

Emanuel stopped the horse outside of Shana's house. He helped her out of the buggy and walked her toward the door. For a brief moment, they both smiled shyly at each other. Neither spoke at first, Shana wishing she could find the words to thank him for forgiving her Englischer ways. But, too embarrassed to speak what came to her tongue, she finally reached for the door.

"Thank you for my buggy ride," she said at last.

Emanuel took a step backward, thrusting his hands into his pockets again. "Shana, if you really want to learn about the Amish, perhaps you'd accompany us tomorrow to my grandparents' farm. I believe Mamm had intended on asking if you'd like to go."

Shana's face lit up. To accompany the Lapp's to the grandparents' was certainly an honor most *Englische* people would rarely have. "I would love to go, Emanuel. That sounds like a lot of fun."

The horse neighed loudly, shaking her head and stamping her feet, too impatient to stand around for idle chatter. "Be ready about eleven then," he said. He hesitated before quickly adding, "If you'd like, you can ride with me." Then, he took the horse's reins and lead Lucky Monday away, pausing to spare her a final wave from the edge of the cow barn.

Shana opened the door to her house, feeling warm and pleased with herself. You've made a good friend in Emanuel, she told herself as she hung her hat up on a hook in the wall. Standing in the doorway, she stared outside at the cow paddock. Already Jonas was milking the cows with the help of Samuel and David, his two younger sons. She could see Steve and Daniel walking from the horse shed toward the dairy barn, waving at Emanuel as he unhitched the horse from the buggy. She watched them for several minutes before, content and happy, Shana shut the door.

For a moment, she looked around the plain room, seeing nothing but the memories from the ride back to the farm. The schoolhouse waiting patiently for the return of the local children, the young foal racing across the field after its mother, Emanuel's eyes lighting up as he reached back into his memory to share his past life with her. Finally, Shana's eyes lingered on the book, still resting on the kitchen counter. She picked it up and leafed through several pages. This book, she realized, came so close to ruining the friendship that developed. Too close, she corrected, allowing her thoughts to linger on Emanuel before, taking a deep breath, she dropped the ill-fated book in the garbage.

Chapter Four

The backyard of the grandparents' house resembled an elementary school yard at recess more than a family picnic. The younger children, mostly grandchildren and a few great-grandchildren, chased each other around the yard, laughing and playing. Most of the children were dressed in similar clothing, the girls in simple homemade dresses and the boys in black pants held by suspenders and a simple blouse. Yet, even in their simplicity, they stood out with the vivacious colors, blues, purples, or rich greens, of their dresses or shirts.

Shana gave up trying to count them, finally settling on thirty or more, if she included the older girls who stood around the back porch watching. Turning to Katie, Shana asked, more out of disbelief and amazement, "Are all of those children your nieces and nephews?"

Katie stared at the Englischer girl, the Amish woman's large, sorrowful eyes hidden behind her plain, wire-brimmed glasses, as she replied curtly, "Ja, some. Ana and Lea's families couldn't make it today. And Steven's are too far." Katie brushed past Shana and disappeared into the house where the other women were already busy in the kitchen preparing the midday meal.

Shana stood by herself in the shade of the large tree, watching the children for a while. The ride had taken almost an hour. Young David and Samuel had ridden in the back of Emanuel's buggy, their two older sisters with their parents, and Daniel rode along with Steve.

The long journey had lacked the fun of the previous evening's ride since Emanuel hadn't pointed out sights for her or shared his memories. Instead, he drove Lucky Monday in silence, his back straight and his eyes focused ahead, as though setting an example for his ten and eight year old brothers. But Shana had enjoyed Emanuel's soothing presence, if nothing else. The younger boys had chattered happily in the back, mostly in Deitsch, while they shyly waved at the thrilled tourists who drove behind the buggy along the winding country roads.

Shana had worn a black, sleeveless dress with a crisp, white shirt underneath and she had French braided her hair away from her face, trying to look as inconspicuous as she could. But she still felt out of place among the plain Amish people. They stared at her, probably in disapproval of her dress, and occasionally, Shana heard someone repeating her name as they passed on what they knew of the background of Jonas Lapp's live-in Englische guest.

"*Wie gehts?*" someone called out in a deep, demanding voice. Shana saw an old man with a long, white beard hobbling toward her with the assistance of a thick, wooden cane. He stopped before her, planting his feet wide apart as he stared her over, his gruff nature unable to hide the kindness in his twinkling blue eyes. "Don't look very Amish to me!" he snapped, his bare upper lip twitching slightly.

"My name's Shana Slater."

"That sounds like a Hollywood name!"

Shana laughed. "I can assure you it isn't."

He shut one eye, still staring her over. "You the Englischer from Jersey? The restaurant worker, ja?"

Shana glanced over his shoulder, hoping to catch Sylvia or Emanuel's attention. Unfortunately, no escape was in sight. "Yes, sir." Faced by the demanding old man, Shana forced a smile as she said, "And, let me guess. You must be Jonas' father."

"That I am. And all those young'ns you been staring out at are my grandchildren. The whole herd of them and there're more! What do you think about that, Englischer?"

Shana glanced back at the children before answering slowly, "I'd say you're one very lucky man, although it must be difficult to remember all their names."

This time, the old man laughed, clapping her good-naturedly on the back. "I'd say you're right!" Then, his eyes still twinkling, he limped over to join a group of older men with gray beards by the picnic table set in the yard.

Alone again, Shana wandered inside the house. The women busied themselves with the preparation of the midday meal. They spoke softly to each other, mostly gentle requests for help rather than actual conversation. No one noticed Shana as she tried to help. Each woman had her own job to do, setting plates of food on the table, heating up pies in the oven, or shucking corn on the porch. The younger women, once out of the disapproving sight of their elders, chattered happily among each other, mostly in Deitsch, enjoying their time among friends and family, even as they worked.

Frustrated, Shana retreated outside. The men stood together, talking about the unusually good weather they were having that summer and where the next Sunday's worship service was being held. The smaller children played in the yard with a small kitten. And the group of young girls had disappeared. Having no one to talk to, Shana drifted toward the enormous garden. By herself, she admired the fine plants, wishing she knew something about gardening, or anything for that matter, that might affiliate her with these people's lives.

Feeling as though she shouldn't have been so eager to

accept Emanuel's invitation, Shana sat down on the grass and rested her head on her knees. She was getting homesick. Homesick for her parents, her friends, even the people from work. Yet, no one had appeared too upset about her leaving for so long and Shana reassured herself that they weren't sitting home at nights, missing her. Suddenly, she felt like crying, hating the loneliness she felt.

"Bored?"

Shana glanced up, not surprised and a little thankful, to see Emanuel hovering over her. "I have a lot on my mind."

"Anything to share?"

Shana shook her head. "Nothing more than problems at work. Boring stuff," she said with a sad smile.

His knees cracked as he knelt beside her and began plucking at the grass. "Saw you met my grandfather."

Shana smiled at him. "He's a character, huh?"

"Ja! He is that. Got married when he was eighteen to my grandmother and they had thirteen children. Four of them died young. Can't imagine so many children." Emanuel laughed, nudging Shana with his arm. When he saw her cheeks flush with color, he sobered and continued, "Several years ago, he lost part of his foot in an accident."

She had noticed the grandfather's limping with the cane but hadn't thought anything of it. She didn't know what to say in response, especially after their conversation earlier that week about Emanuel's finger. After a brief hesitation, she replied, "Certainly is bound to make a person strong."

Emanuel stuck a piece of grass into his mouth. "He liked you. He likes anyone that can make him laugh." They both fell silent again. Shana's thoughts raced to her family and friends, the sadness returning to her eyes. "Are you homesick, Shana?"

Torn from her thoughts, Shana sighed. "It's tough to be far away from friends and family."

His gaze steady, Emanuel softly replied, "Now you have friends and family here."

She laughed good-naturedly at his comment. "I'm not so sure they'd think of me in those endearing terms." Shana tossed a small pebble into the garden. It rolled next to a ripe watermelon. Aware that Emanuel was still looking at her, she met his gaze and was surprised at the concern in his eyes. "I'm an outsider in your world, Emanuel. I don't understand your traditions or customs or where I belong." As she spoke, she realized that she was sorry that she had come, not because she didn't fit in but because she felt as though she almost wanted to belong. "I'm not a little kid that can race around the yard or a young girl that can hang around in gossiping groups. But I'm not married so I feel awkward around the women. Certainly the men don't want me around."

He laid his hand on her arm and, to Shana's surprise, she felt comforted. "You'll find your place, Shana. In the meantime, forget about fitting in and just have a good time, ja?" was his simple solution. The warmth of his gentle grip and the sincerity behind these words touched her.

With a smile, Emanuel stood up and reached down to help her stand. Taking a hold of his hand, Shana noticed his hesitation as he clutched hers. He stared at her, his crystal blue eyes warm and inviting. For a brief moment, his lips parted as though he wanted to say something else. But he said nothing and merely released her hand.

In silence, they walked back to the farm and separated. Shana attempted to help in the kitchen again, this time succeeding after she clung to Katie's side until, to get the Englische woman out of their way, someone found something for Shana to do. Satisfied that she had made her point clear, Shana spent the next hour seated on the porch, helping some of the young Amish wives peel potatoes for the midday meal. She listened intently as they talked to each other, sometimes slipping into Deitsch before they remembered Shana's presence and switched back to English. Yet, they did not draw her into their conversations, much to Shana's disappointment. Still, Shana had managed to feel useful, if nothing else.

Shortly after one, the food was spread out on a blue and white checked tablecloth that covered the kitchen table. Shana stood in the corner, out of the way of the women as they tried to hurry the men inside before everything got cold. She surveyed the table, amazed at the quantity of food that would feed almost sixty people that afternoon. There were homemade sausages, fresh beans, steaming plates full of fresh corn on the cob, and half a dozen garden and pasta salads. Everything, she realized, was the result of their hard work as well as their love of the land.

Before the meal, Grandfather Lapp said a blessing in Deitsch over the food. Then, as the youngest children, eager to eat, single filed past the table, the young girls began to sing a chant like song in German. Soon, everyone was moving about the table, singing the song as they helped the young children dish their food before dishing their own. Shana listened to the sound, smiling to herself when the men joined in with their deep voices that overshadowed the women. Looking around the room, she noticed that everyone sang, from the small children to Grandfather Lapp.

Shana waited until she saw Katie standing in line. Katie smiled and gestured for Shana to join her. Though surprised, Shana felt comfort in her sincere smile and hurried to the older woman's side. Then, as Shana stood next to Katie, the Amish woman handed her one of the plastic plates that she had brought from home for her family. Touched, Shana took the plate and thanked her, her heart beating quickly as it warmed inside her chest.

For the first time, Shana felt as though she belonged. Maybe not belonged, she quickly corrected herself. But she did not feel like a complete outsider to the Lapp family. When she caught Emanuel's eye, she smiled and held his gaze. For a long moment, they stared at each other. Her own smile slowly faded as she realized that he had been watching her, not just for several minutes but ever since she had left him outside. And he had certainly seen the exchange between Katie and her. Shana would have thought him pleased but her smile was returned with a solemn look that disappeared only when he averted his gaze, as though afraid that someone would notice their silent communication.

Shana continued watching him for a minute. If the smile had faded from her face, it now faded from her heart. She had been so proud of herself, finding a small niche in his world. She had thought Emanuel would share her pride. A frown crossed her face. Emanuel had wanted her to fit in and she had, not just for herself, but for him, too. She wondered if he sensed that and if his solemnity came from disappointment. She had truly been curious about the Amish but now, she found herself admitting, that curiosity was more about him. When Emanuel finally disappeared outside with the men, Shana bowed her head, ashamed at her feelings.

After everyone finished eating, Shana helped the women clean up. There were dishes to be washed, food to be put away, tables to be wiped down. Quietly, Shana did as she was instructed, shooing the younger children outside to play while the women cleaned the kitchen. She had noticed how the children had lost their shyness around her. Instead, it had been replaced with curiosity and they had started to get underfoot, especially when Shana teased them and would lean over to tickle the youngest ones. But, with so much work to take care of, the children' place was outside and Shana was needed in the kitchen.

When everything was cleaned up and put away, the women sat down to gossip. To Shana's surprise, Ana motioned for her to join them. "You enjoying your stay here, Shana?" Ana asked when Shana sat down. Ana's head was bowed over a crisp white pillowcase that she was cross-stitching.

"When I'm not working," Shana replied.

Melinda, Katie's mother, leaned over, placing a strong hand on Shana's arm. "And what kind of work was that?"

"I manage a restaurant."

"A restaurant, I see."

"Mamm, did you hear about the Isaac's?" Sarah, one of Katie's sister-in-laws, asked. "Their youngest just died."

"*Schrecklich*," she whispered.

Shana wondered if Melinda was thinking of her own four children that had died. It amazed her how calm everyone seemed to take tragedy. Sarah nodded her head. "Only three years old. They aren't certain what it was. Just took ill one day."

The women began talking about another family. Slowly, Shana drifted into her own world. She watched Ana, sitting contently in the warm summer sun, embroidering her pillowcase. Certainly life as an Amish woman was hard, she imagined, with constant children underfoot and continual work to be done. Shana had also noticed how gruffly the men treated their wives, barely showing any affection and rarely addressing them by name. Instead, the men sat outside, discussing the upcoming hay season while several women served them coffee and dessert.

The grandfather clock had just struck four when Katie said good-bye to everyone, explaining that by the time they got home, it would be milking time. Quickly, Shana followed, telling the ladies how much she had enjoyed meeting everyone. To her surprise and delight, both Ana and Melinda replied by asking her to come visit them at their farms whenever she could during the long winter months.

Shana noticed the women's casual insinuations about how long she would be living with the Lapps and the backward glances she received from the men as she followed Katie outside where Jonas and Emanuel were already next to the buggies, waiting patiently for the women. Shana hurried over to Emanuel's buggy and let him help her in, his touch once again lingering. With a sigh of relief, she settled back for the long, silent ride home, her leg gently brushing against Emanuel's and her heart pounding fiercely within her chest.

Back at the farm, Shana let Emanuel help her down from the buggy. She noticed how he clasped her hand, waiting until she met his gaze. Shana opened her mouth to say something but thought better of it. "Thank you for inviting me," she heard herself whisper, withdrawing her hand from his and quickly disappearing into her house. She shut the door and leaned against it, breathing heavily.

The way she started to feel around Emanuel frightened her, but what frightened her the most was the way the tranquil, peaceful Amish lifestyle appealed to her. No competition or complications. They lived day to day, pleased with whatever they accomplished and enjoying the fruits of their labor. The women enjoyed cooking, cleaning, and raising families for their husbands. And the men enjoyed working hard in the fields and pleasing their families. But it's not just a lifestyle, she corrected herself. It's a faith. Disappointed in her typical tourist attitude about which Emanuel had chastised her the previous day, Shana quickly buried herself in some paperwork from the restaurant.

Half an hour later, she was sitting at the table, reviewing the last month's P & L statements when a soft knock at the door startled her. She glanced at her watch. Six o'clock. Obviously not expecting anyone, she quietly set down her pencil and, getting up from the table, hurried over to the door. When she opened it, she was even more startled to find Steve, Emanuel's younger brother by two years, standing outside. He resembled Emanuel in appearance but his eyes were far less worldly and extremely shy.

"There is a phone call," he mumbled softly.

"Is there a phone?" she asked, raising her eyebrows. She had thought that the Amish didn't use phones. "I mean, I didn't know you had a phone here."

Steve shook his head and pointed to the neighboring farm. "Over at the Hostetler's," he explained.

"Steve!" someone called from the barn. They both looked up to see Emanuel walking from the darkness of the open doorway. His hands in his pockets and his head tilted forward, he seemed preoccupied. "Daed needs your help in the milk house."

Steve glanced back at the barn. "Shana has a phone call."

Emanuel nodded toward Steve, and then turned his attention to Shana. "I'll show you where the phone is, then." He didn't wait for her reply and started walking briskly down the lane toward the road. Steve was already hurrying toward the barn so Shana found herself quickly catching up with Emanuel.

At the edge of the road, Emanuel reached out and touched her arm. "Watch," he said as an old blue Chevy whirled around the bend in the road and sped up the hill. Checking the other direction again, which was clear, he released her arm and crossed the street.

The Hostetler farm seemed more active than the Lapps. Two young girls trudged through a muddy field, rounding up the herds. The younger girl slipped and almost fell headfirst into the mud but her older sister grabbed her arm and steadied her. Emanuel chuckled to himself and even Shana had to suppress a smile at the sight of the two girls flaring their arms and chasing the lazy cows. One of them, noticing Emanuel and Shana, shouted out and waved. Emanuel waved back.

He pointed to a small gray building on edge of the farm. The door was swung halfway open and Shana could see a broken stool propped against the inside wall. She hurried over the small building, curious as to who could have tracked her down.

Picking up the phone, she placed it against her ear. "Hello?"

"You don't know how hard you are to find! There must be two hundred listings for Lapp in the directory."

"Jeff?" she asked as she recognized the familiar voice of the other manager from her restaurant. As he rambled on about how he had lost his keys, Shana glanced at Emanuel. He stood a few feet away, his back to her and his hands thrust in his pockets again. He shuffled his boots in the dusty lane, stared at the girls stomping through the mud, and occasionally glanced at Shana through the half open door in the phone booth. "I guess you want me to trek out there?"

"Well, no one can get into the office or the liquor cage."

She laughed. "On a Friday night?" That would be disastrous. Friday was one of their busiest nights.

"Never fails," he replied.

"I'll be there in thirty minutes." She hung up the phone and stepped outside. She shut the door but it swung halfway open after she released the handle. "That's nice of the Hostetler's to let your family use their phone."

"Three farms share the phone," he explained in a matter-of-fact voice as he started walking back toward the road.

"Why don't you just get your own?" she asked as she walked next to him, wondering how Jeff had located the phone number. She figured that the Internet had played a key part but she made a mental note to ask him when she saw him.

"The Hostetler's need it for business. We don't." He didn't look at her but stared straight ahead. His face seemed more somber than usual. "Problem?" he asked, casting her a quick askew glance.

"The manager on-duty at the restaurant misplaced his keys." She said with a gentle shrug of her shoulders. She dreaded the thought of driving into the restaurant after such a wonderful day. "I'll have to take my set to him."

Emanuel nodded once as if to say that he understood. The somberness lifted and his shoulders looked less stiff. He glanced down the road before, his eyes catching hers, he spared a quick timid smile and crossed Musser School Lane.

They had turned past the mule stable and approached her small porch when Emanuel finally spoke again. He cleared his throat as he stared straight ahead. "Elijah and Jacob Zook are having a volleyball game tomorrow evening. Perhaps you'd care to accompany me to it?"

Her heart pounded inside her chest and she felt her palms grow sweaty. She wanted to go, wanted to spend more time with

Emanuel. But she couldn't help wondering if spending so much time with him was misleading. "I'm not much of a volleyball player," she started to decline but she didn't finished. Emanuel glanced at her, his eyes sparkling in the dim light from the fading sun. Swallowing, Shana fought her fear and followed her heart. "But, that sounds like fun, Emanuel."

Emanuel stopped in front of Shana's small house. "Then I'll see you at seven." He waited until she had disappeared inside to retrieve her car keys before he started walking around the barn toward the Lapp farmhouse. He hesitated briefly as Shana started her car, the engine loud against the stillness of the Amish. She backed up, her eyes catching sight of him in her rearview mirror. Then, he was gone, his silhouette vanishing around the corner of the barn and engraving itself in her thoughts.

Chapter Five

Brilliant flashlights and kerosene lanterns lit up the Zook's barn, full of Amish youths standing around a volleyball net set up between several bales of hay. The young girls stood to the sides, lingering in small groups as their shadows reflected against the walls. They talked quietly to each other, glancing over at the men and, occasionally, giggling. The men, however, pretended to pay no attention to any of the girls as they practiced tossing the ball back and forth. Some of the men leapt up, spiking the ball over the net. Then, as their friends congratulated them, their eyes would wander over to a particular group of girls as though making certain their prowess had been witnessed.

As they approached the doorway, Shana stopped and grabbed Emanuel's arm, her insecurity making her reach out for something real to bring back her self-confidence. He turned around, his eyes searching her face for the cause of her hesitation. She felt his warm skin quiver beneath her fingertips and immediately, she jerked her hand away, casting her eyes down in a silent apology.

Most of her day had been spent in turmoil over what to wear to the volleyball game. While she knew that the other Amish girls would wear their regular, plain dresses, Shana had nothing simple and plain enough for an Amish social event. Yet, for all of her agonizing, as she stood there in her plain black skirt with her embroidered white pull-over, staring inside at the people in the artificial lighting, she knew she had decided wrong. No matter what she had worn, she knew that she would have stood out among the plain dressed Amish girls with their hair pulled back and tucked neatly under their white organdy prayers caps.

"Something wrong, Shana?" Emanuel asked politely.

For a moment, Shana stared up at him and almost blurted that she wanted to go home. She dreaded walking inside the barn, hating herself for not listening to her instinct. But, when she saw the glow in his eyes and the concern in his expression, oblivious to her discomfort or reasons behind it, Shana merely shrugged and forced a smile. "It's so bright in here. It took me by surprise," she mumbled; then, following his lead, she entered the barn.

She noticed at once that a general hush fell over the group. The girls, most of them appearing to range from sixteen to twenty years in age, stared at her. As odd as their lifestyle seemed to Shana, it was she that was the outcast and outsider to them. On the ride over, Emanuel had briefly mentioned that many of the Church members didn't approve of his parents renting to Englischers, especially a single, young woman. He had quickly added that most of the younger Amish people in the community didn't share that sentiment. In fact, they were often quite curious about the Englische people that rented the small apartment on his family's farm.

However, Shana knew that curiosity did not mean they wanted the Lapp's tenant to intrude on their social life. She didn't need Emanuel to tell her that. Instead, she sensed it as the young women gawked at her and the young men began murmuring among themselves. In that single instance, Shana understood the implications of what Emanuel had just done and she couldn't help but wonder why he had chosen to do it. Certainly the repercussions were not worth the effort on his part. But, rather than questioning his reasons, she took a deep breath and said, "Well, it looks like we haven't missed much after all."

A tall Amish youth, not much younger than Emanuel, took the initiative to break the uncomfortable silence that followed their arrival. "*Ach vell*, we were just beginning the game. You want to play, then?"

Emanuel nodded. "Which team needs more players, Jacob?"

"Elijah's has room for you."

Emanuel turned to Shana. "You want to play or watch?"

She glanced at the two teams. One of the Amish boys stood in the back corner, holding the volleyball under his arm. They were all staring at her, a stranger amongst them, as they waited to hear her response. With the realization that she would be the only girl playing, Shana lifted her chin and said to Emanuel, "I'm not much of a watcher, so I might as well give it a try."

"If you get tired, just say so," he replied before they took their places among the other players.

Shana didn't have to listen to hear what Emanuel's peers, especially the young girls, were saying about her. But she didn't really care, either. Her idea of fun was not sitting on the sidelines, admiring the men for their physical skills in a game they probably didn't understand. I'm not Amish, Shana reminded herself, so I'm certainly not expected to act like one. It dawned on her that Emanuel probably invited her there for that very reason. So, rather than disappoint him, Shana helped shock them, instead.

Half an hour later, a few more young men wandered into the barn. They stood close enough that she heard their whispers and one youth mumbled her name. Even though it took every ounce of restraint, Shana refused to listen. She wondered what they were saying as they spoke in their private Deitsch language. Certainly asking why Emanuel had brought her there, a question that lingered in Shana's mind as well. Knowing his reasons were anything but malicious, she continued to hold her head high and tried to play the best game of volleyball she could in order to make

Emanuel proud that he had asked her to accompany him. But the uncertainty rang in her ears, confused about her role as Emanuel's friend and what she felt inside.

The game ended forty minutes later. The teams regrouped, some of the men stepping aside to let the latecomers join in. Shana walked with Emanuel over to the pitchers of lemonade on some bales of hay near the door. Quietly, he poured a glass and handed it to her. Feeling a hundred eyes on her, Shana merely returned his smile and accepted the drink. The barn was hot and stuffy and the cool drink quenched her thirst. But as she sipped it, to her dismay, Emanuel left her side and retreated to where the men stood, their backs to the women.

Alone, Shana clung to her glass of lemonade. The clusters of young Amish women stared at her but no one ventured to welcome her into their group. They talked softly among themselves, some of them occasionally looking at her as though wanting to invite her to join them. But no one dared. For several minutes, Shana waited to see whether Emanuel would return but, when she realized he was engrossed in a conversation with some of his friends, she took a deep breath, hid her discomfort, and walked to the nearest group of girls.

"I hope you don't mind if I join you," she started.

For a long moment, none of the three girls spoke. They averted their eyes and glanced at each other. But, determined, Shana allowed the silence to continue until someone replied. Finally, after a lengthy awkward silence, the tallest of the three spoke up. "You must be the Englische woman living with Emanuel's family."

"I rent a small house over the mule barn, yes. My name's Shana," she said, taking the initiative to introduce herself. In turn, the girls replied by telling her their names. Then, the ice broken, the girls began to talk again, this time in English to include Shana in their conversation.

Shana noticed one of the girls, Ester Ostenberg, glancing at Emanuel. Something in her eyes caught Shana's attention. Perhaps it was the youthful look of curiosity or envy for having an Englische woman living on their farm but, when the young girl looked back, Shana wondered if it weren't something else. She was a pleasant looking girl with a ruddy complexion and strong hands. While Shana had realized that she often underestimated the ages of Amish youth, she guessed the girl to be no more than nineteen. And throughout the half-hour Shana shared with them, Ester's eyes were continually drawn to whichever group Emanuel seemed to be joining.

The other two girls, Ana and Marie, asked Shana some polite questions then, began talking about their upcoming day trip to Washington D.C. to work at a market. Shana listened intently, amazed that these young girls, so innocent of the world that embraced their culture, would travel by themselves to a city so far away to work for a day's wages.

"That's a long way to D.C.," she observed to Ana and Marie.

"Not too long by bus," Ana replied. Then, lowering her voice, she leaned forward and added, "Besides, with the weather so hot, I like spending the time in air conditioning."

Shana laughed softly. "I guess that is an added bonus. Especially since it's so hot. I hadn't noticed it before because I'm at work most of the time. But, since I have this weekend off and I've been at my house, I do miss the air conditioning." They stared at her, as though amazed that she could miss something that they could never have. "It was nice tonight," Shana added, starting to change the subject. "We rode over in Emanuel's open buggy. Those are much nicer to ride in than the closed box-buggies."

Ana raised an eyebrow and Marie mirrored her girlfriend's startled expression. Shana noticed the silent communication between the three girls as the silence fell over them. Shana wondered what she could have said that made Ester looked so crestfallen and the other girls shocked. Finally, it was Marie who broke the silence. "Most Englischers would envy your buggy-riding experience, especially in an open buggy," she said slowly.

"Why's that?" Shana asked, curious about the stiff, stilted words that Marie spoke.

"Usually Englischers have to go into Intercourse and pay a man to ride them around in a carriage. It isn't often they befriend a real Amish man," Ana answered for Marie, her emphasis on the word real.

Marie raised an eyebrow. "Nor do they ride in a courting buggy."

The conversation quickly shifted as two other girls joined their group and, her feeling still stinging from the unusual hint of hostility in Marie and Ana's voice, Shana replayed the conversation in her head to see where she might have offended the three girls. She also wondered what they had meant by a courting buggy.

It was close to ten-thirty when Emanuel came over to find Shana. He greeted the other girls with a pleasant hello before he nodded to Shana and asked if she was ready to leave. Trying to hide her relief, Shana bid the small group of girls' goodnight and, to her pleasant surprise, they replied that they hoped to see her again. Shana wondered if that was for her benefit or Emanuel's but quickly decided that she didn't care. She was just glad to be leaving.

"I hope you don't mind leaving so soon," Emanuel started as they walked to the buggies. "We have church tomorrow and I must get up early to help Daed with the milking," he explained.

"That's fine," Shana said softly, hoping he didn't ask about her evening. She hadn't spent much time with him and she wondered if he was curious about how she had gotten along with the Amish girls. But she had so many unanswered questions that she was thankful that he didn't asked.

Instead, they walked in silence down the lane to the place where he had left the buggy three hours earlier. The night air was cool and the sky was clear. Overhead, the moon lingered, surrounded by the clearest stars Shana had ever seen. Between the moon and the stars, there was a brilliant glow of silver cast over the twenty or so buggies by the silo. It was a pretty sight and Shana sighed softly at how peaceful everything seemed.

"You go to church?" he asked, breaking the silence as he helped her into his buggy.

She waited until he was seated beside her before she replied, "Not recently." She wondered if that bothered him.

For a long time, Emanuel remained silent. The buggy lurched forward as Lucky Monday, at Emanuel's urging, slowly began the long trip home. In the darkness, the buggy felt safer and more comforting. The creaking of the wheels as they rolled along the roads soothed Shana and, had the seat been more comfortable, she would have drifted off to sleep.

"Do you believe?"

His question startled her. "In what?"

"God."

Shana laughed. "Of course! Everyone believes in God."

"Then why don't you go to church to worship Him?"

"Well, I..." she began. Then, not being able to think of a reason why, she shrugged her shoulders and admitted, "I don't know. We used to go a long time ago but when we moved to Connecticut, my father traveled a lot and my mother had never been very religious. I guess you could say that we fended for ourselves and eventually lost touch with the church."

"We?"

"My sister and I."

Emanuel took his eyes off the road long enough to cast a sideways glance at her. "Don't you have any other sisters or brothers, then?"

Shana laughed again. "I guess that must be hard for you to imagine since you have ten children in your family."

"You must get lonely without anyone around," he replied quietly, returning his gaze to the road. A car passed along side of the buggy and Lucky Monday lifted her head at the noise. The lights quickly faded down the dark road until, once again, the buggy was surrounded in darkness, broken only by the dim lighting thrown onto the road by the battery-operated headlights.

"Those girls that I met tonight," Shana started slowly. "They seemed quite friendly."

"You sound surprised," he replied solemnly.

"Ester seemed a little quiet, though," she continued cautiously. She didn't want to mention that brief moment of tension but her own curiosity was getting the best of her. When Emanuel did not reply, Shana asked, "Do you know her family well?"

"They live on the farm down the lane."

Again, the buggy filled with silence. Shana fought the awkwardness of the moment and her mind whirled in a thousand directions. On the tip of her tongue lingered dozens of questions but the silence, while uncomfortable, seemed the most appropriate. She let it hang over them as the horse trotted down the road. Another car passed them and, feeling the vibration from its speed, Shana cringed.

"Does that bother you?"

She snapped out of her daze and looked at Emanuel. "What?"

"Every time a car passes, you jump."

"Do I?"

He nodded, a hint of a smile playing on his lips, something she sensed even in the darkness. "I thought you'd get used to it by now. Perhaps one day," he said softly.

"There are a lot of things that I doubt I'd ever get used to," she heard herself blurt out. Her heart began to pound inside her chest, startled and ashamed of herself for always speaking before thinking.

"Such as?"

Had Emanuel not sounded genuinely curious, Shana wouldn't have answered. But his question was asked earnestly, as well as honestly. So, she decided to answer his question in the same manner. "Courtship, for one," she replied to which Emanuel laughed quietly but he did not respond. Taking the lead, Shana continued. "These men invite the girls to play volleyball but none of the girls actually play. They stand in the shadows, watching and giggling, never once interacting with their dates until it's time to go home."

"And this confuses you?"

Shana sighed. "When do they actually get to know each other? How can they ever marry? I mean, have you ever dated?"

He hesitated for a moment, then slowly responded, "If that is what you consider dating."

"What did you learn about your girlfriend? Her desires? Her wants? Her dreams?"

Emanuel cleared his throat. "Shana," he began. "We learn much more than that. We learn her strengths, her values, and her character. The rest, the little things, we learn those qualities after we make the decision to marry."

"Is that what you consider important?"

"Don't you?" he quickly answered. "Dreams and desires can change throughout the years. You cannot count on those things, Shana. But a person's inner strength, their inbred values, and their entire character won't change. Does she worship the Lord? Practice His wishes as He commands of us? Does hard work frighten her? Or does she tackle her chores head on? Does she strive to be good and follow the Ordnung? Does she shun evil and worldliness? These are things that can be counted on forever. These are qualities that a man looks for and considers important."

For a short time, Shana feasted on his words. Perhaps he was right, she thought. Too often, people stress the unstable qualities of a relationship rather than the constant and more important characteristics, she realized. "Does Ester meet those standards?" she heard herself ask, immediately wishing she could retract those horrible, jealous words that had slipped from her lips.

"Ester?" Emanuel repeated. For a few seconds, he frowned as if confused by her question. Mortified by the anticipation of what he was thinking, Shana watched his reaction. He slowly realized what her question had really meant and smiled in the dim reflection from the battery operated buggy lights. "On several occasions, I've offered her rides home after singings and other gatherings," he softly explained. "But that is only because of the proximity of her farm to ours, Shana."

Had it been daylight, he would have seen her blush. Thankful for the cover of darkness, Shana turned her face away and stared at the moonlit fields of green corn. She didn't know why she cared, but she only knew she did. And now, he knew too.

Sensing her discomfort, Emanuel let the rest of the ride finish in silence. Enough had been said for one night, they both silently agreed. And, when the wheels of the buggy finally stopped before her small house, Shana thanked Emanuel before gratefully retreating to the safety of her home.

Chapter Six

Early that Sunday morning, Shana laid in bed, listening to Jonas and his sons feed the cows. The cows shuffled back and forth on the cement floor in the barn, occasionally stomping one of their hooves impatiently. She could hear the Lapp men working in the barn, cleaning the manure and spreading lime on the freshly cleaned floors to kill the germs. As the men worked inside, the younger sons pitched hay into the feeders for the cows. The hay swooshed through the air, the noise blending in with the soft chewing from the cows. Every once in a while, she'd hear someone call out in Deitsch. A voice would reply then silence, except for the cows.

In the dim early light, she stared at the ceiling, her eyes traveling along a narrow, crooked crack in the faded white paint. It wandered across the ceiling and down one corner of the room, finally disappearing behind the crumpled blankets, which she had kicked off during the previous sleepless night, at the foot of her bed. She had memorized that crooked crack, watching it first in the silver glow of the moon then in the golden brush of dawn. Focusing on it, she had tried to escape the turmoil of thoughts that dashed in and out of her mind. It hadn't worked. Shutting her eyes, she rolled over and clutched a flat white pillow to her stomach, the pressure relieving her pangs of anxiety.

It was almost an hour later when she finally heard the rattle of the buggies as they headed down the lane to a neighboring farm for church. Three buggies filed past her small house before the noise disappeared down the lane and, finally, over the hill. The sound echoed in her ears and, when she could no longer trace it, she dropped her feet to the cold, wood floor and forced herself to face the day.

Downstairs, she stood at the old gas stove, her silk robe, a dark paisley print, wrapped around her. She gazed out the window, watching as the cows, one by one, wandered away from the feeding troughs and out into the open pasture. As they spread out among the field, they staked their claim around a small patch of grass, some of them dropping to rest and other arching their necks as they bellowed softly. As she watched, a thin stream of steam escaped from the chipped yellow metal teapot and, the warmth rising to caress her cheeks, she shut off the stove with a quick snap of her wrist and poured the water into her waiting mug of instant coffee.

Carrying the cup over to the table, Shana set it down on the pale pastel tablecloth. She climbed onto the kitchen chair, one leg bent with her knee pressed against the tabletop. For several long minutes, she stirred the coffee in her cup, her spoon clinking softly against the sides. Then, resting her cheek against her palm, she lifted the cup to her lips. Outside the window, a bird chirped from a nearby tree. It was answered by another bird, the melody of their conversation a welcome distraction on this morning.

Shana leaned back in the chair and glanced around the room. Her eyes fell upon a blank pad of paper next to the sink. Seconds later, she chewed on the end of a pencil, the pad of paper next to her coffee cup. She scribbled an amateur flower on the upper right hand corner then turned the pencil over to erase it. The wet eraser left a smudge where the four-petal flower had once been.

She drummed the pencil against the tabletop, her eyes drifting from the blank paper with the smudge then back to the window. A sigh escaped her lips and she forced her attention back to the pad of paper. Straightening her shoulders, she jotted down four words: "Clean house" and "Wash clothes." For a long moment, she stared at the blotchy writing on the paper. Then, a frown crossing her face, she tossed the pencil onto the table, leaned back, and covered her eyes with her hands.

Get with it, Shana, she told herself. All night, she had relived their conversation from the buggy ride home. She had berated herself a thousand times over for assuming. For assuming that, maybe, he had taken her there for more than just friendship. That maybe she had seen something in Ester's eyes whenever the young Amish girl had sought out Emanuel. That maybe the feelings inside of her, the ones she just couldn't understand, were real.

Several hours later, after her return from the local laundromat, Shana found herself walking among the tall rows of corn, most of them just empty, fading green stalks. The corn had ripened earlier that summer and now, by mid-July, most of it had been picked and sold. A small brown mouse dashed across the row up ahead and, startled, Shana felt her heart jump and she quickly retraced her steps through the field and toward the empty barn buildings.

She stopped at Lucky Monday's stall but it, too, was empty. A layer of fresh straw covered the floor and the water trough in the corner held clean water, with the exception of two pieces of hay floating on top. Shana reached in, plucked them from the water, and let them fall back onto the floor. The dog barked once as she walked out of the barn. Shana spared the growing pup a friendly scratch behind the ears before she headed out to the gardens. A car raced down the road, its momentary roar breaking the peacefulness before fading away into the outside world.

For a long time, she stood on the outskirts of Katie Lapp's garden, lost in thought as she surveyed the farm before her. The scarecrow in the garden, dressed in typical Amish fashion, was faded and the clothing torn. In the front yard of the house, a small flowerbed needed to be watered but the flowers, though dry, bloomed a brilliant red. Further in the distance, she noticed that the barn needed a fresh coat of paint and the driveway a fresh layer of gravel. But, wherever she looked, she saw life and love mixed with the beauty of nature.

The pains inside her chest hung heavier and her palms grew increasingly sweaty as she stood there, the summer sun beating on her back. For a moment, she felt faint and then, to her own astonishment, she started to cry. At first, she fought it, but as she stood there, the tears rolled down her cheeks. She tasted the salt on her lips and, with the back of her hand, wiped them away. Yet, they continued to fall and soon, even though she didn't understand why, she released her emotions and, sinking to her knees, covered her face with her hands and wept.

She was still kneeling there when the family returned from church. Lowering her head as she stood, Shana barely caught sight of the three buggies as they pulled into the driveway and past the barn. As the first buggy rolled by, she thought she saw Jonas wave but, as Emanuel's buggy passed her, she avoided meeting his eyes and quickly escaped from the farm, wandering further down the road and away from the Lapp farm.

She spent the next two hours walking, the fresh air soothing her rattled nerves but not her whirlwind of thoughts. She ignored her confusion, listening only to the soles of her shoes against the street. She held her head high, ignoring her inner turmoil as she blocked out every thing but the beauty of the country surrounding her. While she walked, several buggies slowly passed her, all of the drivers, semi-hidden behind the black walls that surrounded the tiny side window, waving to her. To her surprise, from one of the buggies came a pleasant, "Good day,

Shana."

Pausing by the narrow bridge, Shana stared across the fields. A narrow creek weaved through the fields like an ugly, brown snake, the murky water ruining the freshness of the ripe, green corn. Almost a quarter mile downstream, a black and white Holstein waded through the creek, stopping only to lower her head down to the water and take a long, slow drink. Then, its thirst quenched, the cow lifted its head and spared any listening ears a sorrowful loud cry.

Shana leaned against the stone bridge wall and watched the cow for a while, her thoughts slowly returning to what she fought so hard to avoid. She dreaded having to go back to work the next day. The anger, the tension, the stress. It beckoned her to run and hide. After living in the peace and tranquility of the Amish for three days of pretense, her stomach twisted into a knot at having to step outside the realm of fantasy and face the world of reality. My world of reality, she corrected herself.

She returned down the lane to the Lapp's farm. She kept her eyes downcast as she heard footsteps approaching but, when she realized it was Emanuel's younger brother, David, she spared him a forced smile and soft "Hello". Then, with a forlorn glance in the direction of the large farmhouse, Shana disappeared into her own small house.

It wasn't until much later that evening when she heard the familiar sound of a horse's hooves and the humming of buggy wheels. She had already cooked a light supper for herself and, the dishes drying on a damp towel next to the sink, Shana sat at the table and forced her to complete the following week's work schedule. The gentle knock at the door startled her. Quickly, she hurried to the door and opened it, equally surprised to see Emanuel, still dressed in his Sunday best, standing before her.

"Good evening, Shana." He shuffled his feet and glanced at the ground. It was dark outside and the crickets were busy singing their communal summer song. An occasional firefly would sparkle in the air, disappearing as quickly as it flashed its brilliant, yellow-green light. "I know it's late but I wanted to take my other horse for a quick drive and thought that, maybe, you'd join me."

When he lifted his eyes to meet hers, the timid expression on his face startled her. Had he been experiencing the same turmoil, the same rush of emotions that she had been fighting all day? One look at his face added to her suspicions and she understood that what he really wanted was to talk. Without saying a word, Shana nodded her head and closed the door behind herself, not bothering to lock it. Instead, she followed Emanuel to the waiting gray-topped buggy and let him assist her inside.

When he was seated beside her, he carefully slid the door shut. He paused to spare her an uneasy glance before slapping the reins against the back of the horse and clicking his tongue. When the buggy lurched forward, Shana's arm brushed against Emanuel's and she felt a thrill race through her blood. He let his one hand touch her knee, unnecessarily steadying her as she settled back into the seat. The color rose to Shana's cheeks as she stared out the window, too aware of Emanuel's presence next to her and the emotions raging inside her heart.

Whatever bothered Emanuel became more apparent as they rode down the lane. He kept glancing at her, clearing his throat, then remaining silent. He held the reins with one hand then, uneasily, took them into both of his hands, as though uncertain of what to do with his free hand. He leaned behind her, turning on the small battery operated radio and fiddling with the dial. Then, the only clear stations cracking with static, he changed his mind and turned it off.

"Emanuel," Shana softly started. If she had once thought that maybe her imagination was running wild, she now knew reality was Emanuel sitting next to her, his own uncertainty challenged only by hers. "I think we should talk." To her horror, he nodded but said nothing. Forced to read his mind as well as sort her own misplaced thoughts, Shana took a deep breath and said, "I'm not Amish and I never will be." She looked at him, waiting for him to reply. Please, dear God, she prayed silently, don't be letting me read too much into this.

When he finally glanced at her, he straightened his back and quickly returned his eyes to the road. "Shana, I understand that," he replied gruffly.

"And," she slowly continued. "We both come from different worlds. In my world, women are independent and worldly. In your world, women are obedient and sheltered. I'm afraid if you got to know me any better, I'd shock you."

"Perhaps," he agreed.

"I'm a product of my world. An independent woman, Emanuel. I work in a restaurant with ungodly hours. I have a long career ahead of me," she said, although in her heart she knew that after experiencing the Amish tranquility, her career was not going to be managing restaurants for the rest of her life. Then, softly, she added, "I'm not even religious."

Emanuel hesitated then, slowly, he said, "That doesn't matter."

"But it does," she countered, turning to face him, all doubt vanished from her mind. Even in the sheltered darkness of the buggy, she could see the blazing of his blue eyes, the sparkle of life that she dreaded because it meant only one thing for Emanuel: Shunning. "You have a life here, one that is centered around religion and faith. If we continue this little game, Emanuel, you'd have to leave everything because they'd never accept me in your world."

"Not at first," he argued slowly, appearing to choose his words slowly.

"Emanuel, my curiosity about your lifestyle does not mean I've accepted its faith. No matter how many weeks, months, or years it took, could you expect your community to open their arms and accept me?" she asked, her words trembling from her lips. "Accept an Englischer that belongs to no faith, especially not one that is the focal point of their lives?"

He stared at her. Her long, wavy hair hung over her shoulders in loose, gentle curls. Her large brown eyes danced as though daring him to ignore the words she said. Instead of answering her, Emanuel slowed the horse down until the buggy was stopped alongside the road. Then, very slowly, he leaned forward, reaching one hand out to touch her cheek as he gently lowered his lips onto hers. For one brief, bewildering moment, their two worlds collided as they kissed. To Shana's shame, she gave in to his kiss, closing her eyes and leaning back in the seat. She felt him pulling her close, one arm slipping around her waist, holding her tight to him. His lips pressed gently against hers, a forbidden passion emerging from his kiss. She answered back, allowing herself that one dangerous moment that confirmed everything she had been fighting. Then, to both her disappointment and surprise, he quickly released her and pulled away.

Diverting his eyes from hers, Emanuel stared straight ahead, urging the horse forward again. He neither spoke nor looked at her. Instead, he quickly turned the buggy around and headed home. Each sway of the buggy caused Shana to brush against him. But this time, she did not feel a thrill but a growing sense of shame.

Certainly he was angry with her, hating her for creating the turmoil he was feeling. A turmoil that was, apparently, driving a wedge in his beliefs and values. For the rest of the ride, Shana bit her lip and choked back her tears, wondering how she could have let herself lose the friend she had in Emanuel.

Chapter Seven

For the next month, Shana threw herself into her work at the restaurant, spending every waking hour at work, organizing and managing, in order to escape from the Lapp farm. She forced herself to forget about that nightmare ride in Emanuel's buggy and the sweet memory of his lips pressed against hers. When she returned to the house late at night, he was certainly asleep. In the mornings, when she left the house, she knew he was in the fields. Occasionally, she would see him behind the reins of the mules as they pulled a plow or a wagon, usually with two of his brothers following on foot as they shocked the fallen corn or tossed up the bales of hay. But Emanuel was too far away to see her.

"Shana, phone call for you."

Wiping her hands on her dirty apron, she glanced down the cook line. "You guys ok back here?" She didn't wait for their response as she carefully walked along the slippery floor to the small office in the back of the restaurant. "Hello, this is Shana."

"How you doing out there in farmland?"

Sinking into a chair, Shana shuffled some papers on the desk. "How good to hear from you, Robert," she replied dryly. In the six weeks she had been in Lancaster, he hadn't contacted her once. Slowly, it occurred to her that her promotion had upset him, and his way of dealing with it was to transfer her as far away as possible. "I'm doing just fine out here. Beautiful country."

"Heard from the top that you're doing a great job. Much better than they had hoped." His double-bladed compliment did not go unnoticed. "They're planning to make a trip out there. Probably not until early next month. Make sure you're consistent."

Shana leaned back in the chair, her fingers entwining with

the phone cord. "Robert, why did you call?" She picked up a paper, her eyes quickly glancing over the P & L figures before tossing it back onto the desk.

"Just wanted to make sure you were happy since you're probably going to be there for a while."

Shana felt her heart lunge forward in her chest. "I thought I was coming home in another couple of weeks."

"Couple of weeks?" Robert laughed on the other end of the phone. "Maybe for a Thanksgiving visit. Look, I'm real busy. I'll give you a call in a week or so." He hung up, his laughter echoing in her ears.

Annoyed, Shana slammed the phone back on the cradle. She knew she couldn't keep hiding from Emanuel by killing herself at work. Already, she was burning out. Ever since that weekend when he had taken her to the Amish picnic and volleyball game, she hadn't been able to concentrate on anything, especially not work. Nothing felt the same since that buggy ride and his kiss, she corrected herself. Still furious from Robert's phone call, Shana stormed out of the office and back to the kitchen line.

It didn't take long for the summer night air to grow increasingly chilly as the days began to slowly shorten. The staff at the restaurant turned over, the summer staff being replaced by returning college students. The other two managers insisted that Shana take some time off, noticing her increasing lack of enthusiasm. Reluctantly, Shana had agreed. She knew there was no purpose in making herself sick over a job she no longer loved. Especially now that Robert had so chivalrously informed her that her stay in Lancaster was to be extended. So, a week before Labor Day, Shana left work for an extended week's vacation.

The following morning, she slept as late as possible,

enjoying the lazy feeling of getting out of bed at ten o'clock. After a quick breakfast, Shana took a long, hot shower and dressed in a light summer dress. She sat outside on her porch, reading a book as the heat from the sun dried her hair. She wasn't certain what she was going to do with her time off. Part of her wanted to get away from the farm, perhaps go to the shore or return home for the weekend. But something inside nagged at her to stop running from Emanuel and her emotions.

Some time later, she heard someone approaching. Looking up from her book, she noticed Emanuel's sister-in-law walking slowly toward the house, her one-year-old daughter on her hip. "*Gude mariye*, Shana! How good to see you!" Lillian called out.

Jonas Jr. and Lillian had married two years earlier and lived in the *grossdaadihaus,* a smaller house attached to Katie and Jonas'. Unlike his father, Jonas Jr, didn't farm. Instead, he had started a carpentry business on his father's property. In time, he would move his growing family into the main house and then, eventually, they would build a house closer to the carpentry shop. One of the younger brothers' would inherit the Lapp farm and pass it down to his own children. For now, the slight bump in Lillian's expanding waistline announced that Jonas Jr. and Lillian were working at adding onto their family, even though Lillian looked to be no more than nineteen.

Setting her daughter on the ground, Lillian stopped at the edge of Shana's porch. "You've been busy recently and no one has seen you. If it wasn't for your car, we'd never know you were still here."

Shana returned Lillian's pleasant smile. "Well, my employers have given me a little vacation, although I'm sure I'll end up popping into the restaurant every couple days to keep an eye on things."

"You'll have to come for supper this evening if you're to be home all alone."

"I don't know, Lillian," Shana started, hating herself for wanting to accept but knowing in her heart that she couldn't. How would Emanuel react to her unexpected intrusion in his life after she had worked so hard to forget that night? "I have a lot of work to do and..." A lie that Lillian was certain to sense.

Lillian smiled, "You said you're on vacation. That means relaxation, not work." Picking Linda up, Lillian smiled. "Supper's around seven, after the milking. We'll see you there, ja?" Then, with a friendly wave of her hand, Lillian continued walking up the lane toward the mailboxes.

Shortly before seven, Shana forced herself to wander through the farm toward the big house. At least, she thought, I'll be able to talk with Jonas about extending my stay here. She tried to forget about having to face Emanuel but she knew it was inevitable. The heavy emptiness in her stomach tightened as she neared the house, each step bringing her closer to confronting the memory of that night. She had to get it over with. Running away had never been her style.

Katie and Sylvia welcomed Shana with friendly yet distanced smiles. Then, to Shana's relief, Katie set her to work husking some fresh ears of corn. If nothing else, it kept her busy. She listened to them talking about church the following Sunday and learned that the worship service would be held in their house. Katie listed the various chores to Sylvia that needed to be done by Sunday. "Almost wish Susie hadn't gone away this week. We could have used the extra hands. I don't know how we'll ever get the extra cleaning and cooking done."

Shana looked up as she set the last ear of corn on the table.

"If you need some help, Katie, I'd be more than happy to volunteer," she heard herself say, instantly regretting her lack of foresight. If Katie accepted her offer, Shana would most certainly run into Emanuel all week.

Katie scooped the corn into her massive hands and dumped them into a pot of boiling water. She didn't have time to answer as the men began to stomp up the porch steps, brushing the dirt off their clothes before entering the house. "Looks like the men are finished." While Katie looked anxiously out the window, she did not move toward the door to greet her husband and sons.

Jonas smiled at Shana as he set his hat on a peg on the wall. He walked over to the sink and washed his hands, Katie obediently moving out of his way. "Off from work, Shana? Seems we never get to visit anymore," he said pleasantly.

Shana stole a quick glance at the door, waiting for Emanuel to appear. "They gave me time off for good behavior," she replied with a nervous smile. Two of the younger boys hurried into the house, following their father's example as they hung up their hats and washed their hands. One by one, they slowly sat on the hard, wooden benches at the table, Jonas at the head and the boys on his right.

Shana stood by the oven, waiting for an invitation to join them when she felt a gentle nudge at her shoulder. "Glad you made it," Lillian smiled as she moved past Shana to set some food on the table.

Shana hadn't seen Lillian enter, nor had she noticed Emanuel, standing in the doorway. He hesitated then walked into the room. He ran his fingers through his hair before he sat down at the table, his eyes following Shana as she helped Katie take the corn out of the water and began chatting cheerfully with his sister-in-law.

Still unaware of his presence, Shana returned Lillian's warm smile. "After you insisted, I couldn't pass up the offer." Lillian's daughter tugged at Shana's skirt. Bending down, Shana tugged playfully at Linda's pigtail. "What a pretty young lady you are! Did you visit the kittens today?"

Cheerfully, Lillian laughed and picked up Linda. "Oh yes. We went down this morning then later this afternoon. Those are fine kittens, aren't they, Lindy?" The little girl giggled as Lillian lovingly tickled her daughter's chubby stomach. Then, Linda reached out for Shana. "Looks like you found a new friend, Shana."

After taking the little girl into her arms, Shana bounced her up and down several times, laughing with the child until Sylvia and Katie headed for the table. Shana turned around to follow when she noticed Emanuel. He was staring at her, his eyes glazed over as if deep in thought. Nonchalantly, Shana carried Linda over to the table. She tried to avoid his gaze but it followed her wherever she went as though accusing her of invading his world. She remembered their kiss and, for a brief moment, longed to be alone with him again.

"Shana, come sit." Lillian motioned for Shana to take her seat on the bench. The women sat opposite the men, Jonas and Jonas Jr. seated at the heads of the table. While they bowed their head in prayer, Shana stole a quick glance at Emanuel. His lips moved in the silent prayer but his eyes were still upon her. She felt the color rising to her cheeks and quickly lowered her eyes as though in prayer.

During the meal, the men talked about filling the silo and harvesting the rest of the hay while the women remained silent. Occasionally, Jonas would ask one of the girls a question, either about school or Ana's day in the market. Otherwise, the conversation was strictly male-oriented, much to Shana's satisfaction. It gave her time to sort her thoughts, free them from the web of confusion that seeing Emanuel had created.

"After supper, Emanuel, I need you to drive out to the Amos Smucker's farm. Bought two heifers from him. Might as well pick them up."

Katie looked up from her empty plate. "Is Miriam still ill? Last I heard she caught a dreadful end-of-summer cold." Without waiting for an answer, Katie turned to Sylvia. "Perhaps you should go along with Emanuel and bring her that fresh pie I baked today."

"Ja, Mother," Sylvia obediently answered.

For the first time since he had walked into the kitchen, Emanuel spoke up. "Sylvia has school work she must do. By the time I return, it'll be late."

For a moment, no one spoke. Jonas Jr. scraped the rest of his food off his plate, the fork clinking against the porcelain plate. The two younger boys leaned forward, apparently hoping they were told to skip the evening chores to ride with their big brother. Shana glanced at sixteen year-old Ana. Ana kept her eyes glued on her plate, obviously not wanting to take Sylvia's place since she had spent the entire day in the farmer's market selling canned fruits, jams, and vegetables to tourists. But, now that Katie had spoken, someone had to take the pie to Miriam Smucker.

Lillian glanced around the table as she held Linda on her lap, smoothing down the little girl's solid pink polyester dress. The little girl, her eyes drooping shut, nodded in and out of sleep. Innocently, Lillian smiled at Emanuel. "Perhaps Shana could ride along. I'm sure she'd like to get out for a spell."

This time, Shana felt the color drain from her face as she

glanced at Emanuel. Certainly he'll find a good excuse to take one of the boys, she thought. Her mouth almost dropped when Emanuel nodded, setting his napkin on his plate. *"Ja vell,* I'll be ready as soon as I harness the horse."

Twenty minutes later, Shana found herself in Emanuel's buggy, a blanket over their legs and an apple pie on her lap. They rode in silence with only the steady pulse of the horse's hooves to break up the monotony. The night air chilled her blood, although the pounding of Shana's heart kept her warm. I don't even know Miriam Smucker, Shana thought as she stared out the windshield, nodding at the passing buggy.

"Cold?"

"No," she replied softly.

The silence hovered over them for a few uncomfortable minutes. After they were on the road and away from the farm, Emanuel slowed the trotting horse down to a walk. He glanced at Shana before he cleared his throat. "You've been busy at work."

Ja, she thought to herself before she replied with a simple "Yes."

"Not even one day off for the past few weeks. It's good you have vacation now."

Again, she agreed with a simple, "Yes."

Another moment of silence fell between them. She could tell that he had something he wanted to say but he seemed to be struggling with how to say it. He hesitated, clearing his throat before he announced, "My parents are pressuring me to take my baptism this fall."

Shana gasped as she realized what he was actually saying. "Take your baptism?" She turned to stare at him. "Why, Emanuel, you've never been baptized?"

He laughed nervously. "Better to never take the vow than to take it and break it."

"Then you aren't Amish!" Children of the Amish were never truly Amish until they took their baptism. If they never made the promise to obey the Amish church, they could not be shunned for doing non-Amish things, including buying cars or using electricity or socializing with the Englische. In fact, Amish youth were encouraged to participate in a period of time called *rumschpringe*, a period of time when they were permitted to explore the world prior to making the decision to join the church. Shana hadn't realized that Emanuel hadn't been baptized and was, in fact, in his *rumschpringe*. "Why didn't you tell me?"

"Is it that important?"

"Well, I thought that..." She stopped, hesitant about telling him the truth of her feelings.

He laughed again, the nervousness gone from his laughter. She could tell that he was pleased with her concern that he had stepped outside the faith by that simple kiss that had lingered in both of their minds. "A commitment so great as baptism into the Amish faith is not something I should wish to make in haste." His laughter faded and he boldly enclosed his hand over hers. "Shana," he said, his voice soft but strong. "Is that the reason you have been working so hard? Did you think I had broken my vow?" He did not wait for her answer. "I find that very admirable. But now that your conscience is cleared, you must not hide in your work." He hesitated, slowing the horse down again, pausing to glance at her. "Or from me."

At the Smucker's farm, Shana noticed a growing energy in Emanuel's step. He helped her down from the buggy, his hand gently squeezing hers as he disappeared into the barn to find

Amos while Shana, still getting over the shock from his announcement, carried the homemade apple pie into the farmhouse where Miriam Smucker, a robust woman in her mid-forties, greeted Shana with a warm hello, took the pie and thanked her. Shana soon found herself seated at the table with Miriam. They talked about the harvest and the upcoming Sunday at the Lapp farm. Miriam's pleasant conversation blurred together and Shana barely heard one word. Instead, she thought about Emanuel.

It was almost an hour later before Emanuel came into the house to fetch her. Two young heifer cows were tied to the back of his buggy. Shana paused to scratch the one's neck before she waved good-bye to Miriam and let Emanuel help her inside. Before they started down the road, Emanuel spared her a reassuring smile then slapped the reins against Lucky Monday's back. As the buggy lurched forward, Shana jerked against Emanuel's arm. He steadied her with a soft hand before slipping his hand beneath the blanket and giving her hand a quick squeeze. And suddenly, the ten days that she had been dreading on the farm didn't seem as though they'd be long enough.

Chapter Eight

For the rest of her vacation, Shana spent her days helping Katie prepare for the upcoming Sunday church service; and her evenings in Emanuel's company. Whether Katie knew of Emanuel's secret liaison, Shana never really knew. In the morning, shortly after she heard the men harnessing the mules for a day in the fields, she'd hurry out of her house, usually in time to sneak a smile and a wave at Emanuel, then headed for the farmhouse.

During the sunny days, Katie put Shana to work outside, weeding the garden and the flowerbeds. Shana didn't mind the isolation since the hot sun warmed her back and soul, even if she wondered whether Katie assigned her the outside chores to keep the Englischer out of her way. But Shana liked being able to sit in the grass and smell the freshly cut hay. She'd often gaze out into the field, her eyes seeking the silhouettes of the men on top of the hill, Emanuel behind the mules and the boys trailing behind. Sometimes she imagined that, perhaps, she might have caught him at a moment when he, too, was searching for her figure, crouched over the flowerbeds as she weeded.

During that week, Shana spent every night at the Lapp's house for the evening meal. As the women prepared the meal, Shana would catch herself continually glancing out the window, hoping to see the men retreating from the barn; and, each night, she tried to avoid appearing too friendly toward Emanuel when he followed the rest of the men into the house, just after the milking. Yet, his eyes always sought hers and she hoped that no one else noticed that his baby blues seemed to twinkle just a little more than usual whenever she was around.

Most evenings following supper, shortly after Shana had

helped clean up and bid everyone goodnight, Emanuel would emerge from around the corner of the barn, either driving the buggy or riding Lucky Monday. He'd stop at Shana's door and knock, patiently waiting for her to answer. Then, when she appeared in the open doorway, he'd take a step back and ask her to accompany him, either for a made-up errand into town or a brisk ride in the cornfields.

On the evenings they rode around the fields, Shana sat in front of Emanuel on Lucky Monday's back. Emanuel wrapped his arms tightly around her waist, holding the reins firmly in his hands. She'd lean against his chest, her hands often resting lightly on top of his. His warm breath on the back of her neck excited her as did his strong arms wrapped so protectively around her. Gradually, she found herself yearning for more than his proper goodnight kisses.

When her vacation was over, so were the nightly rides after supper. At work, her mind wandered back to the pleasant talks she shared with Emanuel or to his self-controlled kisses. If she longed for more, she never pushed him. Indeed, she found herself racing home early, hoping to just spend some time with Emanuel, talking on the front porch. On the nights she managed to break away from the restaurant early, always he would appear as if he stood in the shadows, waiting for her arrival. The nights grew colder but still, they sat on her porch, sharing secrets and dreams.

"I always wanted to live in the country," she once confided in Emanuel. The cows stomped through the paddock as they clamored to the troughs of hay. "I love the animals and the peacefulness. It's so unlike my life at the restaurant."

"How is your work?"

She shrugged her shoulders. "Work is...work. My review is

next week. I doubt I'll make the promotion." If she felt any remorse, she didn't show it. "The best week of my life was when I helped Katie prepare for that Sunday church. At night, I went to bed and realized that all the work I did that day was important and appreciated. We worked hard and it showed. Unlike the restaurant, where the results take weeks, sometimes months to show."

"Planting takes a season to show. Raising a cow or a horse takes time."

Shana smiled even though he couldn't see her in the darkness. "That's different. I'm talking about weeding the garden. Afterwards, you can feel good about a job well accomplished. Or baking a pie for the family. Your mother knows that the pie she makes will be eaten that night. She also hears how much everyone enjoys it."

Emanuel frowned. "Such little things to take pride in yet they mean so much. She is deaf to the compliments, Shana. All she hears is that the blueberries God grew in her garden tasted fresh. Her only pride is seeing her children grow up Amish and join the church."

For a long moment, they both fell silent. They both wondered how Katie and Jonas felt about the extra attention their eldest bachelor son showed toward Shana. As much as Shana and Emanuel tried to hide their clandestine friendship from his family, the attention as well as the affection was too obvious to have gone unnoticed. Certainly by now his parents feared that Emanuel's baptism would never occur. Perhaps that was the reason for their increased pressure on him to decide.

A cool autumn breeze blew. Shana shivered and drew her jacket closer around her neck. Emanuel glanced at the sky, seeing the clouds covering the moon. "Soon it will be too cold for our talks, Shana."

She understood what that meant. It was improper for Emanuel to enter her house and when the cold weather came, they could not sit outside. "Then what?" she asked, her worried eyes searching his. The thought of not being able to share her daily events with Emanuel depressed her. On the nights when she worked the closing shift, she often came home and stood outside on her porch, staring at the massive shadow of the farmhouse and wondering if Emanuel's dreams were about her.

Emanuel met her gaze. She sought the answer from him. Sighing, he gently squeezed her hand. "We will find a way. Now, I must retire for the evening. You go inside before you catch a cold." He leaned over and gently kissed her cheek before he stood and helped her to her feet. "Good night, Shana," he whispered before he disappeared into the darkness.

For the next three days, they did not see each other. Shana closed the restaurant each night, the usual sparkle in her eyes gone. Her employees noticed the change in their favorite manager but no one dared question it. Instead, they avoided the quiet Shana and went about their work. The day of her review came and, to Shana's surprise and ...disappointment, it went much better than she had anticipated.

She sat in the booth with Jack and Robert, listening to them reiterate all that she had accomplished over the past few months. Then, with a broad smile, Jack leaned back in his chair. "Seeing how well you've handled everything, we've decided to transfer you with a minor promotion to a more challenging store in South Philly."

If Jack's announcement was supposed to please Shana, it

failed. A transfer meant relocation and relocation to South Philadelphia meant leaving the peacefulness of the Lapp farm. Five months ago, she might have jumped at the opportunity. But now, with her growing feelings toward Emanuel and their friendship, the thought of leaving Lancaster County was the furthest thing from her mind.

Shana stared at both men before she leaned back, scratched the side of her nose, and shook her head. "I cannot agree to that immediately. I'll need a couple of days to think it over." Her reluctance to accept their offer shocked both men but they only nodded their heads, giving Shana the weekend off so that she had time to consider their offer.

She arrived home that evening at six. The sky was dark but the kerosene lamp still flickered from the kitchen window in the Lapp house. Shana parked her car and hurried through the bitter cold air to her house. She warmed some leftovers in the oven, wondering if Emanuel would visit. By the time she had changed out of her work clothes and sat at the table to eat, she heard his light knock at the door. Quickly running her fingers through her loose hair, she walked to the door and tossed it open.

"Home for the evening?" he asked.

A smile lit up her face. She leaned against the doorframe and held the door open with her hand. "Two day vacation," she said.

"I see." He glanced up at the sky. "Nice night."

Shana wondered why he was acting so proper and distant. "Indeed."

"There's a fair in New Holland tonight."

"Is there? I hadn't heard."

Emanuel shuffled his feet, glancing over his shoulder

toward the barn. "You've been working so I must've forgotten to mention it. Brother Steve and I are in the rope pull. Thought you might want to take a ride out there."

Delighted, Shana could hardly hide her enthusiasm. "Sounds like fun."

"Ja," he replied. From the other side of the barn, the dog began barking and the kitchen door slammed shut. Emanuel cracked his knuckles, avoiding Shana's eyes. "Thought maybe you could pick up Steve's girl, too."

In the four months Shana had been living on the Lapp's farm, Emanuel had never asked her to drive him anywhere. Usually they took his horse and buggy out, snuggling under a lap blanket, sometimes holding hands. "That sounds fine. Just come get me when you're ready to go." He nodded and walked away, his head bowed over and his hands stuffed into his pockets. For several minutes, Shana stood in the doorway, wondering what was so heavy on his mind.

Half an hour later, Steve and Emanuel were waiting for her by her small sports car. Shana unlocked the door for them, suddenly nervous about driving with Emanuel. She always felt so secure and protected whenever he drove the buggy. She had grown used to his being in control. She liked leaning on him for support and wisdom. Now, she was the one being leaned on, even if for something as simple as picking up Steve's girlfriend across town.

In silence, they picked up Liddy May and drove over to the fair. Shana noticed how quiet Steve and his girl talked, when they talked, with their heads bowed close together and their voices soft murmurs. Their conversations were short and to the point, mostly about church and the harvest. How different they are from

Emanuel and I, she thought. Then, she suddenly wondered what Emanuel's family thought about her relationship with their son. Certainly they didn't consider Shana to be Emanuel's "girl." What did they consider her?

The fairgrounds, large for such a small town, were packed with people. Shana found a parking space as close to the front lot as possible. Then, zippering her black leather jacket, she braced herself for the cold October night. She walked close to Emanuel, wishing he'd put his arm around her but knowing he wouldn't. Steve and Liddy May kept a proper distance from each other, probably shocked at Shana's boldness. Finally, at the corner of the fairgrounds, Emanuel squeezed Shana's arm then disappeared with Steve into the crowd. Left alone with Liddy May, Shana quickly sized up the quiet Amish girl. She looked not more than sixteen, although Shana knew she was older. Her skin was clear and her complexion rosy, almost like a plain little china doll.

Liddy May's dark eyes stared uneasily at Shana. "I suppose we should go stand by the rope pulling area if we want to catch a good view."

Shana nodded and followed Liddy May through the crowd. Emanuel and Steve had joined their teammates near the announcement stand. Shana caught a glimpse of Emanuel but, with all the people shoving past her, she quickly lost sight of him. So, content with Liddy May, Shana waited patiently for the rope-pulling event to start.

It was almost an hour later before the men began to crowd into the blocked off area. Shana and Liddy May shivered in the cold, straining to see Emanuel or Steve. The announcer clicked on the microphone and said a quick "One, two, testing." Satisfied that it was properly working, he looked around the crowd. "Welcome to New Holland's annual rope-pulling contest!" The crowd cheered. "Tonight, we have our finalists: Teams from Bird-in-Hand, Goodvale, Farmersville, Intercourse, and Blue Ball will compete against each other for the championship!" The crowd roared. Shana jumped as a small crowd of Mennonite girls behind her screamed.

The rope-pulling officials unraveled a long and thick rope down the middle of the street. In the center of the rope was a piece of white tape. One of the officials set the portion of the rope with the tape on it over a white line in the street. The first two teams piled into the area, one team on either side of the rope.

Disappointed because Emanuel's team wasn't on first, Shana turned to Liddy May. "What are they suppose to do?"

Liddy May, equally disappointed, explained, "One team has to pull the other team's rope over that white line. Last night, there were ten teams. Tonight, whoever beats two teams is the champion."

"What do they win?"

"Fifty dollars goes to the town's fire department."

While the stakes didn't thrill Shana, the sudden blast of a whistle and the roar of the crowd did. She looked back at the men, ten on either side of the rope. They pulled, leaning as far back as they could. "Lord! They look as though they're going to topple over!" Shana exclaimed. Liddy May laughed at her.

The Blue Ball team slid along the pavement, quickly crossing the line. The next two teams were Bird-in-Hand and Intercourse. Shana and Liddy May perched on the curb, joining the dozen of screaming Bird-in-Hand fans. They yelled and screamed, watching as the ten men leaned back, their arms wrapped around the thick rope, and their muscles bulging out of their arms. After thirty seconds, the Bird-in-Hand team won. Goodvale played

Farmersville, then Intercourse against Blue Ball. Forty minutes later, Bird-in-Hand played for the championship title against Goodvale.

This time, Shana and Liddy May fought the crowd until they were standing on the edge of the crowd near the Bird-in-Hand team. Emanuel and Steve, both in the rear, wrapped their arms around the rope. They leaned back with the other men, their feet planted firmly on the ground, and, when the official tweeted his whistle, they pulled. Shana held her breath, urging them on as loudly as her voice allowed. Both teams pulled, one slowly sliding toward the line then the other losing their ground. After two minutes and seventeen seconds, Bird-in-Hand crossed the line. The crowd cheered but, disappointed, Shana didn't.

After the awards were handed out to the three placing teams, the crowd moved further down the road for the Women's Bucket Brigade, another contest sponsored for the benefit of the various local fire companies. Shana stood with Liddy May, waiting patiently for Steve and Emanuel to appear. Neither looked half as disappointed as Shana had felt earlier.

"We placed second, Shana," Emanuel announced. He held up the small wood and brass plaque with a fire hat engraved on front.

"I saw." She took the plaque, carefully handling it as she read "Bird-in-Hand's Annual Tug-o-War's Second Place Winner." A fingerprint smug over the fire hat caught her attention and she wiped it away with the edge of her skirt. "Did you hurt your hands?"

He stretched out his hands and looked at his palms. "Just a little burn." He showed her the brilliant red insides of his hands. "I'll live," he teased in his quiet, gentle manner.

The main street of New Holland, temporarily transported into a colorful, vivacious carnival, seemed loud and rowdy for Shana. In God's country, she had grown accustomed to the quiet tranquility and peacefulness of the Amish. The gentle sounds of the farm and the people who lived there had spoiled her appreciation for the lights and noise. Together, they fought the crowds, most of the passing people casting curious glances at the Amish man with the Englische woman at his side.

As Emanuel and Shana walked through, several men called out to "Step right up and try your luck at the..." Emanuel kept walking. Several times, he had to stop, retrace his steps, and wait for a curious Shana. Occasionally, she did try her luck at various games. At the dart booth, Shana's fourth game, Emanuel stood patiently by Shana's side, watching as she carelessly threw her darts at the red star hanging on the cork board in back of the booth. Instead of hitting it, all three darts fell in a scattered pile on the floor.

The game over, Shana pouted as she turned to Emanuel. "I wanted one of those cute bears," she playfully whined.

"Which one?" he asked. She pointed to a large brown bear with a pink nose and tongue. Emanuel sighed, digging into his pockets for a wrinkled dollar bill. Shana stepped back to make room as Emanuel slapped the dollar on the counter.

"Three darts, please." He took the three darts the attendant handed him. "How many darts have to hit the star for that bear?"

Bored, the man held up his two fingers then looked over Emanuel's head as two pretty farm girls walked by. Emanuel glanced at Shana, shrugged his shoulders, and then turned back to the game. He held the one dart between his fingers, aimed, and carefully threw the dart into the center of the star. Shana clapped her hands and cheered him on. The second dart hit the upper point of the star and the third dart landed just below the first one. The attendant handed Emanuel the bear. "Can also have any one of the mirrors down there."

Emanuel leaned forward, staring at the line of square mirrors. Finally, he pointed to one with a black stallion decal in the middle. "That one," he said. The attendant grabbed the mirror and thrust it into Emanuel's hands. He thanked the man whose attention was already diverted to two teenagers with shorts leaning against the booth. Emanuel shrugged and showed the mirror to Shana. "For David," he said.

Clutching her bear, Shana smiled at Emanuel. "Thank you," she whispered into his ear.

He replied by squeezing her hand. Then, he glanced around the crowd. "We better find Steve and Liddy May. It's close to ten by now."

The car ride back to Liddy May's was quiet and peaceful. Shana had the impression that Emanuel wanted to talk with her alone but, not having the opportunity, stared solemnly out the car window. Steve and Liddy May sat next to each other in the back of the car, neither speaking until they drove up Liddy May's lane. "You coming to fetch me after church?"

Glancing in her rearview mirror, Shana saw Steve nod. "Ja. The singing's at James' so I'll be over earlier than usual."

Liddy May leaned forward, touching Emanuel's shoulder. "You coming, too?"

Squirming in his seat, Emanuel shrugged off her hand. "Haven't decided yet," he answered.

Shana pulled into Liddy May's driveway and bade her goodnight. While Steve walked his girlfriend to the door, Shana turned to Emanuel. "There's a singing tomorrow night? Why aren't you going?" she asked, taking advantage of the few minutes alone with Emanuel. He didn't answer. "Is it because of me?" Shana asked. While she had accompanied him to several social events, she knew a singing after church was strictly for Amish youths, especially since the songs were sung in Pennsylvania Dutch or German. Emanuel's silence confirmed Shana's fear but she didn't question him further as Steve returned to the car.

At the Lapp farm, Shana dropped both men off by the farmhouse. Emanuel thanked her while Steve thrust money into her hand. Quickly, Shana pushed the money back at him. "Don't be silly," she said. "That's what friends are for." She noticed the askance look Steve gave her but, politely thanking her, he shut the car door. Both men walked into the house. Shana watched Emanuel, his head hung low and his shoulders hunched over, until the kitchen door shut behind him.

Chapter Nine

Shana hadn't heard the buggies leaving in the morning for church. When she awoke, they had already left. In the solitude of the farm, she spent the day wandering around her small house and the farm, thinking about a decision concerning her job and Emanuel. To take the promotion meant leaving the Lapp farm and that meant she would not see Emanuel anymore. She had come to depend on his friendship and she found her thoughts constantly drifting to him whenever they were apart. Yet, she had gone through college to have a successful career and she couldn't see throwing away everything she had worked for.

Early in the morning, she ventured into the dusty attic, the stairs creaking under her weight. Boxes and crates were piled around old furniture and trunks. She let curiosity get the best of her as she poked through the old, tattered clothing and books. She wiped the cobwebs off a faceless child's doll and, cradling it as she tried to imagine how many girls had loved this doll, pretended it was a real child nestled in their arms. She shut her eyes, trying to imagine what it would be like to be an Amish woman, dedicating her life to caring for her husband and raising a family. Then, ashamed of herself, she tossed it back into the trunk and hurried downstairs.

Around noon, she had driven along the country roads to clear her head. Yet, everywhere she looked was a constant reminder of what she tried so hard to forget. Farms, horses, cows, even a small, man-made pond with a patch of daisies nearby. She drove past one farm with over fifty buggies parked by the barn, apparently where the local Amish district was meeting for services. For a long moment, she sat in her car, staring down at the gray-topped buggies. She wondered whether the Lapp family was worshipping at this particular farm. Shutting her eyes, she sat in the car and tried imagining how it felt to sit in the barn for three hours, listening and feeling the gospel of the Bible. But, the image never entered her mind and, feeling no better than she had before, she eased the gearshift into first and drove on.

When she finally returned home, the Lapp's buggies were in the driveway. The dog barked at a brown striped cat sleeping in the sun by the nearest buggy. Shana glanced at the farmhouse, quiet as usual, before she hurried into her own house. As she shut the door, the evening cold touched her and, shivering, she hurried over to the kerosene heater and clicked it on. It glowed orange, small amounts of heat quickly warming her outstretched hands. For the rest of the day, Shana lounged on the sofa by the heater and read the local Sunday paper that she had picked up at a nearby convenience store. But, the words blurred together and not even the black and white pictures caught her attention. Setting the paper down on her chest, Shana shut her eyes and let an uneasy sleep calm her.

After a short nap, she awoke to a door slamming. Sitting up, she glanced around sleepily. The sun was setting, casting shadows through her lacy window curtains. She looked up at the old, wooden clock over the sink: 6:45pm. Startled at the time, she forced herself to get up and fix herself some supper. While her supper simmered on the oven, a buggy rolled down the lane. The wheels creaked as it turned around the barn. For a brief moment, Shana held her breath. She waited, her hand motionless on the handle of the wooden spoon, but no one knocked at her door. Then she realized it must've been Steve off to fetch Liddy May for the singing.

She had just finished washing her supper dishes when she

heard Jonas barking an order to one of his younger sons. Shana glanced out the window, wondering if Emanuel was helping with the milking. The cows stood in the paddock, some swaying back and forth, their bony rumps hitting the cows next to them. Daniel, David and Samuel were busy pitching hay into their troughs. They didn't speak to each other and their faces seemed solemn in the silence as they worked. Not seeing Emanuel, Shana let the curtain fall back.

It was almost nine o'clock when Emanuel finally knocked at the door. She could tell it was him by the two short, quick raps that echoed against the closed door. Shutting the book she had been staring at without reading for the past half an hour, Shana sat up and looked at the door. Her heart pounded, as she contemplated not answering his knock. But, when he knocked again, she set the book aside and got up.

He wore his Sunday outfit, his head covered with his black felt hat. "I need to talk to you, Shana," he said, his tone as soft as usual. Yet, there was urgency in his voice and a strain in his eyes. "Put on a jacket and let's go for a drive."

Without questioning his demand, Shana reached behind the door for her long winter jacket and hurried outside. He helped her inside the buggy before he climbed in beside her and shut the door. Carefully, he wrapped a thick, black winter blanket over her lap.

"Comfortable, ja?" he asked. She answered with a serious nod. Then, he slapped the reins against Lucky Monday's back and the buggy lurched forward, slowly rolling down the lane toward the road. He stared straight ahead. "I hadn't asked before about your review yesterday."

"I got the transfer and the promotion." She noticed his grip on the horse's reins tighten and the muscles in his jaw twitched. Then, she slowly added, "I told them I needed to think about it." She waited until he looked at her. "I thought about it, Emanuel, and I've decided to refuse."

He nodded once. Then, for a long while, he did not reply. They drove up the hill and Emanuel turned the buggy down another dimly lit road. The horse's hooves gently clippity-clopped against the macadam, the noise soothing Shana as she leaned back, her hands warming under the blanket. The silence frightened her and with each unspoken minute that passed, her heart pounded fiercer within her chest. A car sped past and Lucky Monday lifted her head. Shana watched as the red taillights of the car faded down the road before them. Eventually, the motor was just a low roar and the lights a faded memory.

Finally, Emanuel cleared his throat as he slowed the horse on the dark road situated between two empty cornfields. "Soon is the fall baptism." He looked at her, his eyes clouded with worry. She had never seen him this serious, this intense before. Her heart pounded harder and she almost wondered if he could hear it over his next words. "I've told my parents that I am not going for my baptism this fall." He hesitated before he spoke his next words, staring straight ahead again. "Nor will I ever."

Shana felt goose bumps on her arms and legs. "I...I see," she managed to say.

"I could never leave the Amish way of life. I was raised to believe in certain things, things I've done all my life." He raised the reins to make his point as he continued talking, "Like driving a horse and buggy. I have an inner peace in being Amish, of working hard, and believing in God."

The goose bumps faded away. "So why are you refusing

baptism?"

"I cannot make a commitment that great when I am not certain I can abide by all of the traditions of the Ordnung." Emanuel took a deep breath, as though his words exhausted him. "And because of you." He refused to meet her frightened gaze. "When you first moved onto my father's farm, I thought you were a beautiful woman." He quickly added, "I still do." Then he paused, as though searching for the right words. "We've become good friends, Shana. More than friends in many ways but we're good friends above all." He chewed on his lower lip as he contemplated his thoughts. "You've continually impressed me. Hard working, strong, loyal, and fun. These are what a man looks for in a woman." He leaned forward to turn on his blinker. Stopping at the corner of Groffdale Road and Scenic Drive, he looked both ways before he turned right. "I will always be a farmer, Shana."

Suddenly feeling lightheaded, Shana leaned against the side of the buggy, staring at him. He was waiting for a response. But she wasn't certain what he wanted her to reply. Swallowing, she finally said, "There is nothing wrong with being a farmer, Emanuel."

"Ja," he agreed. Then, he took a deep breath, hesitated, then asked, "But do you believe you could leave your world to be..." He glanced at her. "*Vell*...to be a farmer's wife."

For a moment, she did not say anything. A farmer's wife, she repeated to herself. How many nights had she laid awake in bed, staring at that lonely crack in the ceiling as she asked herself that very question? She had watched Katie and wondered if, in twenty-five years, that would be her. Yet, she had never thought that Emanuel would be seated next to her, his face pale in the dim glow from the moon and stars as he awaited her response to that anticipated question. Shana felt the color drain from her own face as well.

Again, he cleared his throat, sounding more certain of himself. "In late October, we could marry."

"In October?"

Suddenly, Emanuel stopped the buggy and turned to her. He grabbed her hands and stared into her bewildered eyes. "I want to marry you, Shana. You are the most exciting woman I've ever met." He paused as though ashamed of his confession before he softly continued. "My tenant's lease runs out the first week in October, and now that I've told my parents I intend to refuse my baptism, it would be best to leave their house. I want you to come with me." Again, he paused. "But I want you to come with me as my wife."

Shana stared at him, her lips slightly parted. "As your wife," she repeated softly, her heart fluttering within her chest.

Emanuel didn't let Shana say anything else as he pressed his lips gently against hers, the kiss slowly releasing all the passion they had hidden for the past months. Warmth flooded through her body and she felt as though everything was surreal, not happening. As he kissed her, his arm around her shoulder and pressing her tight against his chest, she relaxed and responded with everything that she felt in her heart. And, as she melted against him, they both knew what her answer would be.

When Emanuel finally pulled away, he smoothed her hair back from her face and smiled shyly. "October it is, then?"

"That's so soon," she whispered, afraid to break the magical spell of the moment.

Emanuel nodded. "Ja. Four weeks from last Thursday." He urged on Lucky Monday. Under the blanket, he clutched her hand while, with his other, he held the reins. "I'll have to ride out to the house and tell my tenants the news. As soon as I fix everything up, we'll marry and move in."

"What about your parents?" she asked softly.

"My parents? They are aware of my decision, Shana." He hesitated before he added, "Soon they will get over it and things will return to normal. In four weeks, we'll be married. One of the Mennonite ministers will perform the ceremony and my family will have a small supper for us afterwards."

"What about me?"

Emanuel ran his fingers through his tousled, curly hair, clearing his throat as he quietly said, "You'll have to leave your job."

She realized that she'd have to quit her job but the reality was suddenly hitting her. In four weeks, she would become someone's wife. For the rest of her life, she would probably live on the same land in the same house and certainly with the same man. She would, indeed, be a farmer's wife. "I don't know if I'll be able to do nothing all day, Emanuel."

He laughed nervously. "Being a farmer's wife won't be easy, Shana, nor boring. Come spring, you'll have a vegetable garden to tend. Plus, cleaning, mending, shopping, cooking, and washing. You'll have plenty to do."

For a moment, the thought sank deep into her stomach. In all her life, she had seen herself attempting many different things; domestication had never been one of them. But, as Emanuel stared at her, she knew that she could never work in a restaurant for the rest of her life. If I have to do something forever, she thought, loving Emanuel will be the easiest and most rewarding. "It's going to take me some time to adapt, Emanuel."

"I know that."

"You'll have to be patient with me."

"I know that, too."

"I'm scared of failing you."

He brushed his fingers along her cheek, admiring the softness of her translucent skin. "You won't."

"I do love you, Emanuel," she whispered.

They rode in silence until they returned to the farm. Shana stood in the stable while Emanuel unharnessed Lucky Monday. Stroking the horse's nose, Emanuel stared thoughtfully at Lucky Monday. Then, he turned to look at Shana. In the darkness of the stable, she could not see his expression, but she heard the catch in his voice. "We should tell my parents that you've agreed." Together, they walked up the dark path to the house.

The gas lamp in the kitchen burned bright as Emanuel opened the porch door. Shana followed him, aware of the two pairs of eyes waiting for Emanuel to speak. Emanuel glanced at his parents, both seated on the hard benches and facing each other. His mother stared ahead, her eyes swollen and red. His father's face was taunt and pale. Shana stood in the shadow of the doorway, her heart breaking as she saw the pain in the faces of her future in-laws.

Emanuel stood silently by the old cast iron wood stove, his fingers toying with the blue and white speckled kettle on the closest burner. Katie exhaled loudly, raising her eyes to the ceiling as she said a German prayer. Emanuel lowered his head in respect, waiting patiently. The prayer finished, Katie looked at Shana. "You're taking my boy away, aren't you?" Upon hearing his wife's words, Jonas shut his eyes, folded his hands and lowered his head. Katie gave a stiff nod as she said, "I saw it coming. Can't say I'm surprised anyhow." Then, she stood up and, shoulders hunched over, walked out of the kitchen.

Jonas did not speak but sat at the table, his hands still folded before him and his own German prayer escaping his lips. Emanuel lowered his head again, listening respectfully to his father's words. Then, the prayer finished, Jonas stood and faced his son. "Let us not pray for lighter burdens but stronger backs." He, too, left the kitchen.

The dog barked outside. Emanuel glanced out the kitchen window. A buggy stopped outside the stable. He looked at the grandfather clock in the corner by Jonas' favorite green chair. It read eleven-fifteen. "Must be Steve, back from the singing." He turned to Shana. She hadn't moved from the doorway, her face deathly pale. He reached for her hand and gave it a reassuring squeeze. "I'll walk you home."

Outside, the fresh, cold air caught in Shana's throat. She fought the rush of tears brimming in her eyes. Taking a deep breath, she tried to relax. She knew she should be happy, brimming with love for the future that she would share with Emanuel.   But the sorrowful look on Katie's face and the somberness of Jonas' words haunted her. When she began to cry, Emanuel stopped walking and took her into his arms. They stood on the shadow of the barn until her quiet sobs ceased. The dog barked again as Steve walked from the stable to the house, unaware of Emanuel and Shana's presence in the darkness.

When the porch door slammed shut, Emanuel released Shana and wiped her tears away with his fingers. He tried to smile, to reassure her that it would be all right. "You shouldn't cry, Shana. This is supposed to be a happy time."

"They looked as though you had died! They'll never forgive me for this!" she sobbed.

"In a way, I have died. But there is nothing to forgive," he tried to explain. "My refusal to become a baptized member hurts them because they believe it reflects my upbringing. But, Shana, they will get over it." He tilted her chin and lovingly kissed her lips. Her tears stopped and her lips parted, receiving the warmth of his kiss. His arms held her tightly and the tenderness of his kiss calmed her. When he finally lifted his lips off of hers, he gave her a reassuring smile. "Now, you must get yourself a good-night sleep as must I. I'm helping Daed fill the silo tomorrow. And tomorrow night, I must ride out to my tenants."

At the porch of her house, she let him kiss her again. She shut the door and locked it after Emanuel had wished her good-night. He was right, she thought. This is supposed to be the happiest time of my life. Turning off the kitchen light, she climbed the narrow staircase to her bedroom. For a long while, she sat on the edge of her bed, staring at her bare ring finger. There would be no engagement ring or wedding announcements. Just a simple ceremony and a quiet supper. In less than four weeks, I will become Emanuel Lapp's wife, she thought as she undressed. The smile faded from her face as she remembered Katie and Jonas' reaction. That night, their faces lingered in her dreams.

Chapter Ten

Shana clutched the basket of food Katie had given her when they left the Lapp house only forty minutes before. The simple gold band on her finger felt awkward. She glanced at it, noticing how shiny and new it looked. She twisted it with her thumb. Her eyes drifted to Emanuel's hands, holding the horse's reins as the buggy rolled down the road toward their new lives together. While the Amish frowned upon jewelry, Shana had insisted that they both wear wedding rings. It was a piece of her culture that she refused to give up. Reluctantly, Emanuel had relented, knowing that such a little sacrifice on his part would not hurt.

The ceremony had been performed on the front yard of the Lapp house by a pastor from a nearby Old Order Mennonite church. Shana, dressed in a simple pale blue dress with a white apron, typical of the Amish style, had stood by Emanuel's side, holding his hand tightly in hers.

The pastor had placed his hands on their clasped hands as he said, "The ordinance of Christian wedlock has been spoken. Having heard them, are you, Emanuel Lapp, willing to enter wedlock with Shana Slater as, in the beginning of time, God commanded? Before the Lord and this church, do you promise your wedded wife that you will never depart from her and will care for her, guiding her spiritually through life and in any circumstance in which, as a Christian husband, you are responsible to care for your wife until the Lord separates you?"

"Yes," Emanuel said, his voice raspy and hoarse.

The pastor had smiled as he turned to Shana. "Shana, are you willing to enter wedlock with Emanuel Lapp..." he started as he repeated the same vows.

Shana had hesitated long enough to glance up at Emanuel. He squeezed her hand and she took a deep breath as she replied, "Yes." And they were married.

Afterwards, the newly wedded couple shared their first meal with over two hundred of Emanuel's relatives. Shana felt lost in the introduction of all of her new uncles and aunts and cousins and finally gave up on remembering anyone's name. For once, the women insisted that Shana meet her new family while they worked in the kitchen on the simple but pleasant wedding meal of cooked ham and roasted chicken with mashed potatoes, coleslaw, chow-chow, celery, bread, and plenty of freshly baked pies. With so many people to serve, the family ate in shifts, with the newlyweds enjoying the first serving. After they ate, the rest of the family, from oldest to youngest, found their chance to sit at the tables in the Lapp house for their meal.

While the family appeared joyous for Emanuel's sake, Shana knew that it was hard for everyone to accept a non-Amish woman into their family. The hurt was still obvious. Jonas had stood alone most of the evening, avoiding all contact with his son's bride. Shana had stuck by Lillian's side while Emanuel talked with his uncles and male cousins. Emanuel's aunts smiled pleasantly at Shana, some talking to her about different recipes or what awaited her in her new life on Emanuel's farm.

Finally, to both Shana's relief and dismay, when the meal was over and the younger, unmarried adults had disappeared to the barn to play games, Emanuel signaled Shana that it was time to leave for their hour ride back to his farm. The rest of the family bid them farewell. No hugging, no tears. Just a simple "May God bless you" and the celebration was over. Shana was glad to leave the tenseness of the celebration but knew that, in doing so, she would be starting a new journey. For the first time, they'd be alone as man and wife and she couldn't deny being nervous about that.

For the past four weeks, she had rarely seen Emanuel. After working all day, he disappeared at night, fixing up the farmhouse so, after the wedding, he could bring his young bride home. One evening, he had taken her with him. Together, they had walked hand-in-hand across the bare fields and brown pastures in the dying light of the day, talking about their future lives together, the crops they would plant and harvest, and the herd of cows they would raise. But the air was cold with winter threatening to show its force so they had retreated back to the buggy after Shana had a quick, initial assessment of her future home.

Now, an outline of their farmhouse and barn forming on the horizon, Shana felt her stomach twist into knots again. The small brown river that cut the fields in half had dried up from lack of rain. The fields were empty, last year's crops having been harvested only three weeks prior. The entire barn had been freshly painted, except for the black trim which was chipping around the doors and windows. On this day, while everything appeared familiar, the small farm was no longer a place in her future. This is my home, she thought as Emanuel turned the buggy into the long driveway. Our home, she quickly corrected.

Emanuel stopped the buggy outside of the barn. Unlike the Lapp farm, there was no dog to bark a greeting or cats lazing around the early fading sun. Emanuel slid back the buggy door and got out, the buggy jiggling under his shifting weight. He reached up to help Shana down, holding her hand for a moment before he reached for the basket. Neither spoke, each wrapped in their private world of thoughts as Shana followed Emanuel to the two-story farmhouse with the wrap-around porch. He unlocked the kitchen door then held it open for Shana. She hesitated, wondering if she should mention the non-Amish tradition of carrying the bride over the threshold. Noticing his serious expression, she quickly decided against it and simply walked into the kitchen.

The tenants had moved out two weeks prior to their wedding day. In that time, Emanuel had repainted the main rooms inside the house. The kitchen's walls were sky blue. On the wall over the water pump was a pretty country calendar. The four windows were covered with simple dark green shades, each pulled down halfway. Shana looked around, amazed that this was now her kitchen. No longer would she have to work outside of their farm, she realized. Instead, she would spend the rest of her life in her own kitchen, preparing meals for her own family, rather than complete strangers. She'd care for her home, plant her own garden, and help Emanuel during harvest-time in the fields. This was her new job and her new office, she realized.

Emanuel set the basket on the counter. The quiet echoed in their ears. He watched as Shana started taking the food out. Her hands trembled and she did not meet his gaze. The ring on her finger caught a glimmer of sunlight. Reaching out, Emanuel took her hand in his and held it for a minute. When she finally looked at him, he smiled. "Plenty of time for putting things away, ja?" She nodded. "There's a present for you in the living room," he said quietly.

Together, they walked into the living room. He had taken down the partition that separated the living room from the kitchen. Since he could never be baptized in the Amish faith with a non-Amish wife, there was no reason to keep the living room closed off for those annual Sunday sermons that they would not be hosting in their non-Amish house.

In the living room, there was a simple sofa and a rocking chair. The walls gleamed from the fresh coat of beige paint. The windows overlooked the fields, which, come spring, would ripple with young, green corn. As her eyes adjusted to the shadows, she scanned the room and stopped as her gaze fell upon the corner of the room with a beautiful, oak grandfather clock. Emanuel quickly went to it, opening the glass door and winding the long, brass chimes. He stood back, admiring the splendid workmanship.

"It's beautiful," Shana whispered.

"Ja," he said softly. "I bought it for you."

She fought her tears and averted her eyes. "I don't know what to say."

Emanuel squeezed her hand, understanding Shana's feelings. They stood in their living room for the first time as man and wife, unsure how to react to each other on their first evening alone in their house. As Emanuel had said the night he proposed, they were, indeed, good friends. But now, they had to adapt to an intimacy reserved only for those wedded. For a long while, they stood in the middle of the living room, holding hands as they listened to the steady ticking of the grandfather's clock.

After several silent minutes passed, Emanuel finally sighed. "Guess I better milk the cows, then."

She nodded and followed him as he walked out of the living room and through the kitchen to the staircase. The stairs were high and narrow. Each wooden step creaked under their feet, the sound breaking the increasingly unbearable silence of the house.

Once upstairs, Emanuel led her into the master bedroom. The large double bed with the dark oak headboard threatened her and she lingered in the doorway. Against the wall, Emanuel had put a mirrored dresser. Some of Shana's personal belongings were spread out on the top. The sight of familiar things made her feel slightly more comfortable. Her eyes darted around the typically Amish room. Emanuel's suspendered pants and colorful Amish shirts hung from pegs on the wall. There were no closets in her new home. He quickly undressed from his Sunday outfit and put on his work clothes, ignoring Shana's eyes on his naked back.

"I haven't any furniture for the rest of the bedrooms," he said as he sat on the edge of the bed to put on his boots. "Figured we needn't worry about that for a while." His insinuation brought a blush to Shana's cheeks and he smiled to himself as he tied his boots. Then, standing up, he walked to her. "You get familiar with your new home while I milk," he said softly as he leaned over to kiss her. She clung to him for the briefest of moments, unsure of what to say or do. He smiled into her eyes and gave her one more soft kiss before he disappeared down the dark stairwell. She heard the door shut as he ventured outside to start his evening chores.

Shana quietly picked up the small pile of clothes Emanuel had left scattered on the floor by the bed. She hung them on the wall next to his other outfits before she followed his example and undressed, folding her wedding dress neatly and placing it on the bed. Though plain, it was a beautiful dress that had brought a glow to Emanuel's eyes when he had first seen her early that morning, even if his family had disapproved. Shana reached out and touched the soft fabric, realizing that she would never have an opportunity to wear such finery again. Her heart fluttered and she pulled away her hand, forcing herself to redirect her attention to exploring the dresser until she found a plain black skirt and a white sweater that Emanuel had unpacked from her trunks, which she had sent ahead the day before.

After she had changed her clothing, she turned around and caught a glimpse of her reflection in the oval mirror that hung over the dresser. She stopped for a moment, staring closely at the woman who gazed back. She ran her fingers through her bangs.

The rest of her hair was pulled back in a tight French braid. Her cheeks were flushed and her eyes bright. "You're somebody's wife now," she told herself. In the mirror's reflection, her eyes lingered on the bed behind her. A shiver ran up her spine and she quickly retreated out of the bedroom, nervous at the thought of her first night alone with Emanuel.

Downstairs, she finished putting away the food Katie had given them. Shana could still remember Katie's reaction that night to Emanuel's decision of a bride. For several days after their announcement, Emanuel had seemed extra quiet and serious. Shana knew it was because of his family's disapproval. But after the initial shock, the family had accepted Emanuel's choice, trying to acknowledge the hardworking Shana as their future daughter-in-law, while hiding their disappointment in her religious background.

Shana examined everything inside the gasoline-generated refrigerator, which was stocked with store-bought necessities such as butter, condiments and a neatly stacked row of eggs. Emanuel had even prepared a glass pitcher with homemade iced tea. She shut the door, wondering how she was going to prepare supper for him every day for the rest of her life. Everything she knew how to prepare was cooked with spices and sauces, unlike the natural and plain cuisine on which Katie had raised her Amish family. The cabinets were neatly supplied with canned vegetables, serving dishes, and cooking utensils. Most of these items had been donated by Katie and Lillian, sharing the fruits of their labor to help the young married couple get started at the new farm. Shutting the cabinet doors when she finished with her indoor exploration, Shana ventured outside.

The sky was dark and the sun sinking over the fields. Shana stopped by the fence and watched as the sun set in the sky. It glowed a brilliant reddish-orange over the desolated cornfields. The trees that lined the dried river appeared like skeletons, their empty branches reaching to the sky. As the reddish-orange blended into a deeper, more solid reddish-blue, the cold began to seep into her bones.

Shana shivered and hurried into the barn where she could barely see the bright glow from the kerosene lamp Emanuel was using as he milked the cows. The stench of fresh manure rose to her nostrils and she crinkled her nose. The cows were mooing and she could hear Emanuel talking quietly to them. She smiled. Stepping over a fallen shovel, Shana walked down the long line of cows. Emanuel was crouched by one, sitting on a three-legged stool.

He looked up when he sensed her presence. "Come to meet our family?" he asked cheerfully.

"There's so many of them!" she laughed, amazed at the long line of cows, chewing hay while stomping their hooves impatiently.

"Ja! Fifteen. That's a decent size herd. Should have some babies this spring. The ones with chains around their necks were recently impregnated." He noticed another blush cover Shana's cheeks. Laughing, he stood up and walked toward her. "Does that embarrass you?" he asked, leaning closely to her face and reaching for her hand. He pulled her close and brushed his finger across her cheek.

"No," she lied. "Not in the least."

He laughed again and spared her a quick kiss. Then, moving to the next cow in the line, Emanuel sat on the wobbly wooden stool and began milking. Following him, Shana stood by his side, and reached out to touch the cow. She liked the feeling of the cow's warm fur.

"Where did they all come from, Emanuel?"

"Most of them were at Father's farm. Brother Steve and I brought them over just yesterday with the help of two Mennonite neighbors and their trucks. Jacob was kind enough to do the milking this morn."

"Jacob?" she asked.

"The old tenant," he explained.

"And the rest?"

"Gifts from family." He followed her gaze over the two rows of cattle. "We'll buy some more next spring." He met her eyes. "The more cows, the more milk. The more milk, the more money to buy more cows." An awkward silence fell over them. Then, Emanuel stood up and motioned to the stool. "Go ahead. Give it a try."

"Me? Milk a cow?"

Emanuel insisted, showing her how to do it. After the first couple of attempts, milk streamed out of the cow and into the bucket. Shana laughed childishly, delighted with each tinkle of milk against the side of the metal bucket. Emanuel watched, laughing with her. For the next hour and a half, she helped him finish milking the cows, carrying the full buckets to the large, metal storage tank in the back of the barn. Finally, after feeding the two horses for the night, Emanuel and Shana walked, side by side, back to the house.

Inside the warm kitchen, the silence slowly vanished as Emanuel helped Shana prepare their first meal. He showed her where everything was, unaware that she had already gotten the feel of the kitchen. She heated up some leftovers Katie had sent along while Emanuel turned on the gas heater. After several minutes, the warm kitchen grew comfortably hot as the scents of an Amish kitchen began to infiltrate the smell of the fresh paint. They sat at the table, talking quietly about what the next few weeks would hold for them while they picked at the food on their plates.

When they had finished, Shana cleared the dirty dishes while Emanuel sat down with the local farmers' paper, flipping through it quietly while Shana brewed some fresh coffee. When the coffee was ready, she poured two cups and walked over to the table. The steam rose from the cups as she set them down before she sat opposite Emanuel, watching him as he read. "You know, I was thinking."

He set the paper down, not really interested in the news of the local world, and met her gaze. "About?"

"That money I have in the bank. Maybe we could use it toward something for the farm. A present to us from me."

"Well," he started slowly, "we could invest in a new buggy. Still have some left to put in the bank, too."

"Really?" The grandfather clock chimed in the living room eight times.

"A good buggy is no more than two. Since you sold your car, you'll probably want your own buggy. And my buggy is getting rather tattered. If you'd like, we could raise some chickens this spring. My mother never did but I know enough to get you started."

She made a face. "Chickens? Aren't they mean?"

He laughed. "Only the roosters." He watched her think about it. Her eyes clouded over and she stared momentarily out the window. Emanuel sipped his coffee, his eyes still on Shana. "Are you sorry you had to quit your job?"

"No," she answered, looking back at him. "No, I'm not. It

was burning me out and I wasn't getting anything out of it. Just aggravation and frustration. Besides, I have a much more rewarding job now."

"Which is?"

"Taking care of you."

For a long second, they stared at each other. Then, Emanuel reached out and pulled her onto his lap, holding her tightly. He hesitated before he slowly leaned down and kissed her. When their lips parted, he studied her face. Her eyes glowed, anticipating what they both so nervously were avoiding. "Ja, Shana," he started, his voice low and raspy. "You won't get burnt out from that job," he murmured, nuzzling at her neck.

Outside, one of the cows bellowed from the barn. Shana slid off Emanuel's lap, waiting for him to stand up and take her hand. He reached over the table and turned off the lamp, then, sliding his hand into hers, he led her upstairs to that final aspect of their relationship that they had anxiously saved for their wedding night.

Chapter Eleven

The room was still dark when he stirred next to her under the heavy quilt. Lying on her stomach, one hand hidden under her pillow and the other on top, Shana's eyes remained shut. She snuggled deeper under the covers as Emanuel removed his arm from across her bare back, slowly removing his fingers from her one hand. Realizing that he was getting up, her eyes fluttered open and she half-rolled over to look at him.

"Emanuel?" She sat up and leaned against the oak headboard. "What's the matter?"

In the soft glow of the ending night, she saw him glance at her, his eyes lingering on her bare breast. "Five o'clock. Time to milk the cows," he mumbled quietly as he turned his back and dressed.

She watched him, her eyes barely opened. He grabbed a pair of dark green workpants from the wall and quickly slid into them. The room was cold, his breath frosting in the air as he buttoned his plain, long sleeved shirt. Then, an increasing energy in his movements, he pulled up his suspenders over his shoulders and ran his fingers through his tousled hair. Before he left, he leaned over, gently pushed her back into the bed, and tucked the pink, white, and blue quilt under her chin.

With a tender kiss to her forehead, he whispered, "Keep the bed warm."

Out in the barn, he rubbed his hands together to warm them. The morning cold stung his face. "*Gude mariye*, girls," he mumbled before he started. For the next two hours, he milked the cows then shoveled the manure out from their stalls. His mind wandered back to the previous night, the memory warming his heart. As he milked the cows, hearing the soothing tingle of the milk against the side of the cold metal bucket, he could only think of his wife, sleeping soundlessly in their bed, hopefully waiting for him in her dreams.

The grandfather clock was ringing when he finally returned to the house. Half past seven. He stopped in the kitchen, pumping ice-cold water into his hands. Drying them on a towel, Emanuel sat down at the table to take off his boots and set them next to the counter on the floor. Quietly, he stole upstairs, hoping that the creaking stairs wouldn't disturb her. Once inside the room, he stripped his clothes off his body and climbed back into bed with Shana.

Still half-asleep, she curled her naked body around his, one lazy arm tossed over his chest. For a long time, Emanuel stared at the ceiling, holding her. He stroked her hair, listening to the slightly annoying ticking of the pink wind-up clock on her dresser.

"Um," she mumbled, slowly waking from her sleep. "What time is it?"

"Seven thirty."

"So early," she whispered. She shut her eyes, loving the feeling of his hands caressing her bare back. "I should fix you breakfast." But she made no move toward getting up. Instead, she leaned forward and began to kiss his neck and nibble at his ear. Emanuel shut his eyes, awakening to her pleasing demand. He answered her call by gently pushing her onto her back, his lips covering hers in a passionate kiss as his hand ran through her loose curls before he made love to her.

An hour later, Shana finally crawled out from underneath his arm and padded to the bathroom. She took a quick shower, disappointed at the low-pressure trickle that dribbled out of the showerhead. Drying off with a stiff, yellow towel, she hummed a made-up song to herself. Back in the bedroom, she quietly threw on a pair of jeans and a thick sweater then hurried downstairs to make Emanuel a proper breakfast before he awoke.

Twenty minutes later, he stumbled downstairs. The kitchen was alive with pleasant odors of sizzling bacon fat and fresh scrambled eggs. He leaned against the doorframe, watching Shana for several minutes before he cleared his throat to make his presence known.

"Emanuel! You scared me!" she exclaimed as she whirled around. Then, her face fell. "I wanted to surprise you with breakfast in bed."

Smiling, he replied, "A man can't sleep all day." He moved to the table. "Got a lot of work this afternoon."

"Oh?" The disappointment was obvious in her voice.

"Ja. Promised Jacob I'd help him finish hanging his tobacco." He leaned back as Shana set his plate before him. "It should've been done last month but, with the move, it got delayed. I promised that I'd help him since the tobacco's here."

Shana leaned against the counter, watching him take his first bite. "That was nice of you." He made a face. "Something wrong?"

He set his fork down, shaking his head. "Hot." He reached for the glass of milk in front of him. When he finished cooling his mouth, he stared at Shana curiously. His eyes lingered on her clothing as he asked, "Aren't you eating?"

"If I eat breakfast, I'm hungry all day" was her simple explanation. She noticed him staring at her with an odd expression on his face. "Emanuel?"

He smiled apologetically, bending his head down to eat.

"I'm just not used to you in...in pants," he said softly.

Shana glanced down at her outfit. The thermometer outside the kitchen window read forty-three degrees and he wanted her to wear a dress? Adapting to his ideals was, indeed, going to be trying. "I'll change if it's going to bother you."

Someone knocked at the door and, their conversation abruptly interrupted, Shana hurried to answer it. She opened the door and invited Jacob inside. "Come in out of the cold," she smiled, standing back to let him pass. Jacob took off his hat, nodded his head to her, and walked through the washroom into the kitchen. "Care for something to eat," she asked.

Jacob shook his head and sat down opposite Emanuel. Feeling isolated, Shana retreated to the kitchen sink and began to wash the few dishes from breakfast. She glanced over at the two men, noticing how different they looked, Jacob with his strict Amish beard and Emanuel with his clean-shaven face. Jacob toyed with his black felt hat as he talked with Emanuel about the tobacco. Shana half-heartedly listened as she dried the dishes, setting them on the counter. When she finished, she set her damp towel over the top of the dishes. Satisfied, she went to join the men at the table.

Emanuel spared her a smile. "*Ach vell*, we'll be out in the barn for most of the afternoon."

"Anything I can do to help?"

Emanuel quickly glanced at Jacob who raised his eyebrows before turning away. Emanuel smiled at Shana again as he stood up. "Nothing more than an occasional hot pot of coffee." He started to walk out of the kitchen.

"Emanuel."

He stopped in the doorway, reaching inside the washroom

for his hat. Placing it on his head, he looked at Shana. "Ja?"

"You didn't kiss me," she whispered.

Emanuel glanced over his shoulder at Jacob. Standing quietly by the door, twirling his hat in his hands, Jacob stared outside, keeping his distance from the newlyweds. Emanuel shuffled back to Shana and leaned down, quickly kissing her lips. Her eyes glowed at him and he smiled. "See you in a while," he murmured.

Left alone in the house, Shana tried to keep herself busy. Upstairs, she changed into a light blue sleeveless dress with a white long-sleeved shirt underneath. Pulling her hair off her neck, she tied it back with a pink ribbon. Then, she made the bed, lingering near his pillow before she fluffed it up and set it by the headboard, a whisper of a smile playing across her lips.

The stairs creaked as she hurried downstairs. Quickly, she washed Emanuel's plate and put away the dishes. The grandfather clock rang once. Shutting the kitchen cabinet, Shana listened to the chimes echo. Finished with her kitchen chores, she walked into the living room and stared at the beautiful cherry oak grandfather clock with the Old Roman numerals. She walked up to it, running a finger along the smooth wood casing before she opened the door and wound it for the day. The thick weights rose from the bottom of the clock cavity up to the top, each swaying rhythmically as she shut the glass panel door. Stepping back, she stared at it for another minute, smiled, then returned to the kitchen.

Fixing a pot of hot coffee, she sat at the table and leafed through the day old newspaper. Most of the articles were about weather and agriculture. Shoving it aside, Shana leaned back in her chair, sipped some coffee, and stared around the kitchen. It was large, like most Amish kitchens. The old-fashioned water pump looked ancient next to the stove, refrigerator and semi-modern linoleum countertops. The oak table was square and small compared to other Amish kitchen tables she had seen. Against the one windowless wall was an old, dark blue sofa.

In front of the sofa was a portable gas lantern. The house had no electricity. Shana knew that would take some getting used to. She stood up, walked to the sofa, and sat on it. A spring popped under her weight. Startled, Shana jumped to her feet. That was something that would need to be fixed, she thought as she added it to her mental list of chores. From the living room, the grandfather clock struck again. It was nine-thirty.

Shana walked to the pantry and surveyed inside. She pulled out flour, sugar, graham cracker crumbs, and other boxes, setting everything neatly on the counter. Vaguely, she remembered helping Katie bake several pies for that Sunday sermon several months ago. Determined to accomplish something, Shana began to painstakingly make her first pie.

Working from memory, for she had no cookbooks, Shana poured and mixed ingredients together in large bowls. By the time the clock struck ten-fifteen, the pie was baking in the oven. While the kitchen filled with the warm, sweet scent of cherry pie from the canned cherries she had found in the pantry, Shana carried a freshly brewed pot of coffee outside and to the barn.

The cold wind chilled her and she clutched the front of her black, wool cape shut. The Amish cape had been a present from Katie. While Shana had grown up only three states away, she hadn't been prepared for the bone chilling wind that hovered over the Lancaster County farms. She crossed over the driveway, staring out into the pasture where the cows stood in small groups. Even their coats had grown thicker in preparation for the winter.

Inside the barn, Shana shut the sliding door behind herself and called out, "Emanuel?" The barn seemed larger and emptier without the small herd of cows.

"Up here," he answered.

Shana walked over to the ladder leading into the hayloft. Carefully, she held the coffee pot and her skirt in one hand as she climbed the stairs. "Thought you might want to warm up," she said as she set the pot on a bale of hay, noticing Emanuel's approving nod at her change in clothing. Ignoring him, Shana looked around. The barn's hayloft appeared larger than the downstairs without the cow stalls and dairy milk storage container. The heavy wooden floor was covered with stray straw. On the far end of the loft, several massive piles of tobacco leaves waited to be hung up to dry from the eaves. Closer to Shana, at least a hundred, perhaps more, bales of hay were stacked from floor to ceiling.

"Is all that your tobacco, Jacob?"

"Ja," he nodded. "Brings in some good cash."

"Whose hay?"

Emanuel finished stripping the stalk of tobacco he was working on before he poured himself a cup of coffee. "Jacob was kind enough to leave that hay when he moved onto his new farm."

Smiling, Shana sat down on a bale of hay as she asked, "How is the new farm?"

"The addition isn't finished but, with all the *kinners*, it's mighty more comfortable, anyhow."

"Kinners?" she asked.

"Children, Shana," Emanuel explained. "That's Deitsch for children."

She turned back to Jacob. "How many children do you

have?"

Jacob hesitated. "Eight now."

"Oh my!" Shana glanced at Emanuel. He had mentioned once in jest how he wanted a large family. Certainly he didn't expect her to have a typical Amish family of ten children. "So many mouths to feed," Shana commented lightly as she plucked at a loose strand of straw.

After a moment's silence, Jacob replied, "So many hands to work the new farm that God has blessed us with."

The color rose to Shana's cheeks and she lowered her eyes. She felt Emanuel's eyes on her and wondered if he felt her shame. He walked over to her, gently touching her arm. When she looked up, he gave her an encouraging smile. "We'll be in around one. Jacob will stay for dinner with us."

Nodding, Shana quietly walked away, her eyes on the floor and her heart pounding inside her chest. She left the coffee pot on the bale of hay. Once inside the kitchen, she sank into the ugly blue sofa, burrowing her head in her arms. The tears wet her arm and her sobs broke the hateful silence of the house. The men didn't want her in the barn, she didn't know what to do in the house, and she felt alone. The tranquility that had once enticed her to Emanuel was now turning into her enemy. Only if you let it, she began reprimanding herself as she sat up, wiping her tears away with an impatient hand.

For the next two hours, Shana set about making the best supper possible. She cooked a small ham, boiled a dozen peeled potatoes, steamed some frozen peas, and made orange gravy from the ham's juices. She set the table for three, using her own pretty pink placemats and napkins. She went upstairs in one of the empty bedrooms and dug through her unpacked trunk of household knick-knacks. With a satisfied smile, she carried a silk arrangement of pink and white flowers downstairs and set it in the center of the table.

The washroom door slammed shut and the men stomped inside, slapping their arms against their bodies to warm up. Shana glanced at her watch. It was quarter after one. The supper was in the oven and the cherry pie cooling on the counter. She perched herself by the sink, towel in hand as she dried a pot that didn't need it. She waited for the men to come into the kitchen.

Emanuel caught her eye and smiled softly as he set the coffee pot on the counter. "Certainly got cold out. Might even get a flurry or two." He pumped the water pump three times then quickly washed his face, hands, and neck in the cold stream of water that gushed out. Patting his face dry, he stepped aside for Jacob to wash. "Come spring, I'll put in real plumbing down here." Then, handing the towel to Jacob, Emanuel sat down at the table.

Shana stared after Emanuel, watching him sitting at the table, his head bowed slightly. His ears, barely visible under his curly mass of hair, were brilliant red. Feeling ashamed for having felt so sorry for herself while he had been battling the cold to help his friend, Shana quickly brewed another pot of coffee then took the food out of the oven and set it in the center of the table. She watched as the men quickly prayed before they piled the by-now sticky mashed potatoes high on their plates, soaked them in the overcooked gravy, then cut thick slabs of dried ham. She poured them coffee, pleased to see Emanuel filling her plate as well.

The conversation centered around the men's plans for the following planting season. Emanuel expressed his enthusiasm in, perhaps, planting his own tobacco crop. Jacob began explaining about the various problems with raising tobacco. Shana listened, not understanding everything they talked about. Occasionally, the men slipped into Pennsylvania Dutch and Shana understood nothing. All she knew was that Emanuel and Jacob had arrived late and her first supper tasted awful.

When the meal was over, Shana cleared their plates, poured more coffee, and proudly presented her still warm cherry pie. "What a surprise," Emanuel allowed himself to say as he noticed the gleam in Shana's eye when she set it before him. Then, handing him the knife, she waited for him to cut the first piece.

The crust flaked off as Emanuel cut into the pie. Jacob took the first piece, his eyes large and his fork in hand. Shana turned back to the sink, stacking the supper dishes. When she went back to the table, both men were staring at each other but quickly looked away as Shana sat down. She raised her coffee cup to her lips. Slowly, Emanuel took another bite of his pie and Jacob followed. Neither spoke.

Quietly, they finished their pie. Jacob stood up, smiled his appreciation at Shana, and then said to Emanuel, "Tomorrow at eight?"

Emanuel walked with him outside. From the kitchen window, Shana saw Emanuel bid Jacob good-bye before disappearing into the barn to clean the cows' stall. He was gone for over an hour, more than enough time for Shana to clean up the kitchen. She was putting away the last plate when Emanuel returned. He poured himself another cup of coffee and leaned against the counter, watching Shana wipe the sink.

"Shana," he started. She folded the towel neatly and hung it over the side of the sink. "Did you want any coffee?"

"No thank you." She glanced at the pie. "What should I do with that? Put it in the refrigerator? I don't want it to spoil."

Emanuel's eyes seemed to dance at her as he laughed, "No

need to fear that. It should keep for quite a long time."

"Emanuel! That's not very kind." When he continued to laugh, she put her hands on her hips. "What's so funny?"

He placed his cup carefully on the counter and opened the utensil drawer. He took out a fork and stuck it into the pie. Then, he lifted it to her mouth. Reluctantly, for she tended to shy away from sweets, Shana took a bite, confused by Emanuel's actions. Her eyes widened and she forced herself to swallow the salty piece of pie. The tears welled in her eyes and she ran out of the kitchen, sobbing hysterically.

She sat on the edge of the bed, hiding her face behind her hands when he came upstairs. His heavy footsteps sounded outside the bedroom and she heard the door creak as he pushed it open. Patiently, he knelt in front of her, taking her hands in his and pulling them away from her face. "Anyone could have made that mistake, Shana."

"I can't do anything right!" she whined, her shoulders heaving from her sobs.

"That's not true. You made a wonderful supper, Shana."

"You were late and everything was overcooked and dry!" she cried. Emanuel gently laughed, wrapping his arms around his horrified wife. Falling against him, she laid her head on his shoulder, her tears staining his dirty shirt. "Why can't I understand?" she murmured, clinging to him as though afraid to let go. It felt good to finally have his attention.

Emanuel forced her to release him. He smoothed the tears off her face with his thumbs as he stared down into her watery eyes. "What do you mean you don't understand?"

Sniffling, Shana chewed on her lower lip. "I always say the wrong thing and I can't cook the foods you like and I get upset when you ignore me and..."

He pressed a finger to her lips, silencing her. "I don't ignore you, Shana."

"You do!" she cried out, the tears streaming down her face. She felt foolish crying but she couldn't stop the emotion from pouring out. "This is supposed to be our honeymoon, our adjustment period, and you act like we've been married for years. You don't kiss me hello or good-bye or compliment my efforts. You don't want to spend any time with me or..."

Emanuel hushed her again, this time by lightly kissing her lips. When he pulled back, he stared into her eyes. "I do want to spend time with you, Shana, but I have work I must do. A farmer cannot leave his farm nor ignore his work. Come summer, perhaps we can take a vacation, visit your family, or go to a beach. Until then, I promised Jacob I'd help him since we gave him such short notice. Would you have me go back on my word to Jacob?" Through her tears, she shook her head. Emanuel kissed her again. "I love you, Shana. When I fail your expectations as a husband, remember it'll take me time to conform to your ideals."

He held her hands, staring into her eyes. The tears stopped falling from her eyes as she suddenly realized that, throughout their short courtship, Emanuel had never actually told her he loved her. Not the way he had just said those three words to her. Wrapping her arms around his neck, Shana hugged Emanuel, wishing that their life together could always be like this moment, together, alone, and understanding the other. Later that night, after they had made love and Emanuel slept, his head upon her shoulder, she wanted to cry again. She loved Emanuel but, she realized, she hated the non-expressive culture to which he had been born and that she had just married.

Chapter Twelve

Those first several weeks, Shana quickly found herself adapting to the new routine in her life. Every morning at five, Emanuel slid out of bed and dressed in the dark. Shana usually darted in and out of sleep, listening to him move around the bedroom. Several times, she arose with him and helped milk the cows. She knew that he appreciated her help, especially since twice each day, he had to milk the cows and clean the manure out of their stall. Any help eased his burden of caring for the animals that contributed to their livelihood.

Some days, she couldn't bring herself to leave the warmth of the bed and he'd end up milking the cows alone. On those days, she waited another two hours before dragging herself out of the bed and into the cold. After a quick, steaming shower, she'd hurry downstairs to the kitchen. The kitchen was already comfortably warm, Emanuel having started the kerosene heater. After brewing a fresh pot of coffee, she'd make Emanuel a large breakfast, usually consisting of fluffy scrambled eggs, fresh bacon, occasionally burnt toast, and a cup of black coffee.

"You're up," he teased as he walked into the kitchen one morning. He washed his hands in the sink. "Thought I'd have to come pull you out of bed this morning."

"It's so warm under those blankets. Didn't think I was going to get up."

"Ja," he started. "Don't think I wouldn't have considered joining you." He reached for the towel she playfully flung at him. Wiping his hands dry, Emanuel watched Shana set the table. "It's getting colder out there every day. Getting harder to milk the cows alone."

Shana bit her lower lip and made a silent vow to herself. She had to force herself to help him. All of those cows were hard for one man to handle alone. Yet, her days had begun to fill up with her own chores. Cleaning the house took longer without the luxury of Englische products like Pledge and Mop-n-Glow. Three times a week, she spent the entire day just washing floors and windows, dusting and straightening up. Everything seemed to get dirtier quicker on the farm. Indeed, Emanuel had not been lying when he said that her days would be full.

"Plans for today yet?" he asked.

Shana carried the coffee pot over to the table and set it down on a hot pad. "What do you have in mind?"

"*Vell*, tobacco's all hung so I thought to mend some of them fences in the pasture. Maybe you could help."

They both sat at the table, Shana waiting patiently for Emanuel while he bowed his head in silent prayer. When he finished, he smiled at her then reached for the eggs. Shana sipped her coffee. "Thought I'd take a trip to the laundromat this morning. Need to wash some clothes, don't you think?"

Handing Shana the bowl of eggs, Emanuel frowned. "No need for a laundromat. There's a washer here."

The disapproving look in Emanuel's eye had not gone unnoticed. He had the same look whenever Shana slipped on a pair of jeans and a sweatshirt to help with the morning milking or work in the barn. She had seen the piece of machinery that Emanuel called a washer one day earlier that first week. At first, she had thought it was junk that had been left behind. Now, she knew otherwise.

"I suppose I could do the laundry here," she replied as she relented.

The frown faded from his face as he bent his head to eat before his food got cold. Half an hour later, Shana stood in the washroom, a pile of dirty clothes at her feet. She stared at the ancient metal washtub and wringer. For a moment, she chewed on her bottom lip, contemplating an escape to the laundromat. She had known she would have to give up certain luxuries from her world, but they hadn't seemed so important before. Finally, with a determined sigh, Shana filled the washtub with soapy water, watching the bubbles foam up to the edge of the tub before turning off the hose.

She picked up a pair of Emanuel's dirty workpants from the pile and dipped it into the washtub. Suds trickled down the side of the tub. She frowned then took the wet pants and rubbed them against the old fashioned washboard. One of her fingernails caught on the metal and broke. Wincing, Shana quickly withdrew her hands and stuck her finger in her mouth. Stepping away from the washtub, Shana eyed it with hatred while feeling admiration for Katie who, for all her life, had used this ancient piece of machinery for her entire family. Yet, at the same time, she felt sorry for her and all Amish women for never having experienced the convenience of modern laundry facilities. Above all, she felt sorry for herself for having known the convenience but willingly having given it away.

Determined to succeed, Shana dipped her hands back into the cold, soapy water and began to rub Emanuel's workpants against the washboard. Then, after rinsing them under the pump, she wrung them out in the old fashion wooden ringer. She hung them over the line Emanuel had strung diagonally from corner to corner in the washroom. Although she questioned how clean they really were, Shana took a step back, her hands placed evenly on her hips as she evaluated the dripping wet pants.

"Piece of cake," she said to herself before she continued washing the rest of her clothes.

She had just hung up the last piece of clothes to dry on the makeshift clothesline strung from corner to corner in the washroom when Emanuel opened the door and walked in. He smiled at her, pleased to see that she was managing. "*Vell,* look at you! You figured out how to work it, then?" He wiped his feet then walked over to the sink to wash his hands.

"Three fingernails later, yes."

"Maybe after dinner you'd like to help me with that fencing."

Shana bent down to wipe some water off the floor. Her own clothes soaked, Shana realized she had probably spilt more water on herself and the floor than on the clothes she had just washed. "Oh Emanuel, I totally forgot about the midday meal!" She smiled apologetically. "Let me change my clothes and I'll heat up some soup for you."

He was already seated at the table, glancing through the day-old newspaper, when she hurried back into the kitchen. He looked up at her and smiled, despite the fact that she wore jeans. "Thought we might ride into town tonight."

"Oh?" she replied, her back toward him as she hastily prepared dinner. She hadn't left the farm since her arrival and a ride into town sounded more like a night in Manhattan.

"Couple of things I need at the store and maybe you could do any shopping you need."

"Perhaps we could stop somewhere to eat, Emanuel. That way I'll be able to help you all afternoon with those fences and the milking." She glanced at him over her shoulder, hoping to see him nod in approval. But as she faced him, her smile faded from her face and, drying her wet hands on a towel, she walked toward him, both dinner and supper suddenly forgotten. "Emanuel, you haven't shaved today, have you?"

"No," he answered, his own eyes troubled.

"You aren't planning to grow a beard, are you?"

"Shana," Emanuel said softly, disapproving of the tone in her voice.

"You needn't grow a beard to let the world know you're married. You're wearing my ring," she said anxiously.

The look in his eyes darkened. "That is not the only reason we grow beards after marriage, Shana," he murmured but the underlying tone in his voice warned her that she was trespassing on forbidden ground.

"Who are 'we'?" she asked, her temper flaring. He didn't answer her. "You are not Amish, Emanuel," she retorted slowly. "Growing a beard will not make you Amish. I don't think you need to be reminded of that fact."

He sighed. "I told you, Shana, before we married that..."

"I know what you told me, Emanuel," she interrupted. "But I did not marry the Amish. I married you. While we both have to conform to find a happy medium, you have to realize that you cannot have me and pretend to be Amish as well," she argued, trying to keep her voice soft and gentle rather than harsh and reprimanding. But her anger could not be hidden and the look in his eyes told her that she had hurt him with her words.

They ate in silence, Shana too aware of his downcast eyes and her own trembling heart. Her appetite lost, Shana pushed her plate back and watched him, hating the silence as well as her fear. Prior to their marriage, she had laid awake many nights, fighting the increasing anxiety that Emanuel would not be able to abide by his bargain. Now, the shadow of the Amish covering his face, she realized that with each second of silence that passed, he was gathering strength from his upbringing by shutting her out. In her world, man and wife could speak openly to each other. In Emanuel's, a good wife was a non-opinionated wife. She had crossed the line and his disappointment showed.

After dinner, they walked out to the pasture, Emanuel several steps ahead of her. He avoided her eyes and began to work, repairing a section of the rotting fence. When needed, Shana jumped in, holding up the section as he hammered it into the ground. An hour passed and the sky darkened. Before long, a light sprinkling of snow fluttered to the ground. Emanuel raised his eyes to the sky and his brow creased together. He worked quicker but, as the snow fell harder and covered the ground, he tucked his hammer under his arm and reached for Shana's hand.

She took it, surprised by his unusual display of affection. Holding hands and giving kisses were for the privacy of the home where curious eyes could not see. Far from displeased, Shana walked next to him, a new energy in her stride. She did not want to fight with Emanuel but they had both agreed before they married to conform to each other's ways. And while she understood his refusal to own a car and use electricity, things he had been without all of his life, the mustache-less beard so typical of the married Amish men crossed her line.

The rest of the snowy afternoon, Emanuel did his bookkeeping in the kitchen while Shana sat down to write a letter to her family. The kitchen grew darker as the afternoon passed and Emanuel lit the kerosene lantern over the table. He wandered to the window and pushed back the sheer curtain. "Snow's falling good, now. Reckon we won't be making that trip into town after all."

"Why's that?" she asked, slightly disappointed. She hadn't left the farm since she had arrived and had begun to look forward to the shopping trip.

"Dangerous with the buggy." He dropped the curtain and stood for a long moment with his back to her. Shana wondered if he had something on his mind, most probably about their earlier discussion. And, at that moment as he stood there, his curly hair just hanging below his collar and his suspenders tight against his shoulders, she realized that they were worlds apart, even if they had joined their worlds in marriage.

"Emanuel?"

He turned and looked at her. He remained silent then, as though his chain of thought broke, he smiled and walked to her side. "There are two things the Lord gave man over the other creatures. He created the ability for man to think. The other is the ability to love." Emanuel knelt before her and took her hands in his. "I thank Him daily for these gifts, along with all the other wonderful things He created. And I thank Him for sending you to me."

"Emanuel," she whispered, startled at this sudden introduction of his religion to her. In all those months together, he had never openly offered her any insights into the religious aspect of his upbringing. It startled her and, as his words sunk in, frightened her for she suddenly realized that there was another side to the man she had married; a side that, not only she did not know, but that had a stronger effect on his life than his own love for her.

He shook his head for her to let him continue. "There is a reason for everything He does and we must learn to live by His decisions. If He had not wanted our love, He would not have allowed it." He hesitated, giving her hands a slight squeeze. "Had I been baptized, our marriage could never have happened unless you had converted, and even then, that would have created some problems. I cannot ask you to convert to the Amish ways now. But you cannot ask me to convert to your ways."

"I thought our love would be enough," she said softly.

"We have our love but we have His love, too. By trusting in Him, all things will be right, Shana. You must understand that and believe that."

"I do," she mumbled, uncertain as to whether that was true. He kissed her hands and stood up. A smile crossed his lips but it was an unusual smile, so unlike his typical mischievousness that lit up his face. This smile was an inner smile and Shana knew that he was content. Even though his little talk had left her feeling more frightened and alone, apparently Emanuel had eased his own mind and found that inner peace that lingered over every Amish man's home.

Chapter Thirteen

Every afternoon, Shana took long walks around the farm, studying the land. She enjoyed breathing in the fresh winter air while temporarily escaping her household chores. After that first light snow melted, at Emanuel's suggestion, she'd take a bucket with her and collect loose rocks out of the fields that would hinder the spring plowing. When the bucket was full, she carried it to the creek and dumped the rocks into the rushing water.

She enjoyed what Emanuel called helping him in the fields, even though she certainly didn't consider it work. She began to enjoy not being confined inside all day, a freedom that she had never experienced before. Her days were peaceful and quiet, not filled with senseless, false conversation. Instead, she used all of her senses, watching the clouds flutter across the sky or hover low to the horizon. She'd listen to the whistling wind that whipped around her ears, a curious symphony that she had never heard before. She'd take in all the smells of the surrounding flora and fauna. No matter what Mother Nature put before her, Shana began to see beauty and peace surrounding the farm, rather than the isolation and loneliness she had originally feared.

The farm, located off a winding, narrow back road, did not welcome many passing cars or visitors. An occasional buggy trotted by their lane but, otherwise, silence surrounded the farm. When the cows were outside the barn, she could hear them mooing or stamping their feet. The two mules and the horses might occasionally whinny, a momentary break in the noiseless calm. In the house, the steady clicking of the grandfather clock kept her company. Every fifteen minutes, the chimes reverberated throughout the house, reminding her that time was constant and she had plenty of it ahead of her. Occasionally when working in the house, Shana longed for her small radio, more from the constant lack of companionship than for the actual music. But, knowing Emanuel's certain objection, she kept her wishes as quiet as the farm.

Most nights, while supper cooked, Shana would join Emanuel in the barn. She loved watching him milk the cows. He was so gentle and patient. No longer did the thick stench of cow manure offend Shana's nose. Instead, she found it soothing and, whenever she did notice it, the odor welcomed rather than repulsed her. These animals were their livelihood, extensions of their family. Occasionally, she'd try to sneak up behind Emanuel and, standing in the shadows of the doorway, watch Emanuel as he sat patiently, talking in his soft, milking voice to the cow.

"Cold hands, aye?" he murmured to the cow. As if in response, the cow lifted her back leg and stomped her hoof on the cement floor. "Can't be that bad, missy. Come on now. Thatta girl," he cooed. Shana smiled. The milk streamed out of the cow's teat and tinkled against the metal bucket. She sensed Emanuel's pleasure that, as he talked to the cow, she gave in to his gentle pulling.

"Your turn now, Shana."

"And I thought I had been so quiet!" she teased, stepping out the shadows.

"I sensed you." He glanced over his shoulder and smiled, returning her tease. "And your perfume helped, too."

He stood up so that she could sit down at the stool. Most nights, Shana carried the full buckets to the holding container that continually ran off the generator in the back room of the barn. Still uncomfortable with milking, she cautiously reached out and laid her hand on the cow's udder. She laughed and pulled away at first but, Emanuel leaned forward and, taking a hold of her hand, persisted.

"Remember how? Just squeeze it like this," he prodded patiently. A trickle of milk dripped out. "Vell, almost like this. Practice," he announced. "That's what you need." He sat behind her, crouched on the very back of the stool. Shana fit neatly between his legs, her back pressed against his chest. Both of his arms around her, he continued helping her milk the cow. "I think you're finally getting it," he whispered hoarsely into her ear.

His warm breath sent a shiver down her spine and she leaned back against him, his lips sweeping against her neck. The roughness of his growing beard grazed her skin and goose bumps ran up her arms. She shut her eyes and tilted her head slightly, just enough to rub her cheek against his. She breathed in his scent, the all too familiar mixture of the outdoors and Emanuel. Her heart beat inside of her chest and she felt energy pulse through her veins.

The warm stream of milk tinkled against the side of the metal bucket but Shana didn't pay attention. Being near him caused her to have to catch her breath. She felt his hand brush against her leg, reaching up to gently rub her arm. His touch burned her skin in a way that caused her to sigh, enjoying the moment of intimacy. But, as soon as his touch was there, it disappeared. Quickly, he stood up and turned away from her.

"I fully expect all of these cows milked and their stalls cleaned by supper," he teased, his voice still raspy and his face flushed. "Now that you know how, I guess you're hired, then." As if sensing her disappointment, he touched her cheek and smiled, lowering his tone to a serious level. "If you help me tonight, we can get finished twice as quick."

Trying to calm her racing heart, she accepted his hidden apology with a soft smile as the color flooded to her cheeks. Always work before pleasure on a farm, she thought. So, with a simple nod, she took a deep breath and set back to work at milking the patient cow before her.

Most nights after the cows had been milked and the horses bedded down, Emanuel would sit for a while at the kitchen table, reading the paper in the dim light from the kerosene lamp or talking with Shana until they retired to bed. But twice after the first major snowfall had melted from the roads, Emanuel harnessed Lucky Monday and took Shana for a night ride. In the increasing bitter cold, they would snuggle under the lap blanket, Emanuel patiently trying to teach Shana how to drive the horse while Shana just enjoyed being near him.

A month after they had married, Emanuel sold his older horse and purchased a beautiful black Morgan with Shana's money, putting the rest aside for a new buggy in the springtime. "She's beautiful," Shana whispered as she stared at the magnificent creature in the clean stall. The horse lifted her head, neighing loudly as though answering Shana's compliment. With a timid hand, Shana reached out to rub the horse's nose. "Does she have a name?"

"Lady Priscilla," he answered, leaning against Lucky Monday's stall as he watched Shana meeting her new horse. "But you can call her anything you wish."

"I think I'll just call her Lady," Shana mused, running her fingers down Lady's sleek neck. The horse nuzzled at the long, neat braid that hung down Shana's back. Laughing, Shana reached for her braid and backed away. "She certainly is frisky, isn't she?"

"She's only five." Emanuel started to walk out of the stable, waiting for Shana to tear herself away from Lady. For a moment, he stood in the doorway, watching Shana until, a glow on her face, she turned to join him. "Later tonight, we'll go for a ride in the fields, ja? For now, I must finish my chores in the barn."

Taking his cue, Shana hurried into the house and started to prepare supper. She kept glancing at the kitchen clock as she wished Emanuel would finish his chores so they could eat the evening meal and go riding. Even in the cold of winter, she found herself anticipating the ride. With no crops in the fields, she could imagine Emanuel and herself racing each other around the farm.

She thought back to those summer nights during what she now recognized was their courtship, the nights when they had ridden together at night. She had loved the feeling of his arms around her but had always wished for the glory of speed. He had been so cautious, afraid to scare her. Tonight she'd get to know Lady, introduce the horse to the farm and let the animal run free. But the harder she wished for Emanuel to return home, the longer she seemed to wait. Finally, her supper growing cold and the sun already faded from the sky outside her kitchen window, Emanuel stomped into the kitchen.

Holding in her disappointment, Shana dished his plate and carried it to the table after he sat down. With the sky so dark, there would be no ride in the fields. But Emanuel did not seem to notice her silence. Instead, he quickly ate and excused himself to go bathe. With a gentle shrug of her shoulders, Shana cleared their dishes and cleaned the kitchen. There's always tomorrow, she told herself. But the next day was Sunday and there was no horse riding on the Lord's day, regardless of whether it was a church Sunday or off-Sunday.

While Emanuel had refused his baptism, he had talked to one of the local elders in their new church district about attending an occasional service. After two weeks of deliberating, the elders agreed to their attendance at the bi-weekly services as long as they sat quietly in the back of the room and knew they could not participate in the foot washing ceremonies.

Shana had not argued with Emanuel about his wishes to attend church. It was important to him and, for that reason, Shana donned her plainest dress and pinned her hair back in a neat bun. She hurried down to the kitchen where Emanuel waited. He wore his freshly brushed, plain black suit and a black hat on his head. And, even though the clothes seemed slightly outlandish to Shana, she smiled anyway, pleased to see him so happy.

"Do I look plain?" she asked as she shut the door to the stairwell. Her black dress with small black buttons down the front almost appeared to be an Amish dress. Had she worn the white prayer cap and had her forehead not been shadowed by bangs, she knew that she could have been mistaken for an Amish woman.

"Ja, you look plain enough," he replied solemnly, his voice hoarse. But Shana knew from the sparkle in his eye that he, too, was pleased.

They walked down the road to one of the neighboring farms. Several shiny black buggies passed them, young children hanging out of the back open window despite the cold air. The horses neighed and snorted, their breath forming misty clouds around their noses. Their hooves hit the macadam as they raced by the walking couple, the soothing noise fading away as the buggy traveled further down the road. Occasionally a car would slowly pass them, for the most part gawking tourists who would stare at Emanuel and Shana. Apparently, even in the cold, tourists came in droves, eager to learn about the Amish, regardless of the season or weather.

As they approached the farm, Shana glanced nervously at Emanuel. His reassuring calm soothed her, giving her a strength she never realized she had. Pushing her shoulders back, Shana followed Emanuel into the farmhouse as almost a hundred inquisitive eyes met hers. For a moment, she felt as she had that night when Emanuel had taken her to the volleyball game at the barn. Except, this time, there was no hidden speculation about their relationship. This time, they entered the room so steeped with curiosity as husband and wife.

Feeling more confident, Shana held her head high and nodded at the few familiar faces that she saw. Then, as Emanuel had instructed her, Shana sat in the back of the kitchen on a hard bench behind the other women. She lost sight of Emanuel in the sea of people and, as she smiled at a small child who stared over his mother's shoulder at the strange Englischer, Shana wondered if he sat in front of her with the other men. But, all of the men wore the same black hat and Shana could not recognize Emanuel.

For the three hour long German sermon, Shana sat quietly, her hands folded and placed on her lap, her eyes lifted and staring straight ahead. She understood nothing yet she understood everything. The elder's strange sounding words somehow made sense to her and, when everyone else bowed their heads in silent prayer, Shana found herself praying with them. When the people sang, their untrained voices lifting in unison to praise their Lord, Shana found herself wishing she knew the words to join them. The power in this house of unity, of peace, of good will, increased with every syllable in their songs and every word in the sermon; and Shana began to understand, as she looked around at the seriousness on the people's faces, the unquestionable faith reflected in their eyes.

After the church service, the other members readied

themselves for the midday meal. Shana recognized one of her neighbors and, forcing herself to overcome her insecurity, walked over to the stout young woman. "We haven't formally met yet but I've seen you driving past our farm," Shana started.

"You must be the young Lapp's Englische wife, then?" Like other Amish women, her voice was soft yet full of strength. Her casual reference to Shana being Englische did not sound condemning or insulting but, rather, matter of fact. "Shana Lapp."

"Ja, you are Emanuel's Shana," the Amish woman said as though to remember the name. Then, after a brief hesitation, she returned Shana's smile and introduced herself. "Ana Lantz."

"Which farm do you live on?" Shana asked.

"Just up the hill from yours." A young child, no older than four, scurried over and clung to Ana's skirt. "Been a change for you, ja?"

"Just a little," Shana replied to the woman's forward question. But Shana couldn't help smiling. "It's very quiet."

"You were from the city, then?"

"Outside of the city, you could say."

"*Vell*, come visit sometime." Ana smiled one last time before giving in to the child at her side.

Shana retreated, feeling lost in the wave of black clad people. They all looked the same and talked the same yet, Shana knew, each of them lived and loved as individually as the people from her own culture. Her eyes drifted over their freshly washed faces with clear complexions and shiny foreheads. The women congregated together while the smaller children had the liberty to run back and forth between the women and the men until, their laughter too loud, their parents gently reprimanded them.

Shana caught sight of Emanuel, standing in a small circle of older men. Her heart skipped a beat as she watched him. My husband, she thought and smiled to herself. He was talking intently with the man she recognized as the district bishop. The bishop stroked his beard and looked thoughtfully at Emanuel. Finally, he nodded and slapped him good-naturedly on the back. Then, the small circle broke up.

Shortly afterwards, Emanuel found Shana and led her out of the farmhouse. They walked back to their farm in silence. Emanuel seemed deep in thought and, respecting that, Shana wandered in her own revelation. Her back ached and she had a slight stomachache, but her heart felt soothed as though some of the burden she had been feeling was lifted from her shoulders. She realized that, without having understood one word of the sermon, she had understood it all. And, in the process, she had taken one step closer to understanding a side of Emanuel she hadn't been given the chance to learn: His faith.

Chapter Fourteen

Late December's cold weather came with such vengeance that Shana dreaded crawling out of bed in the mornings. Without a heating system, the cold seemed to hover inside the house, digging deep into her bones. She had never known such misery as each morning when she woke up and often wondered how a house could get so cold. She'd lay in bed, buried beneath a high pile of quilts as she waited for Emanuel to start the kerosene heater in the kitchen before he headed out into the winter bitterness to tend to his morning chores.

Most days, after the morning milking and cleaning, he spent time in the house with Shana. With the winter, he couldn't work outside and the barn was too cold to spend any unnecessary time. Twice during those cold weeks in December, they drove the hour ride to visit at Jonas and Katie's farmhouse and to share the midday meal.

Shana silently fought her personal trepidation at going to Emanuel's old home, too aware of the tension with her in-laws. Their marriage had been treated with a touch of distance and a lack of warmth toward her. It was to be expected, she knew, and she couldn't really complain since Katie and Jonas were always hospitable. However, after Katie had offered to share some recipes for canning fruits and vegetables on their first visit, Shana began to wonder if the distance and apparent coldness was typical of the Amish and not to be taken personally. On the second visit, Shana decided this must be the reason especially when, upon learning that Shana had attended an Amish church, Katie invited their son and his non-Amish wife to attend one of the services in their own district.

So, the following church Sunday, they dressed in their best and. leaving the house at quarter to seven, they drove to a farm near the Lapp farm. Shana was surprised to realize that Emanuel was especially elated to be returning to worship with his old friends. He was happier than she had seen him as he was returning home to his former community.

During the service, once again, Shana found herself seated alone on a hard bench in the very back of the kitchen. The men sat in the partitioned room and the women sat in front of Shana. The sermon was, as usual, in High German and she found herself envious as she could not understand the elder. Feeling alienated, she drifted into her own thoughts about God and the reasons behind His ways.

After the sermon, Lillian approached Shana. Her stomach was now swollen enough that her clothing stretched tightly. Shana wondered how long before her second child would be born. "Haven't seen you in a while," Lillian said. The friendliness in her voice warmed Shana. "You mustn't let the cold frighten you away and must come visiting more often."

"And you, as well," Shana invited. She wondered if, had Lillian not been Amish, they would have been better friends. Her gentle way with Linda and easy laughter pained Shana, making her wish they were more alike so they could, indeed, be closer.

"Katie says you've attended church in your district already."

Shana nodded. "Two weeks ago, yes."

"How do you like sitting still for so long on those hard benches?" Lillian asked teasingly.

"Well, I could do without that," Shana replied, reaching down to tug playfully on Linda's pigtail. "But the songs are so beautiful that it makes up for the benches."

"That it does," Lillian agreed. "Katie and I will be working on a quilt early January. Perhaps you could come quilting, ja?" Lillian asked as Linda clung to her hand and twisted around, peering eagerly at Shana as she pressed her face against her mother's hip.

"Quilting? I'm not too handy with a needle." Noticing the disappointed look in Lillian's expression, Shana quickly added, "Yet."

Lillian smiled. "Then you must come and learn!" But there was no more time to discuss quilting. It was their turn to file into the kitchen and eat their meal. Shana followed Lillian and took her plate to the table. Katie smiled at her two daughter-in-laws, stepping aside to make room for them to join her.

The sky hung dark and gray as Shana and Emanuel rode home after visiting with Jonas and Katie. The younger brothers had disappeared after the church meal, most of them to pick up their girls for some social event. Sylvia, too young to date, had sat in the kitchen, listening intently to Katie and Shana discuss spring gardening. But now, the cold beating at the buggy, Shana listened to the gentle sound of the horse's hooves hitting the macadam. It lulled her, soothing her tired eyes and weary spirit, Before long, Emanuel was gently touching her arm. Startled, Shana opened her eyes and blinked. They had reached their farm.

"Oh," she started. "I must've fallen asleep."

"That you did."

"I don't know why I'm so tired," she said softly as she clambered out of the buggy.

She waited patiently for Emanuel to unhitch Lady. She liked to watch him when he worked, his strong hands unhooking the harness and his breath forming misty clouds in the cold. He led the horse into her stall and shut the gate. Then, together, Shana and Emanuel walked up the stone path to their house.

In the kitchen, Emanuel turned on the heater while Shana put on a fresh pot of coffee. The fresh aroma of percolating coffee soon filled the room. She had just set the two coffee cups on the table while Emanuel hurried upstairs to change his clothes. Shana sat at the table and looked around herself. The kitchen indeed felt like home to her. She spent most of her days in it, cooking and cleaning and sometimes sewing rips in Emanuel's work clothes. She shut her eyes, listening to him walking around in the room above her. A drawer shut and she thought she heard the bed creak. Seconds later, he emerged from the staircase.

"What is that smile for?" Emanuel asked.

"Was I smiling?" she asked as she stood up to get the coffee pot from the stove. "I was just thinking about you and our home and how happy I am."

"*Es gut,*" he said as he sat down. He took the pot of coffee from her. "I am happy too," he said, smiling back at her. But he remained quiet, focusing for a moment as he poured coffee into the two empty cups Shana had set onto the table. When he placed the coffee pot back onto the stove, he looked up at her, "My mamm invited us for Christmas worship."

She could tell that pleased him. She hadn't given much thought to Christmas. Without the big tree and exchanging of gifts, it would feel like every other day. Yet, while the disappointment lingered in her mind as she remembered her own family Christmases when she was younger, she found she truly did not resent not seeing her family this year. "Did she?"

"We have a family service and a big dinner in the early

afternoon. I told her we would go."

"When is Christmas, anyway?"

"A week or so, I guess," Emanuel said as he leaned back in his chair and glanced at the calendar hanging on the wall. "Six days, it appears. Perhaps you should call your own family."

"Time flies, doesn't it?" She felt her own shame at Emanuel having to remind her about her family. While they had never been a close family, Shana had written to them about her marriage. "It feels like a lifetime ago that I was a part of their world. They don't even seem real to me, anymore," she said, mostly to herself.

"All the more the reason to call them, then. I'll take you to the payphone this week." He finished his coffee and pushed his cup aside. "Mamm also told me that Steve and his girl parted."

"Liddy May? Did she mention why?"

He shook his head. "I didn't think to ask."

"That's a shame, isn't it? She's such a sweet girl." Shana felt a twang of sympathy for Liddy May. In Shana's mind, Liddy May made the perfect Amish wife. Strong, loyal, a member of the Amish church. And, as Steve had taken his baptism that fall, she was certain that he had found what he was searching for. "I almost forgot, Lillian invited me to join them quilting this January," Shana said, changing the subject. "Maybe one evening, we should have your family here."

He laughed as he stood up. "Just as long as you don't make any of those famous pies of yours."

"A little salt's good for you," she retorted as he slid on his thicker winter jacket and disappeared into the cold to take care of his evening chores.

Three days before Christmas, Emanuel came into the house after the morning milking. To his surprise, Shana was not in the kitchen. Usually she had breakfast ready for him, especially if she didn't help him in the barn. But today, she hadn't even come downstairs yet.

Quietly, he climbed the stairs, the top step creaking under his feet, and noticed their bedroom door open. He glanced in the empty room, the bedcovers still tossed back. A frown crossed his face as he knocked at the closed bathroom door. She didn't answer for several minutes. He could hear her moving around behind the door, the water trickling into the sink, and the flushing of the toilet. When she finally opened the door, her face was pale and her eyes watery. She leaned against the doorframe, clutching her robe around her stomach. Her unbrushed hair fell down to her waist in sweeping waves.

"Shana?" Emanuel glanced inside the bathroom. "Are you all right?"

"Merry Christmas," Shana sighed, her eyes dark and dull. "I think I'm pregnant."

"What?"

A tear fell from her eyes. "I just got sick."

Wrapping his arms around her, Emanuel tried to soothe Shana. He smoothed back her hair, kissing her forehead. "That's wonderful news, Shana. Why are you crying?"

She sobbed into his shoulder, ashamed of her jealousy. "It's too soon for a baby," she said between sobs.

Laughing, Emanuel put his hands on her cheeks, staring into her watery eyes. "It's never too soon for a baby," he smiled before kissing her, the pride swelling from his eyes. "And that is a wonderful Christmas present," he said tenderly.

The next day, he drove her into town to see a doctor where, to Emanuel's delight, Shana's suspicion was confirmed. "I'd say you can expect in late July," the doctor said as he clapped Emanuel on the back.

Shana sat quietly in her chair, hating herself for not being more careful. He would never have allowed her birth control but she should have counted her days better. Two months married and already pregnant. She fought the tears as she followed Emanuel out to the buggy.

She had never seen Emanuel so content. He hummed to himself while he worked, teased her more during supper, and held her throughout the night. If he noticed her lack of enthusiasm or sensed her fear, he never questioned it. Instead, he lived in his own little world where life was as he had planned it. And, Shana slowly realized that, indeed, he had planned it.

Since he was a child, he had been taught that there were three things important to life: worshiping God, farming, and family. She knew that he had lived that life through his parents and watched as his older siblings followed that path. And, while he was not the Amish man with the Amish woman at his side, he had followed in the footsteps of his Amish ancestors; without even realizing it, Shana had fallen into the cycle.

At Christmas, no one mentioned anything about Shana's pregnancy. Shana had noticed the little fanfare that surrounded Lillian's pregnancy and, respecting their ways, she kept quiet about her own. She quickly realized that having children was just the natural course of life to the Amish. Having children was God's will and wasn't necessarily a cause for prolonged celebration.

But, with her family, she knew it would be different. On her next visit before New Year's to Zimmerman's Market, she stood in the phone booth, her hands shaking as she called her parents for the first time since her marriage. As expected, they wanted to come out but Shana had immediately thought better of that idea. Now, when she told them, a sigh in her voice, that she was pregnant, she knew there could be no stopping their imminent visit.

"Just wait until it gets warmer out," she managed to stall them.

While in many ways, she missed aspects of her old life, she was growing accustomed to her new lifestyle. She enjoyed the solitude and tranquility. The few noises that did surround her added to the relaxed atmosphere of the farm life. She was even getting used to attending those three-hour church services every other week. But, above all, she felt a growing sense of belonging, even though, she knew that she'd never be fully accepted by the Amish.

To bring her family into her new world frightened her. They had known her all of her life, seen her through college days, and reprimanded her for staying out too late. Now, they would be coming to visit, to see their youngest daughter in the new environment she had chosen to join. With their fast cars and upbeat energy, her parents certainly would never understand how she could extract pleasure and pride from the domesticated lifestyle she had fought against for so long.

It was the slow season at the market, although a few local residents wandered down the aisles. Out of boredom, they watched as the Amish man with his young mustache-less beard and the obviously Englische woman who accompanied him. He glanced up as she touched his arm. To the strangers, they wondered how they knew each other since most Amish men did not consort with non-Amish women.

"You got through, ja?" he asked.

"I told them to come visit when it was warmer, closer to the time the baby's due," she replied. "Maybe fall."

The eavesdroppers raised an eyebrow but busied themselves in the shelves of supplies, trying to act inconspicuous but curious about the relationship between this mix-matched couple. But as the Amish man and his Englische companion continued down the aisle, consulting about different foods to buy, it became obvious, even to the amazed locals, that the couple was husband and wife.

Chapter Fifteen

If the lone black buggy clattering up their driveway surprised Emanuel, he did not let it show. They had been sitting by the heater, Emanuel reading the local farmer's paper and Shana sewing. The small, rusty thermometer hanging outside the window over the sink read about 45 degrees and a thin layer of clouds flirted with the sun. One of the trees on the edge of the driveway, its bare branches reaching toward the sky, loomed eerily over Emanuel's unhitched buggy. He had driven it into town earlier that day and hadn't put the buggy back into the protection of the stable. They hadn't been expecting anyone so, when the wheels of the visitor's buggy rattled along their driveway, neither knew who could be visiting.

Emanuel set the paper down on the table as he walked over to the kitchen window and gazed outside. "Lillian's coming." He glanced over his shoulder at Shana. "Perhaps I should let you two visit and get to mending some of that fence while the sun's shining and the wind has stopped," he said quietly.

Shana laid down the shirt she was sewing and stood up. She was just under four months pregnant, yet her waistline certainly showed the weight gain. Shana had been concerned about how quickly she was gaining weight but, to her relief, her doctor had eased her fear with a comforting explanation, "Each woman has a different pregnancy, Shana. Some gain next to nothing, others gain a lot. Just watch the foods you're eating."

Emanuel put on his heavy winter coat, covered his head with a black, felt hat, and disappeared into the cold. Shana stood by the window and watched as he greeted Lillian, by the barn. He reached out for the horse's reins until his sister-in-law, herself increasingly large with child, scrambled out of the buggy. They exchanged a few more words then Lillian walked quickly toward the house.

"Hello there," Shana said as Lillian swept into the house, a gust of chilly winter air following her. "Such a long trip for you to make alone on such a cold day."

Lillian shook off her cape and hung it on a peg in the washroom outside the kitchen. She bent down for a moment as though brushing some dirty snow off of her boot. "*Ja vell,* I was visiting my sister three farms up the lane," she said as she walked into the kitchen. The cold had marked Lillian's cheeks with a rosy glow. "She just gave birth. A son. I wanted to stop by before my own time," she said, referring to her own pregnancy. "Besides, the winter's been so cold, I had to take advantage of the good weather."

"Well, I'm glad you thought to stop by."

Lillian didn't reply but looked around the kitchen. Shana watched as Lillian's eyes took in the open living room, no partition to block the entrance. For a moment, she looked slightly confused then she smiled. "How strange it looks," she commented, not unkindly. "There are Englische touches around the house. Yet, everything looks quite plain."

"Does that surprise you?" Shana asked, hurt by Lillian's obvious reservation regarding the decor of her house.

"No." Again, the smile. "After all, you are Englische and Emanuel is Amish. Shouldn't it make sense that you'd blend the two into your home?"

"Emanuel isn't Amish," Shana reminded.

"*Ja vell,*" Lillian replied as she moved toward the kitchen table and sat down. "You can't take the Amish out of Emanuel."

Her smile slowly faded as she returned Shana's curious gaze with complete seriousness. "He was born Amish and he continues to live as though he is Amish." She looked around the room again. "Even the plainness of the decor is mostly Amish, Shana."

"Because of me, he'll never truly be Amish, Lillian. He'd never be allowed to take his baptism."

"No," Lillian agreed. "Not unless you were both to take the baptism. He loves you more than he loves the church, ja? Otherwise, he could have taken his baptism and married a nice Amish girl. Certainly it would have been easier for him in the long run anyway, ja? But there are reasons for everything. God provided it that way. 'Judge not that ye be judged not," she quoted before softly adding, "You were meant to stay on Mother's farm and marry Emanuel. Is it our right to question the acts of God?"

It was the first anyone had spoken to Shana about the conflicts brought on by their marriage. During the past three months, Shana had spent several days at Katie's farm, once for the quilting and another time for visiting with her mother and sister-in-law while Emanuel joined his father at an auction in Lancaster. Neither one of those times had anyone mentioned anything about religion or Emanuel's non-Amish wife. Instead, they had talked about friends and family and the upcoming spring planting. Now, after Lillian had spoken the words, Shana felt relieved, as though she had been holding her breath for this moment. "I wouldn't suppose we should question Him."

"It pleases everyone that you've taken such an interest in the church. Especially Emanuel," Lillian remarked casually.

"Especially Emanuel," Shana agreed. She took the empty coffee pot off of the stove and quickly filled it with water. Shana was slowly suspecting the visit hadn't been entirely unplanned.

"I think I knew that you would marry Emanuel," Lillian continued calmly. "Perhaps from the very first moment I saw you two walking down the lane together, a week or so after you arrived." She hesitated, her eyes dark and thoughtful, as though visualizing that moment in her mind. "His mamm knew it, you know. But she also knew she couldn't stop it from happening. Emanuel's always been a little quiet about the things he wanted in life. But, he acted so different after you arrived." She paused, her eyes glazing over as though thinking back to those days. The memory must have pleased her for she smiled, "I thought the change was rather nice."

"And the others?"

"Some people resist change, the Amish in particular," Lillian began as she sat down at the kitchen table. "They resist change in society and religion. But that does not mean that a person cannot change, does it? Months before you arrived, Jonas Jr. and I wondered about Emanuel. He didn't conform to our ways, ja? He didn't court girls. He didn't attend too many singings. He never used his courting buggy. We often wondered whether he'd join the church and prayed that he'd find the answers to his own questions. He seemed so lost, Shana. We understood and accepted the change in Emanuel."

"I don't think too many people were as understanding when they realized that Emanuel refused his baptism in order to marry outside the church," Shana said softly.

The grandfather clock began to chime from the other room. Lillian waited until it finished before she ventured further. "A refusal of baptism is understood better than a member straying from the Ordnung after accepting baptism. It is easy to find religion; it is salvation most seek. After committing to a life of Christ, salvation is lost in those who stray and do not repent.

Those who have not committed cannot stray." The smile had once again vanished as her light-sided conversation turned serious. Leaning forward, Lillian asked softly, "What religion will your child be baptized into?"

"I...Well, I don't really know," Shana started. Lillian's directness startled her, catching her off-guard. She hadn't even been aware that anyone, besides Emanuel, truly knew about her pregnancy. "I imagine the child will decide when the time is right. We'll teach all of our children Christian values and continue attending the church. But the decision? That has to be theirs."

"And what religion are you baptized?"

"I was baptized as a child, Lillian, from a Christian faith, but not of Anabaptist descent. Although my parents didn't force a particular faith upon me, they knew I'd choose my own when the time was right."

"And what did you choose?"

Shana frowned, curious as to the reasons behind Lillian's questions. Shana didn't respond, ashamed at her answer. Her parents had chosen no religion, not actively. And she, as their offspring, had followed in their footsteps. They did not belong to a church, and neither did she. "The time has not been right," Shana admitted quietly.

The seriousness vanished from her face and Lillian smiled. Protectively, she rubbed her enlarged stomach and said, "My children will certainly follow in my footsteps, although I appreciate the philosophy of your parents. At the foot washing this past season, Lindy cried because she couldn't go. Already she understands that we're more than just a church. We are a community and a family. It's nice to know that they're there for us."

"Your baby is due soon, then?" Shana asked, eager to change the subject.

"End of this month." She looked out the window dreamily. "I hope I never stop having children," she said softly. "I'd be happiest if I was always surrounded by their smiling faces and happy laughter. Children bring such joy to the farm." She met Shana's gaze again. The placid look on her face, so content and serene, almost forced envy into Shana's heart. "You'll see, Shana. For a farm, the springtime is the best time of year; the busiest, too. But add a little child to that, with all of their wonder and curiosity..."

A silence ensued. Neither dared to break it for a moment. Lillian vanished into her depth of thoughts, thinking about the glory of motherhood while Shana watched her, envious of her sister-in-law's self-tranquility. Finally, the coffee began percolating and, the silence broken, Shana got up to pour them each a cup.

For the next half-an-hour, they talked about the crops their farms would yield the next harvest and about the breakup of Steve and Liddy May. Lillian confided that she wondered about an interest Steve had taken in a neighbor's hired girl who was helping the family while the wife had taken ill. When the clock chimed again, Lillian got up and explained that she had to hurry home before Jonas Jr. would worry about her.

She disappeared into the washroom and put on her thick wool cape. Then, to Shana's surprise, she gently handed her a small wrapped parcel and whispered, "I made them myself for you," then hurried out of the house after a quick and distant good-bye. Shana watched from the window, pleased to see Emanuel emerge from the barn to help her with the buggy. Then, with a friendly wave at the house, Lillian drove the buggy down the lane and toward her home.

The buggy slowly disappeared and, with it, the clattering of the wheels against the cold road became just a gentle ringing in her ear. When it was finally gone, Shana turned her attention back to the package in her hand. It was wrapped in what looked like an old paper bag. Carefully, for she could tell that its contents were delicate, she unwrapped the paper and took out the precious present Lillian had made for her.

At first, she was startled. Setting the package on the kitchen counter, she held the lily-white head covering up first. A second one, black, remained in the paper. The handmade organza caps, perfectly round with two strings hanging down the sides, brought tears to her eyes. She knew the amount of time it must have taken Lillian to make these head coverings, especially when she had so many other things to do.

Carrying the white cap over to the mirror, Shana hesitated before placing it on her head. The strings hung over her shoulders and, imitating the way Lillian wore her own cap, Shana tied a tiny bow at their end. Her fingers lingered, her eyes downcast as she touched the bow. The material felt stiff as she gently stroked the thin ribbon-like strings. Then, brushing her hair off of her forehead and holding her breath, she lifted her eyes and gazed into the small mirror over the sink.

The person that gazed back frightened her. She barely recognized herself with the naturally colored cheeks, the large brown eyes and the white prayer cap resting on the back of her head. The neckline of her dress showed off her slender neck, bare of any jewelry. The dark color of the fabric made her skin resemble the color of fresh milk. Yet, as her dark eyes sought the reflection for a trace of the young woman she had once been, she found only a stranger peering back.

"Shana?"

Startled, Shana spun around, the cap falling from her head. She bent down and grabbed it, holding it against her chest as she faced Emanuel's inquisitive gaze. She hadn't heard him enter and wasn't certain how long he had been watching her. But she felt a hot blush covering her cheeks.

He stared at her, his blue eyes taking in the white head covering in her hands. Then, he drifted his gaze to the partially unwrapped black one, the cap worn for baptism, that she had set upon the counter. Emanuel walked over and, gently, picked it up. It looked so delicate in his large, calloused hands. For what seemed like long minutes, he toyed with it, his eyes glazing over as he disappeared into his own world.

She watched him, breathlessly. What was he thinking? The privacy of the moment so suddenly broken, she wondered whether he felt anger or pride. She knew the answer as he returned to the moment and walked toward her, reaching out to set the black covering on her head. Gently, he placed his hands on her shoulders and turned her around. His inquisitive eyes stared into the mirror as he stood behind her, his hands still lightly touching her back.

"I...I don't know if I can do it, Emanuel," she finally whispered into the reflection.

"I don't know if I can't," he replied solemnly. He dropped his hands from her shoulders and turned away. She watched him in the mirror as he headed for the kitchen doorway into the washroom.

"It doesn't mean the same thing to me," she said quickly, her voice still soft yet strong.

He paused in the doorway, his back hunched over as he reached out to open the door. "It doesn't have to," he replied before disappearing out of the house and into the cold winter air, leaving Shana alone to remove the covering that he had placed upon her head.

Chapter Sixteen

Shortly after Lillian's visit to Shana, the cold weather cleared out and signs of spring began to appear. The birds returned from their migration south and two of the cows gave birth. Emanuel began spending more and more time in the fields, preparing for spring planting. It was early for the warm weather to start but the days began to lengthen shortly after the birth of Lillian's second child, a son she named Jacob. There were few occasions for visiting them, although one Wednesday in April, Emanuel and Shana rode over to Katie and Jonas' farm to visit and meet the youngest and newest member of the Lapp family.

By early April, Emanuel was gone for most of the day. Shortly after milking the cows, a chore Shana now helped with daily, he'd harness the two mules and head out to the fields. Shana would finish washing the breakfast dishes before starting her own daily chores. After cleaning the house, something she tried to do every day, and feeding the two horses, she'd take a hot pot of coffee to the chilly fields to provide some relief to Emanuel while he plowed the fields.

From pre-dawn to after-dusk, Emanuel plowed . The farm, a full 65 acres, would allow one man 20 acres of corn crops that year. And Emanuel planned on yielding over 100 bushels per acre. In the meantime, Shana started building her chicken coop and, on a rainy Thursday, Emanuel drove into town and returned with two hens and a cocky rooster. From that day on, Shana never found herself idle for more than a few wishful minutes throughout the day.

By the end of April, along with the fresh sun and warm air, spring brought her the first batch of chicks. Shana heard the peeping before she entered the chicken coop; and, as she carefully entered, she saw her first yellow chick. Born during the night, one chick, still wobbling on its skinny legs, had ventured out from its shell and away from the protection of its nonchalant mother.

"Betsy! Look how beautiful your babies are!" Shana exclaimed. She scooped down and picked up the fuzzy chick. Nuzzling her nose against the warmth of its fresh peach fuzz, she smiled and shut her eyes. The chick peeped a couple of times before Shana remembered that there were more and, after all of their hard work, they must be hungry.

She took longer than usual to feed the chickens that day. She sprayed the feed on the floor, watching as the chicks copied each other as they scrambled for food. Two eggs hadn't hatched yet and, later when she mentioned it to Emanuel, to her tearful dismay, he told her they probably never would.

Twice a week, especially as the chicks grew, Shana chased them outside and washed down the inside of the coop. But, the harder she tried to keep it clean, the messier it seemed to get. Most of the day, the chickens stayed inside their closed pen while the rooster wandered around the farm. But, even though she kept the rooster separated from the hens, another batch of chicks was born shortly after the first batch had lost all of their peach fuzz.

"I don't understand," she complained at night to Emanuel. "I kept them apart and thought I found all of the eggs. How could this have happened?"

Emanuel laughed at her plight. With over fifteen chickens now, twelve of them young, hungry chicks, she had enough chickens to handle and gave up on naming them. The rooster hung around the cages as though waiting for his chance. But Shana, onto his game, was more careful during feedings and cleanings.

As the chilly spring air became warmer, the cats returned to the farm. It didn't take long for Shana to discover that the baby chicks were no longer safe under the careful supervision of their mother hens. Twice, she found evidence of cats in the henhouse and three chicks disappeared. When she finally found the remains of one of them, she spent the next hour in tears until Emanuel managed to calm her down. He couldn't understand her emotions over the lost chicks but he tried to explain that new life on a farm did not mean that death would not follow.

She painted a sign "Fresh Eggs For Sale" and placed it at the end of the driveway. Within a few days, she had a regular clientele of neighbors trickling up her driveway every day. Some neighbors came once a week, others came twice. But they made certain that they always knocked at the door and paused to chat for a few moments before asking for their supply. Some days, Shana had to walk out to the end of the driveway and turn the sign around. Until the chicks turned into chickens, her eggs supply could not meet the local demand.

By early May, Shana shed her shoes and started her garden. She was thankful when Sylvia came over from Katie's for a week to help Shana plan her first garden. Six and a half months pregnant, Shana tired easily and began experiencing back pains. She hated being so overweight and found it hard to bend over all morning. Quiet Sylvia was a relief, especially since Shana was uncertain how and what to plant. Together, they had decided to plant tomatoes, lettuce, carrots, celery, cucumbers, and beans. For Shana, that was all she felt she could handle. "We'll plant more next year," she explained to a disappointed Sylvia.

It was during the last day of planting that Sylvia mentioned the instructional at the church. They were finishing the last row of tomatoes. Sylvia had shown Shana how far apart to plant them and put the stakes in the ground. Tying the last young stalk to the stake, Sylvia glanced up at Shana, a slight sweat breaking on her brow. "Did Emanuel tell you that Ana's attending her instructional this spring?" she asked in her soft voice.

Shana stood back and admired the work of art they had accomplished during that long day. Her back ached and she felt weak. She tired easily but, as her eyes feasted on the long rows of tiny plants in the freshly tilled soil, she felt the inkling of pride. "Instructional?" she replied as she bent down and patted some more earth around a lettuce plant. "I thought she finished schooling."

"Ja," she mumbled as she stood up and wiped her dirty hands on her apron. "But this is church instructional. She has to attend prior to the fall communion."

Shana snapped her gaze to meet Sylvia's. "Church instructional?" Shana repeated softly, her gaze drifting to the rolling hill beyond the barn. "Has Emanuel ever attended?"

"I believe." Sylvia stepped out of the soil and onto the grass. She wiped her feet before bending over to pick up her shoes. "You have to attend before you join. It's called *die Gemee nooch geh*."

"Die gimme what?"

Sylvia laughed at Shana's weak German pronunciation. It was the first time Shana had heard Sylvia's gentle laughter. "*Die Gemee nooch geh*. To follow the church, Shana."

"Die Gemee nooch geh," Shana repeated to herself.

"The next church Sunday is the first meeting," Sylvia added as they started walking back to the house.

"Really?" The baby shifted inside of her enlarged stomach and, for a moment, she paused. Each movement of her unborn child excited her. What was it Lillian had said, she wondered.

"Spring is the best time on a farm," she whispered.

"Did the baby kick again, then?" Sylvia asked anxiously.

Despite having always been surrounded by young children, Sylvia still seemed curious and almost envious of each newborn that entered the world. She delighted in Lillian's children and was eager to help Shana when her baby was born. Shana wasn't certain whether it was maternal instinct or cultural expectations that made her young sister-in-law so interested in babies but she did know that she would be quite glad to have the young girl's help when the baby finally arrived.

"Right here," Shana said as she showed Sylvia where to place her hand. She watched as her young sister-in-law's face lit up when the baby shifted again.

That night, after they had milked the cows and finished preparing supper, Emanuel emerged from the dusky darkness and stomped into the washroom. The kitchen faucet ran and he sloshed water around the basin as he washed his hands and face. Then, reaching for a towel, he rubbed himself dry and walked into the kitchen.

"The garden looks as though it will yield enough food for a family of ten," he teased.

"Then that should be enough to feed this household, if we keep working so hard," she retorted playfully.

"With all that food, I should have enough energy to work twice as many hours in a day."

Shana laughed. "There are twice as many hours in a day, Emanuel. But twelve of them are called night." Even Sylvia smiled at their teasing banter. "I couldn't have done it without Sylvia's help," Shana offered the compliment cautiously.

"Perhaps she will have to help again when you have other

things to tend to," Emanuel said, insinuating that Shana would have her hands full after the baby's birth without actually mentioning Shana's pregnancy. He sat down at the head of the table and let his sister serve him. Shana sat to his right and smiled her appreciation to Sylvia as she finished setting the steaming plates of fresh vegetables, mashed potatoes, and smoked ham on the table. Then, Sylvia sat across from Shana and bowed her head in prayer.

"O Lord God, heavenly Father, bless these gifts that thou hast tenderly given us," she mumbled quietly. "Feed the hunger and quench the thirst of our souls until eternal life and bestow before us thy heavenly table through Jesus Christ. Amen."

Emanuel glanced up and, catching Shana's curious gaze, he winked at her before turning his attention back to his younger sister. "Well done, Sylvia. In case we had forgotten, you did well reminding us."

Startled, she looked up. "Did I pray aloud?"

"Either that or we've become mind readers."

Ashamed, she lowered her head. "Please forgive me."

Laughing, Emanuel reached across the table for the potatoes. "Never ask for forgiveness for seeking the Lord," he replied soothingly and, when she looked up, he spared her a kind smile.

After a brief silence with plates being passed around the table, Shana cleared her throat and said, "Mary Yoder came by today for eggs." Each meal was spent retelling who had stopped by the farm or paused for a visit along the road. Normally, at least two hours of her day were spent visiting with some neighbor who came to buy eggs or stopped by on their way home from some errand. If she wasn't too busy, Shana often invited them in for a glass of lemonade or ice tea. She found most of her neighbors warm and friendly. For the most part, she enjoyed being invited into their lives, to hear the local farm gossip. "Did you know that the farm down the road is for sale?" she asked.

Emanuel looked up from his plate. "The Millers are moving then?"

"The Beilers," she corrected. She noticed the frown on his face. "I believe they're moving to Ohio to be closer to their relatives. I wasn't aware that they were from Ohio." But Emanuel's eyes clouded over and she knew that he wasn't listening to her.

For the rest of the meal, he remained quiet, the wheels of his mind spinning in a direction far from anything else Shana or Sylvia had to say. So, in silence, everyone ate. After the meal, Emanuel quietly left the table and retreated upstairs. While Sylvia washed the dishes and cleaned the kitchen, Shana put away the leftovers and listened to the creaking of the floorboards as Emanuel walked around until, finally, silence prevailed.

The table cleared, the food put away, and Sylvia excusing herself for bed, Shana retreated to the solitude of the living room where she sat at the desk and pulled out a sheet of paper to write to her family. The lantern on the desk flickered as the sun outside set behind the fields. The clock chimed seven times and Shana listened to each reverberation that temporarily broke the silence. She rarely sat in the living room as Emanuel frowned on using the room without need. But, she often enjoyed the privacy and quiet that surrounded her.

Shana dreaded receiving each letter from her parents, fearful of an announcement that they would be visiting. She hated to admit that being reminded of her past and how far she had strayed from her former life style terrified her. Yet, at the end of each passing day, she looked back on everything that she had done and, indeed, she felt pride in just being alive and having survived. From the house to the garden to her small chickens, Shana enjoyed her new role as wife, worker, and worshipper. She didn't even mind the three-hour sermons every other Sunday. In fact, she realized as she sealed the envelope shut, she was actually looking forward the next worship service.

Chapter Seventeen

She stood at the back of the barn, leaning against a stack of bundled hay. Her eyes remained downcast, staring at the swept cement floor. She blended into the strictly female crowd that either sat on hard benches or stood in front of her, all of them dressed in similar blue or green dresses, complete with the same white organza head covering that hid her neatly parted hair, almost one length hair now, pulled back off her face in a tight bun at the nape of her slightly sunburned neck. A few strands of wispy bangs strayed from the traditional hairstyle of Amish women. But her cheeks had taken on the color of a woman who spent a healthy amount of time outdoors, working hard under the spring and summer sun.

Shana listened to the sermon, her eyes staring at a spot of mud on the shoe heel of a woman standing in front of her. With the warmer weather, the bi-weekly services were held in the hosting Amish family's barn. With the doors open, a gentle breeze occasionally filtered into the crowded barn. Shana was thankful that she stood at the back where she was able to not feel so stifled. During the sermon, she caught bits and phrases that she thought she understood. But, surrounding her, the faith of the people in the barn filled her with complete understanding of what she was about to do.

Two rows up, seated on a hard bench, a young child, not quite three years of age, began whimpering and rested her head against her mother's shoulder. The woman with the mud on her shoe reached her hand in her pocket and, leaning forward, tapped the mother's shoulder to hand her something. The mother smiled her appreciation and took what looked like a cookie to silence the fretful child. Shana watched, her curiosity peaked, as the child took the cookie and, quietly, began gnawing on the edges. The mother, satisfied that the child was better occupied, returned her attention to the front of the barn, staring at the man who was preaching the sermon in German.

Most of the women were fortunate enough to sit during the three-hour service. Some of the younger women stood in the back. The men sat in the front, their heads covered with their black Sunday hats. If she watched long enough, she'd catch a black hat slowly dip forward for several seconds, the man obviously having fallen asleep. But his neighbor would usually nudge him enough to jolt him awake. Shana tried to pick out Emanuel, certain that he sat closer to the back than the rest. But, the sea of black rims looked the same to her. Giving up, she returned her own attention back to her neighbor's heel.

The air had grown stale and thick before the five Amish men that stood in the front of the barn finally shut their Bibles, signaling that the service was over and the people began filing outside into the increasingly hot sunshine. As the other women hurried toward the house to begin serving the simple noon meal, Shana searched the crowd of people until she found the man with the long gray beard and sun beaten face.

She pushed her way past the small formations of men and, reaching out to touch his heavy, black sleeve, she softly whispered, "Bishop Studer."

He turned around, his kind, aging eyes searching her face. Then, as he recognized her, he smiled. "Shana, how are you today? Did you enjoy the sermon?"

She returned his smile but her eyes darted away from his gaze. She thought about the restless child and the sea of black hats, some of them bobbing as they fought the Devil's sleep during a Sunday sermon. "What I understood, I enjoyed." Then, she dared to lift her eyes to meet his steady stare. "And what I didn't understand, I felt."

The bishop countered as his blue eyes softened, "That was the Lord opening your heart."

"Bishop," she said abruptly in order to curtail the gentle friendly chatter. "I have a problem that I think you can help me solve."

A moment of silence followed and she sensed he was studying her face, his blue eyes flickering back and forth as they read her expression. Obviously recognizing the seriousness behind her words, he reached for her arm and led her away from the crowds, softly whispering, "Seek and ye shall find, child. I will help you if I am able."

For what seemed like a long while, Shana stood before the bishop and looked out through the open barn doors: The black buggies, the swarms of children, the laughing Amish men standing in cliquish semi-circles as they swapped stories about their friends, families, and farms. Someone shouted out, a woman from the house. Some men looked up and, their circle disbanding, headed for the long table outside the kitchen door where the women were busy dishing out food for their families.

Shana turned back to Bishop Studer, her shoulders pushed back and her chin tilted forward. "I want to raise my children Amish." Noticing the change in his expression, Shana continued cautiously. "It is important to Emanuel to pass along his heritage to his children and it is important to me that my children grow up surrounded by the love of these people and the church. In the past year of my life, I have almost learned to be in complete peace with myself but there is one thing lacking."

The bishop tilted his head, again studying her face. "The Lord," he stated slowly.

She took a deep breath. "I desire to seek Him through the church. I have learned so much from Emanuel and the Lapps and the congregation, it isn't fair that I'd take everything they've offered to me without giving back. If I wish my children to learn the same values, I must dedicate my life to living those values. Otherwise, my faith is hypocritical." She paused, hoping that Bishop Studer would say something. He continued to study her face, his eyes softening as he detected her sincerity. She met his gaze as she said, "I understand that there is instructional right now, die Gimme nooch deh," she said.

The bishop smiled. "*Die Gemee nooch deh*," he said, gently correcting her pronunciation.

"Perhaps I might attend or, if that is not possible," she said, suggesting the complications of her present state with a simple gesture toward her enlarged stomach. "Perhaps we could meet for private lessons. I'm sure I have more to learn than most of the others attending the instructional."

"We never stop learning about the Lord's ways. You have no more nor no less than the rest of us need to learn, ja?" he said. Then, with a twinkle in his eyes, he glanced toward Emanuel who was standing amidst a group of young married Amish men, talking about, Shana assumed, the summer planting. "He would be greatly pleased should you join the church. But you would have to join together."

"Emanuel has never stopped seeking the Lord. Joining the Amish church would not be a hard argument for me to pass with him," she whispered more to herself than to the bishop. "I'll talk to him when the time is right."

"It is always a right time," the bishop chided her. She felt a blush creep onto her cheeks. She had envisioned telling Emanuel in private, surprising him with her announcement in a moment of intimacy. Yet, the bishop had given her a first lesson in what it meant to surrender to the Amish way of life as he casually dismissed such an idea when he said, "I'll see that Emanuel knows where to meet for the instructional." The conversation over, he walked away to join the men.

Since the Sunday midday meal was mostly pre-cooked, there wasn't as much cooking or setting up. The congregation filed through the kitchen to fill their plates. The church elders ate under the shade of a tree in the front yard. Several more tables were set up around the yard. The women and children waited patiently for the men to finish eating before they took their places at the table.

While waiting in the shade on the porch for her turn, Shana visited briefly with her neighbor, Mary Beiler, asking her when they were planning to move to Ohio. "Certainly not until after the summer harvest," she explained to Shana. They began to talk about the crops and Shana felt her own pride when Mary commented, "Your Emanuel works from morning to night, ja? Plowing and planting all those acres by himself. He has the aspiration of a man with seven sons."

Shana laughed with her. "I don't know what he'd do with his extra time if we did have seven sons."

After the midday meal, Emanuel caught Shana's gaze and, without words, made it clear that he was ready to leave. Shana excused herself from the small crowd of women and walked over to join Emanuel as he bade good-bye and headed toward the buggies. He helped her into the buggy, his hand lingering at her touch. When she glanced down at him, he quickly released her hand and jumped up next to her.

Inside the buggy, Emanuel grabbed the reins and, before slapping them against Lady's back, he hesitated. In that hesitation, Shana thought she saw the glimmer of a tear in his eye. She reached out to touch his arm, concern wrinkling across her forehead.

"Emanuel?" she prodded.

He turned to look at her and she saw that, indeed, there were tears in his eyes. But, the smile that crossed his face quickly reassured her that those tears were from joy. Lowering her eyes, Shana realized that the bishop had talked to Emanuel about their conversation. Certainly the bishop had told him about his wife's desire to join the church.

If she had hoped to tell him herself, perhaps even surprise him, she realized that such surprises were the Englische way. And she had just given up those ways. The magnitude of what she had just done began to hit her. Her heart began to pound inside her chest and she felt unreal as though walking through a dream.

"Bishop Studer and Preacher Yoder spoke with me. They've agreed to allow us to attend the instructional next week. Preacher Yoder also expressed interest in visiting this week to assist you in your learning," he said seriously.

"Perhaps you could assist me as well, Emanuel."

"I am flattered, Shana." He met her gaze as he replied, "But undeserving of such a compliment. I need as much instruction and guidance as you." Then, as though sensing her trepidation at her decision, Emanuel urged the horse forward in silence, letting Shana wander in her own thoughts.

Deciding to join the Amish church had been, in some ways,

a harder choice to make than her decision to join her life with Emanuel's and to give up her Englische way of life with electricity and cars and the glory of convenience. Every day that passed, she thought less and less of what she had given up and thanked God more and more for what she had gained in the process. Her love of the land and life was new and fresh. She cherished the wonder of each new sprout of corn that poked up out of the ground. She enjoyed feeding the newborn calves and helping Emanuel milk the cows each day. She loved each one of the new kittens and chickens that were born during the spring. But now, she wasn't changing just her lifestyle but her entire way of thinking and believing. She was changing her faith.

Several minutes passed before, tears forming in her own eyes, she whispered, "I'm scared."

"He will guide you," Emanuel replied evenly. "*Be of good courage, and He shall strengthen your heart, all ye that hope in the Lord,*'" he quoted.

"I've given up everything, haven't I?"

"You've given up nothing, Shana," he reminded her. "You've just begun your ascent into His Kingdom. 'Out of His heart shall flow rivers of living water.' Your life has just begun."

Blinking back her tears, she sighed and leaned back. She raised her eyes to stare at the roof of the buggy. There was no turning back, she realized, not in the eyes of the community. In their mind, the decision had just been made and the baptism, in its own way, had already started. While the unbaptized were not fully Amish, those who desired to take the communion were treated as though they already were.

Chapter Eighteen

Shana walked down the lane, the envelope in her hand-hanging heavily in her heart. The dirt from the lane felt dry on her bare feet. She hadn't worn shoes in weeks, except for church. She liked the freedom and dreaded the upcoming cold months. By the corner of the horse stable, she bent down to scratch the belly of a gray cat, lounging in a warm sunbeam. The cat purred under Shana's touch for several minutes before it rolled over and swatted at Shana's hand, its claws grazing her skin. A thin line of blood immediately appeared.

Shana snatched her hand away and frowned at the scrawny freeloader. "After all the table scraps I've given you," she said to the cat who quickly jumped to its feet and sprang towards the stables. "Off with you then, Mr. Ungrateful," she called after it.

Heading back to the house, she glanced down at the return address on the envelope and sighed. For the past year, she had avoided the inevitable, hoping that the time for her parents' visit would never come. Yet now, she was certain that what she had been avoiding was finally upon her.

There were times when she missed her parents but she had gotten used to living without them long ago, since her early days in college. Occasionally, she daydreamed about seeing them and witnessing their reaction to the changes she had experienced. Her greatest fear was that, by seeing them, she'd be drawn back into the Englische world she had worked so hard at separating from. Yet, whenever she glanced out the window and saw Emanuel working in the fields or milking the cows, she knew that she would never want to leave the peaceful life he had blessed her with.

The walk down the lane had tired her. She sat on the front

porch and held the letter before her, staring at the elegant handwriting that spelled her married name. She dissected the writing, wondering whether each loop was written in anger or love, or maybe both. Initially, their letters had expressed concern about her rapid marriage to a man they had never met. Then, they wrote about her pregnancy. While they never expressed their disapproval, it wasn't hard to read between the lines. Clearly her parents were upset by how rapidly their daughter's life was changing.

During the summer months, she hadn't written as much, trying to avoid the subject. What was done was done and, despite their unhappiness, Shana was quite content with the decisions she had made. She loved Emanuel and loved her new life.

Yet, with the baby's birth being followed by an imminent visit from her parents, Shana knew that she couldn't put off the inevitable task of informing them about Emanuel's Amish upbringing and her decision to join the church. She wanted them to know before they arrived for a visit. After all, their grandchildren would be raised in the same faith. Her hand touched her stomach and, without knowing it, she protectively rubbed her unborn child.

"Letter from your mamm, ja?"

Shana snapped out of her daze and looked up at Emanuel as he walked around the corner of the house. His clothes were covered in mud and his mustache-less beard looked fuller than she had noticed recently. "My mother, yes."

"Say when they're to visit?"

She shrugged. "I haven't read it yet."

"Don't you think that you should open it before you judge what is written?" He sat down next to her, taking his straw hat off his head. With the back of his arm, he wiped the sweat off his forehead and set his hat on his knee.

Glancing at him, she managed to smile before sliding her finger under the back flap and slitting the envelope open. She took out the two pieces of neatly folded paper and began to read the contents of her mother's letter to herself. Emanuel waited patiently, his own eyes staring at the massive field of green corn sprouts. In the sunlight, it glistened like a sea of green crystals. A car drove down the road, its engine breaking the peaceful tranquility of the early summer breeze.

She set the letter down in her lap, covered by a slightly stained floral apron tied around her waist. "Well, they aren't too happy," she sighed.

"What should they be unhappy about, Shana?"

The tears came to her eyes. She rolled her eyes toward the sky, fighting the sudden flow of sadness that streamed down her cheeks. "Oh, me, I guess." She wiped at her eyes with the corner of her apron. "They expected more from me than to settle down to a life as a farmer's wife. And they can't understand why I didn't tell them about you being Amish, about the life we're living."

Emanuel smiled and reached for her hand. He squeezed it gently. "Then they will understand when they come visiting."

A laugh escaped her throat. She felt angry and abandoned; forced to have to make a decision that no person should ever face. Her family couldn't understand why she felt compelled to hide his Amish upbringing and how she could consider raising her children surrounded by the faith of a culture that had, in their opinion, fought so hard and for so many years to regress in time. Yet, if she didn't, Shana knew, she'd never fully have Emanuel nor would she ever feel the strength and love she so admired in Katie and Lillian.

"Oh, they're coming to visit alright," she said. "They'll be here in August." Just two weeks after the baby is due, she didn't say. She didn't cherish the idea of facing her new challenge of motherhood while fighting the ideals of her own parents when she would them that she had decided to become a baptized member of the Amish church.

Emanuel lifted his hat and placed it on his head. "I guess we should get started fixing the downstairs guest room for them, then." He stood up and reached down for her hand. Helping her to her feet, he smiled. "We have a lot of work to do, ja?"

They rode into town that afternoon to pick up some paint and food. The air was dry and the buggy hot. Shana leaned back in the seat, shutting her eyes. Her arms and neck felt damp with sweat and she longed for a cooling breeze. But, the gentle sound of the horse's hooves against the pavement lulled her into a soft sleep, interrupted only by a passing car's impatient honking horn.

Bolting upright, she looked around. Then, seeing the car, an old roadster speeding up the road, she settled back. Teenagers, she thought. She had heard stories of teenagers throwing rocks at buggies, running them off the road, and even trying to hit the horses with their cars. While she couldn't understand the resentment the local people had toward the Amish, the knowledge that it existed frightened her.

Tourist season had started, a fact made obvious by the crowded aisles in the store and the abundance of cars on the roads. Ahead of them was the market, a particularly notorious Amish general store that had been in a popular movie back in the 1980s. It was a must-see tourist attraction for all visitors to Lancaster, a place to stop for a quick walk through the aisles and pause on the front porch for a quick photograph. Shana had learned that the Amish tried to avoid using that store, especially during the peak of tourist season. But it was convenient for quick purchases when other stores were either closed or too far away.

Shana remembered the year before, almost a year to the day, when they had visited the store. She thought of the tourist who had tried to take Emanuel's photo and how she had reacted. Yet, as they were both the center of attention as they climbed out of the buggy, Shana felt startled and confused by the stares and pointed fingers.

She reached for Emanuel's arm and lowered her eyes from the curious gazes. To the outsider, they couldn't tell that she had once been one of them, curious about the Amish way. She wondered what they would think if she stopped to tell them how she had fallen in-love with her Amish man and, in just a couple of months, they would both take their baptism and join the church.

"Good day, Shana," an elderly woman leaving the store said.

Shana looked up in time to see Anna Zook passing her. "How are you, Anna? We haven't seen you since we visited Katie and Jonas' church this past winter."

Anna stood aside as two children raced down the aisle. "I understand you'll be taking the baptism this fall."

"So we plan," Shana replied, her eyes glancing around the store for Emanuel's hat. She spotted him by the household section and knew he was looking for an appropriate color to paint the downstairs guest room.

"Did you hear about Katie's brother's farm?"

Shana frowned. "Which brother?"

"Samuel, I believe. Outside of Intercourse?" When Shana nodded, Anna continued. "The barn burned to the ground just early yesterday morning."

Knowing what that meant, Shana heard herself gasp. "What

happened?"

"Well, there isn't any solid evidence but..."

Shana felt her heart skip a beat. "Arson!"

Anna shrugged her shoulders. "Some of the cattle and mules got caught inside but, otherwise, no one was hurt."

"Well, I'm certain Emanuel will be appreciative for the news, although it certainly isn't good news at that. Say hello to Jacob." They bade good-bye and Shana hurried over to Emanuel's side.

He was standing in front of a row of paint containers, holding out two color patches, one a pale green and the other a light blue. "Which one, Shana?"

"The green," she said quickly, barely looking at the two swatches. "Emanuel, I think we should stop by your parents' farm on the way back."

Sensing the urgency in her voice, Emanuel frowned. "What's happened?"

"Your uncle Samuel's barn burned."

His first reaction was a thickening of his brow and tensing of his lips. He glanced down at the floor and shook his head. Then, returning her gaze, he sighed heavily. "There's been so many recently, it was bound to happen."

"So many what?"

"Burnings." He glanced down the aisle and managed to smile at a passing elderly couple. "Some locals have been burning down Amish barns for over two weeks now. It happens every summer. I never thought to mention it, not wanting to alarm you," he explained quietly. Then, wasting no time, he grabbed two buckets of paint and headed toward the register. Shana followed, more concerned about the local prejudice toward the Amish than the unfinished guest room for her parents.

There were several buggies parked near the Lapp family's barn. Shana glanced at Emanuel but he stared straight ahead as they pulled in behind the other buggies. He helped her out but did not wait for her as he hurried inside. By the time Shana caught up with him, he was already seated around the kitchen table with the men.

Lillian caught sight of Shana as she stood in the shadows of the summer kitchen doorway. Smiling, she walked over to greet her, young Jacob asleep in her arms and Linda at her side, clutching to her skirt. "Isn't it just awful?"

"Who would do such a thing?" Shana asked.

Lillian shrugged. "Some of the local youth must have nothing better to do with their time."

"They know who did it then?"

"Two pick-up trucks were spotted with some Englische boys but nothing otherwise. It doesn't matter anyway. Punishing the boys does not bring back the barn or the animals. It's best to get on with it, ja?" She rubbed Jacob's back as she turned her attention back to the kitchen table where Jonas, Jonas Jr. and Emanuel sat in deep discussion with three other men that Shana recognized but whose names she couldn't remember.

"What will they do?" Shana whispered curiously.

Lillian glanced back at her and smiled. "Why, we'll build Samuel a new barn," she said matter-of-factly. Then, motioning that she wanted to put Jacob to bed, she disappeared through the open partition between the kitchen and the living room that lead to the door opening into her house.

The men talked for another fifteen minutes before Emanuel

stood and clapped his father on the back. "We'll see you at eight o'clock on Saturday, then," he said as he headed to the doorway where Shana stood. He walked past her and waited at the outside door, holding it open for her.

The air had grown thick and heavy, the humidity clinging to her skin. Even though the sun had begun its descent in the sky, it felt hot and clammy. Shana reached for Emanuel's arm and leaned against him as they walked back to the buggy.

"You all right?" he asked as he slid the buggy's door open.

She nodded. "It's so hot and I'm getting sleepy," she complained. "And the baby keeps jumping around."

"We'll be home shortly," he replied, a concerned look on his face. But he said nothing else, merely helping her into the buggy and climbing in beside her. He slid the door shut and turned Lucky Monday around. "We'll be going to Samuel's on Saturday morning, then. A busy day before us, building a barn."

Rather than asking, Shana shut her eyes and leaned her head back. A shallow breeze cooled her face but she couldn't get comfortable in the stuffy buggy. Her excess weight and tight clothing added to the frustration she was feeling; and, with each kick from the baby, she began anticipating its birth. She couldn't wait to rid herself of the extra fifteen pounds she had gained.

"Uncomfortable?"

"Um huh," she mumbled.

"The baby's moving a lot?"

She opened her eyes. "Kicking and fussing a bit, yes." She looked over at him and noticed his concern. It touched her. "The doctor said that I still have three weeks, so don't worry."

"Three weeks?"

"More or less, yes."

Nothing more was said during the long trip home. The sun sank lower in the sky but the air grew heavier rather than cooler. By the time they drove up their lane, Shana could barely force herself awake. Feeling slightly feverish, she was thankful when Emanuel suggested that she'd cool off with a shower and go right to bed. She smiled her appreciation at being allowed to skip the evening chores and disappeared into the house to follow her husband's orders.

Chapter Nineteen

As they rode up the driveway, the massive burnt skeleton of a barn loomed beyond the house, peeling paint trickling down the sides, a silent warning of the dangers beyond the lane. Yet, as Emanuel steered the buggy around the side of the house, Shana saw that, surrounding the burned skeleton, was the busy life of community love. Nearly a hundred Amish men and women scurried around the yard, each with a specific task to perform in their tight-knit organization. Everyone seemed joyous and happy. There were no signs of sorrow or fear.

Several wagons loaded with wood were circled around a bare patch of land near the burnt out shell of the old barn. The men, most with tool belts around their waists, clambered around the timber while the women, aprons covering their dresses, lingered near the front yard of the porch, some peeling fresh corn, others getting ready to serve cold refreshments to the working men.

Emanuel stopped the buggy on the outskirts of the active area. He took Shana's hand and helped her out of the buggy. She stumbled as she crept out but, with a tender hand, he steadied her, sparing her an encouraging smile before releasing his grasp, then hurried toward the crowds of Amish men. Uncertain of her place, Shana lingered by the buggy and watched as several men slapped Emanuel on the back, some of them laughing gaily and others pointing toward the spot where, within the next eight hours, a new barn would be raised.

"Shana," someone called out.

Tearing her gaze from the men's area, Shana gazed toward the farmhouse. Katie and Lillian stood side-by-side on the porch, each waving for her to join them. Her happy face covering her fear, Shana left the familiarity of the buggy and approached the dozens of women, most of whom she did not recognize. Immediately, they welcomed her and set her to work peeling potatoes as she sat on the front step next to Lillian and Sylvia. With over two hundred potatoes to peel, the three women spent an hour visiting while they worked.

During the morning hours, the married women served the men cool drinks as they worked while the older women prepared the midday meal. Some of the younger women, those without children or husbands, helped the men by retrieving tools and fetching lighter pieces of lumber. The children helped as well, picking up bent nails and sawed off pieces of wood. When the potatoes were finished, Shana sat with Lillian in the shade, watching as the bare space beside the burnt rubble began to transform into a new, fresh barn.

Shana watched as the men, using only their weight and thick ropes, began pulling the new walls, just outlined by two-by-fours, up into place. Lillian finished feeding Jacob, her own eyes gazing out as she tried to locate Jonas Jr.

"Quite a sight, isn't it?"

Shana glanced at her, her eyes glowing and her face flushed. "Like poetry," she said breathlessly.

Lillian smiled. "I imagine so."

But words couldn't describe how Shana felt. She watched the men, each doing their own tasks yet each task contributing to the building of the new barn. No one gave orders, but each man knew what to do. She saw Emanuel, atop the highest beams, pounding nails into the structure. He stopped for a minute as the men below him passed up a glass of cool water. Pushing his hat back off his forehead, he pressed the cool glass to his skin.

"Shana!"

Snapping her gaze away from the new barn, she turned around and saw Katie approaching her. The smile on her face was genuine and warm, reflecting the newfound respect she had for her daughter-in-law. "You done with the potatoes, ja?"

Shana motioned to the last bucket and nodded. "All peeled and ready to go."

As Katie picked up the bucket, she noticed Shana press her hand against her side. "The child is restless?"

"Very," Shana replied, trying to smile through the slight tremor of pain.

"I think it will be an early birth. The child moves too much," she said. She hesitated, her eyes darting over the heads of the women. "When you leave today, Sylvia should go with you." Katie met Shana's eyes, a concerned look on her face. "So close to your time, you should not be alone during the day."

Lillian smiled at Shana when Katie left. "You want to hold Jacob for a while? You could use the practice, ja?"

Shana took the baby from her sister-in-law. She stared into his tiny face and felt the emotion swell into her throat. "It's just so amazing, isn't it? In less than three weeks, the baby in my arms will be my own." She looked up at Lillian and returned her sister-in-law's smile.

Shortly before noon, the men crawled down from the top of the barn. The frame was finished, the new wood standing like a friendly skeleton against the horizon. Shana helped the women serve the men by pouring water in their glasses. After a morning of hard work, everyone was thirsty and she found herself busy just trying to keep their glasses full. She moved slower than the other women and found herself stopping to catch her breath every so often. It was too hot and beads of sweat dotted her forehead as she filled the men's glasses. On her third trip from refilling the pitcher, she paused by Emanuel's place and, when he spared her an approving glance, she felt her heart warm. Then, to her surprise, he took the pitcher from her and poured his own water.

"You should sit down, Shana," he said softly, concern in his eyes. "You look tired and one of the other women can tend to the men."

She nodded, reaching to take the pitcher back. But Emanuel's expression changed, a frown clouding his usually good-natured expression. He stood up, touched her arm gently, and led her away from the table. "We'll leave early, Shana. I should have insisted you'd stay at the farm." He handed the pitcher to a young woman, one that Shana did not know. The woman, smiling her understanding as her eyes fell to Shana's large stomach, walked back to the table.

"I think we should stay until the barn is finished," Shana replied softly. "Your help is needed, Emanuel."

He squeezed her hand affectionately, a look of approval at her generosity crossing his face. "Go rest inside where it is cool. I'll come for you when we're done."

She headed into the house, thankful to escape the hot sun. Sitting down on the sofa in the kitchen, she leaned her head back and shut her eyes. The day seemed endless and she was beginning to feel her patience almost at its end. She tried to relax, taking a deep breath. But she felt herself close to tears. The extra weight, her uncomfortable size, the baby's demanding movements stole any relaxation she might have been allowed.

"Shana?" Lillian sat next to her, baby Jacob in her arms. She leaned back into the sofa and pushed aside the front of her blouse to let the infant nurse. "You are not well?"

"Just ready, that's all."

"But you've still some time, ja?"

"You heard Mother Katie earlier. She thinks the child will come early." Shana managed a smile. "She's had more children than I have, so I think I will listen to her."

"It's not unusual to be early. I was with Linda."

"I wish it were tomorrow," Shana replied. "I'm tired, now. Tired of being pregnant, of back pains, of stomachaches. I could complain forever."

Lillian laughed. "Imagine how Katie felt. She gave birth to twelve children!"

"Twelve? But..."

Lillian's smile faded. "They buried two as infants."

"I hadn't known."

"But now, she already has eight grandchildren, soon to be nine. By the time her children are all married, she'll be certain to have many more, maybe even sixty."

Shana forced a breathless laugh. "Sixty grandchildren?"

"Why, I have over eighty cousins. Some of them I've never even met."

"No wonder," Shana answered but her breath came quick as her unborn child kicked again. "I think this baby will take more after me than Emanuel. It seems very anxious."

Lillian shifted Jacob in her arms. "Are you? What about, Shana?"

Having said too much, Shana quickly tried to smile away her comment. "Labor, mostly. I suppose my baby and I are thinking the same thing."

"Thinking of the joy your baby will bring to your life should ease your fear, Shana."

"I suppose it shall."

To Shana's relief, Lillian changed the subject. "Everyone is quite pleased about Emanuel and you taking the fall baptism." Her large brown eyes studied Shana's face. "The instructionals are over?"

"Emanuel took me to two meetings then Bishop Studer and Preacher Yoder rode out to meet with me alone. I suppose the hardest thing for everyone to accept it my lack of knowledge of German." She glanced up at the kitchen door that slowly opened. Little Linda peeked inside then, seeing her mother, she ran across the kitchen floor to Lillian.

"You'll pick up enough to understand eventually," Lillian said. With her free hand, she reached out to brush some sawdust out of Linda's hair. "Have you been helping the women, Lindy? That's a fine big girl." Linda smiled in delight and buried her face in Lillian's lap. "She pretends to be shy, you know," Lillian said to Shana.

"Linda, come sit next to me," Shana said to the three year old. "You've grown so big this summer."

The little girl climbed onto the faded brown sofa and, at Shana's encouragement, leaned against her side and put her head against Shana's stomach. She let Shana put her arm around her but her eyes never left her mother's face.

"I feel your stomach moving," Linda smiled, her angelic face peering anxiously at her own mother. "Mama's stomach moved before, too."

Lillian reached over and tugged affectionately at Linda's

disarrayed pigtail. "That was your brother moving around."

"Is this my brother, too?"

"Your cousin," Lillian gently corrected. Fascinated, Linda returned her attention to Shana's stomach while Lillian changed the subject. "I understand that your parents are to come visiting. You must be quite glad to see them. It's been over a year, ja?" Jacob finished nursing and Lillian wiped his mouth with a yellow cloth.

"A year, yes."

"Are they excited about their grandchild?"

"Excited about their new grandchild?" Shana started to stand up, Linda scampering over to Lillian's side. Her back was aching the worst that she had felt yet. Sitting only made it worse. "Their excitement has been masked by their confusion when I told them Emanuel is an Amish man; and, when they visit, they'll be horrified to discover their daughter's being baptized Amish. I may as well have never existed."

Once on her feet, Shana put her hands on the small of her back and turned to face Lillian. She was startled by the expression on her sister-in-law's face. She hadn't meant to sound bitter when she answered Lillian's question. But, she was certain the words had come out that way.

"Imagine how you would feel if Linda left the faith. But that is a possibility, isn't it?" she tried to explain. "The Englische society surrounds the Amish youth, pressuring them to conform to their ways. They make it especially attractive with fast cars, convenient laundry machines, and fancy clothing. Imagine how the Englische would feel to lose their child to the Amish. No more weekly phone calls, no surprise visits, no family Christmases. Most Englische don't even know what the Amish are. They aren't touched by us. But this is something my parents will be faced with and I fear they will find it hard to accept."

"I wasn't aware they didn't know," Lillian apologized, sensing the hurt and frustration that Shana felt. "Perhaps once they visit and see how happy you are, they'll understand that you've married into a community of love and faith. Perhaps experiencing your peace will make it easier on them."

Shana doubted it but did not comment. At the present moment, she wasn't certain she was feeling any inner peace over her increasing pains. "I must lay down," she said more to herself than to Lillian as she started to make her way toward the door but halfway there, she stopped and clutched at her stomach.

Katie and several other ladies were carrying in large trays of dirty dishes as Shana stood at the center of the room. Noticing the deep frown on Shana's face, Katie quickly handed her trays to one of the other ladies and hurried over to her daughter-in-law. "Shana, you're sweating," she said as she touched Shana's arm.

"I think I need to go home," she whispered weakly.

Katie glanced around until her eyes met with a young woman standing nearby. "Fetch Emanuel, Sarah."

The woman, taking one look at Shana's pale face dotted with sweat, hurried past them and rushed out the kitchen door. Katie directed Shana back to the sofa. Lillian handed Jacob to Sylvia and hurried to the kitchen sink to get a glass of cold water. "Sit down, child."

"Where's Emanuel?"

Katie felt a tug at her arm and turned around as Lillian handed her the glass. Katie sat next to Shana and forced her to sip some of the cool liquid. "Sarah went to fetch him. Do you feel pains?"

"A little."

"I think He is about to send us your baby, Shana."

"It's too early," Shana replied, suddenly frightened.

"That's not for us to decide," Katie gently reminded her.

Emanuel hurried in through the kitchen door, his hat in his hand and his hair disheveled. "*Was gehts,* Mamm?"

Katie rose to meet him. "You best bring around the buggy. Ana, Sylvia and I will follow. If you want your child born at home, we better get started at once."

Emanuel glanced over her shoulder at Shana. She sat alone on the sofa, the glass of water held tightly in her hands. She stared at him, her eyes wide and frightened. He walked over to the sofa and knelt before her. "It'll be fine, Shana. I'll get you home." He squeezed her hands and helped her to her feet, holding her tightly as they walked toward the door. "She's been feeling it all day, Mamm."

"She's probably been in labor all day."

A momentary wave of admiration swept over Emanuel, which was quickly replaced with concern. "Will we make it home?" he asked softly.

"With plenty of time to spare, Emanuel. Now hurry," Katie instructed.

Outside, Jonas had already pulled the buggy around, having overheard Sarah calling for Emanuel. Emanuel smiled nervously as Jonas clapped him on the shoulder and reached out for Shana's hand to help her inside the buggy. Once seated next to him, she leaned her head against his shoulder, her breath coming in short, uneven waves. She felt her pains grow and spread as though a vice was pressing against her midsection. But, just as quickly as it came, it disappeared.

"Isn't it remarkable?" she whispered, more to herself than

to Emanuel.

"What is remarkable?"

Shana wrapped her arms around her protruding stomach. "Lillian was right, you know. The inner peace..."

Emanuel pulled the buggy to a short stop at the end of the driveway, looked both ways, and quickly slapped the reins against the horse's back. "Inner peace?"

"I thought I'd be more afraid of the pain," she whispered. "But even that isn't so bad." She laughed softly. "I thought I had a stomachache all morning."

"You are remarkable," he corrected. Then, reaching down with one hand, he covered her folded hands with his.

Eight hours later, Shana gave birth to their son, Noah Lapp.

Chapter Twenty

The Lapp family welcomed the birth of Noah Lapp with little fanfare or celebration. Emanuel cried when he first held his son in his arms, the baby's face still puffy red and his hair damp from birth. Katie and Ana had left the room, leaving the new parents to enjoy those precious moments.

Emanuel held Noah, sitting on the edge of the bed, the room hot and humid. Emanuel stared down into the face of his first-born son, amazed at the small button nose, puckered lips, and tiny creases. Finally, lifting his eyes to stare into the face of his exhausted wife, Emanuel smiled through his tears, "He's a blessing. A beautiful blessing," he whispered; and then, he placed the newborn baby in Shana's arm to let the two of them drift to sleep.

Shutting the door as he left the guest room, Emanuel started down the short hallway into the kitchen. His mother sat at the kitchen table, watching him as he approached. He stood by the kitchen table, half turned away from Katie's gaze. "He is truly amazing," he said softly.

Katie quietly replied, "Your son is that."

Emanuel glanced over his shoulder at her. When she looked up, he spared her a smile as he said, "I meant God." Then, bowing his head, he retreated from the kitchen, pausing only to grab his hat by the door, and escaped to the barn where he prayed his thanks to his Lord.

The next day, early in the evening, Emanuel had driven to town and, his hand shaking, shoved three dollars in quarters into a payphone to call Shana's parents and tell them about their new grandson. He spoke to them briefly, his heart pounding inside his chest, as he told them about the home birth and the beautiful baby boy that resulted. Then, his fears allayed, he confirmed their visit in three weeks and hung up the phone.

Sylvia stayed at the farm immediately after Noah's birth for which Shana was thankful. While Shana tried to return to her daily routine, she moved a lot slower and tired too easily to tend to all of her chores. During the day, Sylvia managed the chickens and helped Emanuel with the milking, allowing Shana some solitude with her son.

In the evenings, after supper, Sylvia helped her sew some new dresses for herself, showing Shana how to sew typical Amish women's garb. They also sewed some clothes for baby Noah. A week after his birth, they tested his miniature versions of Emanuel's clothes. Shana laughed as they dressed Noah, even though he slept through the fashion show.

"He'll grow into them soon enough," she said as she dressed him in a soft, cottony sleeper.

During those first days, Shana could hardly keep her eyes off of him. She cherished the early morning hours when he cried to be fed. Slipping on a robe, she padded across the floor and lifted him out of his crib. She'd sit by the window in a rocking chair that Emanuel had made for her. By the dim light from the moon and stars, she cradled him against her breast, staring into his sweet face as he fed. It was their private time, alone, to share together.

During the day, when Emanuel and Sylvia worked the fields cutting and spearing the tobacco, Shana would hum softly to Noah, walking him from room to room while he slept in her arms. She loved to hold him, to talk to him, to watch him while he slept; and when he awoke, his unseeing eyes searching her face, she smiled to herself, fighting tears of pride.

After that first week, the rest of Emanuel's family began visiting their newest family member. Early evening on most days, someone would stop by for a visit. Some of the family, mostly uncles and aunts from further distances, asked their Englische neighbors to drive them to Emanuel's farm. Whoever came was welcome in Shana and Emanuel's kitchen. They'd sit for a while, drinking tea or coffee which Sylvia usually prepared, each taking a turn at holding Noah as they talked about crops, their own farms and other relatives. Then, when the sun finally set over the farm, they'd hand the baby back to Shana and wish the Lapps goodnight.

"He smiled," Sylvia told Shana eagerly one evening, as they sat alone in the kitchen. Supper simmered on the stove, the kitchen full of the thick smell of roasting ham. "Did you see him smile?"

Shana set the damp kitchen towel down on the counter as she hurried over and stared down at Noah as he lay in Sylvia's arms. "Did he really smile?"

"Just a little one."

Emanuel finished washing his hands at the kitchen sink, his evening chores just completed. "Three weeks is too young to smile, Sylvia," he said as he dried his hands on a kitchen towel.

Hurt, Sylvia looked up, defending her observation. "I said it was a little smile."

Shana reached out and took the baby. Snuggling his head against the crook in her arm, Shana sat down on the kitchen sofa. "Let's see," she began to coo. "Does Baby Noah have a smile for Mama?" Instead of responding, Noah tried to focus his eyes but ended up blinking twice and rolling his head to the side. A small spot of saliva drooled out the corner of his mouth. "I don't see too much in favor of a smile," she said teasingly to Sylvia who had retreated to the sink to wash and bleach her organdy prayer cap.

"Visitors," Emanuel announced, setting the damp kitchen towel on the counter.

Shana glanced out the window. The sky was turning silver and they would be retiring to bed right after supper. Between the hard work during the day and Noah's crying at night, everyone was extra tired. "Bit late for visitors, wouldn't you say?"

Emanuel leaned forward. "Connecticut plates. I think it's your family." He turned around and asked, "Is it Friday already?"

She didn't answer as she stood up, Noah drifting to sleep in her arms and, a stiff tilt to her chin, she walked toward the kitchen door. Both Emanuel and Sylvia started to follow but Shana hesitated at the door. "Sylvia, perhaps you'd be kind enough to set two more places at the table. I'm sure they'll be hungry after their travel."

"Let me take Noah," Emanuel said softly.

The car stopped in-between the barn and house. Shana carefully handed Noah to Emanuel before, a quick hand soothing back any hair that had strayed from her pulled back bun, she opened the door and stood outside on the porch. The air, warm and thick, carried the stench of ripe manure. Shana wondered if it would offend her parents but, as the car door opened and a tall, sinewy man stepped out, she forced a smile and waved.

"Hello there!" she called out, wondering if her strength had evolved. She stepped off the porch and made her way across the lawn to properly greet them. Her bare feet treaded along the cool, dewy grass, each step bringing her closer and forcing her heart to pound louder. She stopped a short distance away and found herself startled when her father leaned over to kiss her cheek. "Find it ok, then?" she asked, her back stiffening and her temples starting to throb.

Her father's eyes quickly tried to recognize the young girl he knew as his daughter in the woman who stood before him. "Look at you," he started, his gaze taking in her neatly parted hair and plain blue dress, but his voice trailed away and he left his sentence unfinished. Everything about her was Amish, from her dirty bare feet to the cape covering the front of her dress. The only thing missing was her prayer covering.

"Hello Mother," Shana said as her mother, not nearly as tall as her father, walked around the side of the car. "You look well."

"Shana," her mother started. But she stopped, her troubled blue eyes quickly darting around the farm. "This is home?" The confusion and, perhaps, disgust in her mother's voice angered Shana. She hadn't wanted this to happen. Her peaceful world was suddenly tossed upside-down in those three simple words that had slipped from her mother's tongue.

"This is our home," Shana confirmed with a warm smile as she tried to maintain control over her beating heart and quickening pulse.

"*Willkumm*," came a soft, gentle voice from behind her.

Shana turned around, relieved that Emanuel had stepped forward. She noticed her parents staring at him, taking in his black suspendered pants, dirty white shirt, and mustache-less beard. Their shock was apparent by their silence so Emanuel approached them, clutching Noah tightly as he, too, quickly studied his in-laws. While their clothes struck him as too fancy, their expressions softened as they noticed the baby sleeping in his arms.

"You want to meet your grandson, ja?" and he quickly relinquished Noah to Shana's mother. He touched Shana's arm lightly as he watched the barrier between her and her parents slowly melt, their emotions overwhelming as they cradled Noah in their arms.

After supper, they all sat around the table, sipping at their iced tea. The cows shuffled around noisily in the fields and one of the horses neighed loudly. Sylvia sat quietly in the corner, Noah sleeping soundlessly in her arms, as she watched Shana's parents with wide eyes. Occasionally, Shana would glance at her, appreciating her young sister-in-law's encouraging smile, before returning her attention to her parents. Emanuel sat at the head of the table, listening as his in-laws, mostly Shana's mother, droned on about everyone's shock when Shana left her career to marry a farmer. While her mother spoke kindly, both Shana and Emanuel noticed the disappointment in her voice. But, rather than comment, Shana smiled meekly and offered them more iced tea.

Finally, after the grandfather clock struck ten times, Emanuel took Noah from his younger sister with a gentle reprimand. "So late for you, Sylvia. You should have retired earlier."

Shana quickly came to Sylvia's defense. "No more so than you or I, Emanuel."

He nodded at Sylvia who, taking his cue, softly bid her goodnights and retreated upstairs. He waited until he heard her bedroom door shut before he turned to Shana. "We should retire too. After all, we must get up early for chores. Besides, we have plenty of time to visit tomorrow."

Shana stood up from the table. "We've fixed the downstairs guest room for you," she said as she walked toward a door off to the side of the kitchen into the room where Noah had been born. She decided to not mention that fact until another time, if at all. She disappeared into the room and, seconds later, a flicker of light glowed inside the room. The orange illuminated around her as she returned, a smile on her face. "I left some clean towels on the bed. The water pressure isn't very consistent but it gets hot enough," she said, waiting for them to get up from the table and retire.

They bade her good night, her mother pausing to give her a stiff hug and whisper "It's good to see you, Shana" in her ear.

Upstairs, Shana checked on Noah as he laid in his cradle. She tucked the thin blanket under the baby's chin and smiled to herself. "He's a sleeping angel," she whispered.

Emanuel remained quiet as he stripped off his clothing and, with a heavy sigh, climbed into the bed. Shana glanced over her shoulder at him. He lay on his side, his brown curls spread out on the white pillow. His mustache-less beard appeared a thick shadow across his face in the flickering light of the kerosene lantern.

"Emanuel?"

"Hum?"

"What's wrong, Emanuel?" she asked, moving over to the side of the bed. "You've hardly spoken a word all night and then only to reprimand Sylvia."

"We have a lot of work to do tomorrow," he said sharply.

"She's old enough to know when she's tired. Besides, I think she was curious about my parents."

He rolled over and leaned back in the pillow. "Her curiosity tonight will make her lazy tomorrow," he snapped.

"Emanuel!" For a long moment, her shocked expression countered his own obvious anger; and, indeed, she was shocked for she had never heard him say an unkind word about anyone.

The clock downstairs rang a quarter past ten, the chimes

reverberating throughout the quiet downstairs and floating up the stairs to the second floor. The flame from the lantern danced against the glass, its glow casting shadows across the plain white walls. Finally, Emanuel broke the silence. "I'm sorry, Shana," he apologized as he sat up. "I'm not used to such tension and hostility in my home."

Her expression softened as she sat down on the bed next to him. "You mean my parents?" She folded her hands in her lap, staring at the dancing shadows for a long moment. She had felt it, too. She had tried to prepare Emanuel that their visit would not be as amicable as he imagined. But she had hoped that once they held their first grandson in their arms, they would have forgotten that their daughter would raise him Amish. "I don't think meeting their hostility with hostility toward Sylvia will ease the tension," she said softly.

He leaned his head in her lap and sighed as her fingers began stroking his curls. "If they knew your new life would shock them, why did they insist on visiting?" He wrapped his arms around her waist and exhaled loudly. "I don't understand the Englische, Shana. Your ways are so different."

"No different than your parents' initial reaction to our marriage." She ran her fingers across his cheek. "It isn't our place to always understand, only to accept."

Emanuel smiled up at her and gave her a gentle squeeze. "Your wisdom shames me, Shana."

"It shouldn't, Emanuel." She smiled back. "I've learned it from you." She leaned down and kissed the top of his head. "Now, you should sleep. We have a busy day tomorrow and Noah will certainly wake us early."

Twice during the night, Noah woke for his feeding. Shana

sat in the straight back chair by the window, staring out into the darkness at the fields in the moonlight. Soon, the tobacco would be all speared and hung to dry. By then, it would be time to cut the alfalfa and bale it for the upcoming winter months. Shortly after that, Emanuel would continue harvesting the corn and start shredding the drying stalks. He would also start harvesting the second set of tobacco plants that he had planted just weeks before Noah's birth. And then, the winter months would settle in again. While she looked forward to spending more time with Emanuel, she dreaded the thought of the cold.

When Emanuel awoke in the morning, Shana had just finished nursing Noah. She dressed quickly and woke Sylvia up with a gentle touch to her shoulder. "I'm going to the barn to help Emanuel. Will you watch Noah?" Within minutes, Sylvia was dressed and in the kitchen, Noah asleep by the open window in his crib, a gentle warm breeze blowing across his back. Sylvia stood in front of the small mirror over the sink in the washroom. With expert fingers, she rolled her hair back over her ears and pinned it in a careful, neat bun.

Shana smiled at Sylvia as she touched her own hair. "You do that so quickly. It always takes me ten minutes and I usually have to do it twice."

"It'll get easier in time," Sylvia replied modestly as she opened a kitchen cabinet and reached for a pan. "Should I start breakfast for your parents, too?"

"I'll fix theirs later, Sylvia. I'm afraid it's too early for them."

Her parents awoke around eight-thirty. By that time, the early breakfast dishes had been cleaned and Emanuel was already out in the fields, checking on his tobacco plants. Shana greeted her parents with a warm smile and hurried to fix their breakfast, conscious of their constant gaze on her back. She tied an apron around the waist of one of her plain green dresses that Sylvia had helped her make after Noah's birth.

"I'll help you, dear," her mother started but Shana quickly discouraged any help. She needed to keep busy, force herself to work in order to ease the tension. "You're so busy, Shana," her mother replied as she joined her husband on the slightly tattered sofa.

"Mother, Noah was born over three weeks ago. I can't be idle forever."

"But you should take it easy."

Shana broke five eggs into a large bowl. She tossed the broken eggshells into a garbage bag before whipping at the eggs with a bent fork. "Sylvia's been a great help while I've been getting back onto my feet." She looked up at Sylvia and smiled. "Of course, it's Sylvia who's been doing most of the chores. Washing the clothes, weeding the garden, cooking the meals."

"How long will you be staying with Shana, Sylvia?" her mother asked as she leaned over to pick up Noah. Sitting back on the sofa, Shana's mother shifted the baby in her arms, her one hand expertly patting her grandson as he slept.

Sylvia lowered her eyes, avoiding the gaze of Shana's parents. "As long as I'm needed." She glanced up at Shana. "I like being around the babies."

The eggs sizzled in the heavy cast-iron pan. Shana began stirring them, her wrist moving quickly and the iron prongs of the fork scrapping against the pan. "I thought after breakfast we could go for a buggy ride," Shana said. "I figured you hadn't been on a buggy ride before."

"Can't say that we have," her father answered.

Shana turned around, her wrist still scrambling the eggs. "Well, if you're out here in Lancaster, visiting your daughter, I guess we better remedy that," she replied lightly. She noticed the darkness that crossed their faces and quickly changed the subject. "We'll go to the store for some apples and, this afternoon, Mother, you can help Sylvia and I make applesauce. Maybe Father can help Emanuel in the barn. You can clean some stalls to get the city out of you," she teased and, noticing their frowns turn into surprise, she laughed. "Or you can just watch," she added.

Later in the afternoon, with over twenty quarts of applesauce stacked neatly on the shelves in the washroom outside of the kitchen, Shana walked through her garden with her mother. Emanuel had taken her father into the fields after the noon meal and Sylvia had opted to watch over Noah while she completed her school journal entries for the day. So, the sun beating down on them, mother and daughter walked through the garden, Shana occasionally stooping to pluck some weeds from the dry ground.

"I wish it would rain soon," she said wishfully, her eyes scanning the cloudless sky. "It's been such a dry summer, the crops are behind."

"Well, you can't control the weather," her mother replied.

Shana stood up, wiping her hands on her skirt. Then, reaching her hand up to shield her eyes, she searched the horizon for the men. "Emanuel's showing Father the young tobacco plants," she said. "We'll be cutting that some time next month. Jacob Zook, the old tenant here, grew tobacco. That's how Emanuel learned about it. The first crop was successful. He hung them to dry in the barn's loft. It smells wonderful in there."

"They can grow tobacco?" Her mother shook her head as she asked, "But they don't smoke!"

"Not cigarettes anyway," Shana answered, smoothing back some stray hair from her face. She hadn't started wearing the Amish Kapp yet, slowing easing herself into it on Church Sunday and when they went visiting family. "Isn't it peaceful here?" She looked at her mother. For a long moment, they simply stared at each other, both searching for the words to describe how they felt. "You realize that I'm joining the church this fall."

"What does that mean, Shana?"

"It means that I will be baptized as an Amish woman. There are a lot of rules surrounding their religion, most of them against conforming to the ways of your world."

"My world," her mother repeated softly.

"No owning cars. No electricity. No telephones."

"I don't understand how..."

Shana smiled. "How I can give that up?" she finished her mother's question. "I don't see how you can't understand. I love Emanuel, I love Noah, and I love this farm. Have you ever seen the birth of spring? Have you ever known the exact moment when a plant breaks free from the earth to reach for the sky? Or the baby chicks that are born? Have you ever seen them as they peck their way out of the shell and stand, for the very first time, on their two wobbly legs? Did you know that they immediately start searching for food? It's fascinating that they know that. It's born within them. I'm surrounded by wonder and glory and miracles every day. Giving up the cars and the phones and the television isn't giving up anything. It's gaining everything." Shana reached out and touched her mother's arm. "I know you don't understand. Just know that this is what I want and I'm happy."

Her mother lifted her chin, fighting the urge to cry. Forcing a smile, she quickly added, "And you have a beautiful son, a caring husband, and a wonderful farm." She hesitated, her eyes drifting in the direction that the men had disappeared. "When you first told us about Emanuel being Amish, we didn't know what to think. Maybe it didn't really hit us or maybe we just didn't know what that meant. But, when he called us..."

Shana tilted her head and frowned. "He called you?"

"After Noah was born," her mother replied. "His voice was so strong, so in awe of everything that had happened. It was hard to believe that it was real. Our baby girl was gone." Her mother met Shana's eyes. "But now I see that it is a woman who has replaced her, not the stranger we had feared."

"Thank you for coming, Mother," Shana whispered. And, blinking back her tears of relief, she found herself in her mother's arms, returning the hug of love with her own thankful hug.

Chapter Twenty-One

Her parents stayed until the following weekend. During their visit, Shana's father helped Emanuel in the morning with milking the cows and for the rest of the day, spearing tobacco in the hot, stuffy barn. Shana kept her mother busy assisting Sylvia in the garden and, after dinner, the three of them spent the afternoon canning peaches and pears for the winter.

In the evenings, after Shana and her mother finished cleaning the supper dishes, Emanuel and Shana would smile to each other over the nodding head of her father and drooping eyes of her mother. If there was tension among them in the beginning of the visit, by the time they left, Shana felt satisfied that they had truly glimpsed a piece of her new life that helped ease their confusion over her decision.

By that time, Sylvia had reluctantly agreed that it was time for her to return to her parents' farm. So, mid-afternoon on Saturday, Emanuel hitched up the buggy and, with sorrowful eyes, Sylvia gathered her few belongings and said good-bye. Shana watched as they drove down the lane, emotion welling up in her throat. During the past several weeks, she had grown used to Sylvia's quiet presence that had been her only company during the long days, except when her family had visited.

Alone for the first time since the baby's birth, Shana spent a few minutes cooing over Noah before she started gathering up the dirty clothes for the wash. For the rest of the afternoon, she washed the clothes and hung them to dry on the clothesline that ran from the side of the house to the corner of the barn. Afterwards, she sat on the edge of the porch and fed Noah while she watched the cloud formations against the blue backdrop of the clear sky.

The chickens talked noisily amongst themselves from the chicken coop, the rooster impatiently hanging around as though waiting for its chance to dart inside the forbidden pen. The herd of cows wandered in the pen, several of them lingering near the gate into the barn. One of the cows, a large black one with a heavy chain around her neck, stood to the side, arching her neck as she mooed, over and over again. Each cry dragged out in a soulful bellow as she slowly moved away and disappeared behind the barn.

"Isn't she noisy?" Shana asked Noah. He gurgled in response, his head rolling to one side as he blinked his dark eyes. Shana smiled to herself and wiped some milk from his chin. "Messy eater, you are," she said.

A buggy pulled down the lane and, looking up, Shana squinted as she tried to see who it was. "That can't be your daed," she said to Noah. Standing up, she walked to the edge of the porch and raised her one hand to cover her eyes. "Hello Mary Beiler," she waved as she recognized her neighbor. "Thought you had left for Ohio already." Stepping off of the porch, Shana walked toward the buggy that had stopped in front of her house.

"Another two weeks, yet. Waiting for the papers to be finalized," she explained. "Must be proud of Emanuel. Adding on like he did."

Shana tilted her head as she shifted Noah in her arms. "Adding on?"

"To the farm." Mary reached down and ran a calloused finger over Noah cheek. "What is he, a month yet?"

"A month, yes," she confirmed before pressing Mary. "What do you mean that Emanuel is adding onto the farm?"

Mary smiled, the wrinkles under her eyes deepening from

behind her round glasses. "Why, he purchased most of our land between your farm and ours, Shana. And several of the cows, too."

Shana stared at her for a moment until the realization of her words sunk in. There were almost fifty acres between the two farms. Amos Beiler had lost both of his sons, one in a farming accident and the other at birth, and their daughters had married and moved to their husbands' farms. While Emanuel's farm was by no means considered small, the additional land would provide for several sons in the future. "And the rest?" Shana asked, trying to cover her surprise at Mary Beiler's announcement.

"Young Mennonite couple bought the farm and the land on the west side." The horse stepped backward and Mary steadied the buggy. "Stopped by for some of your eggs, Shana. Good half dozen will do fine."

After Shana hurried to the barn and gathered up a half-dozen fresh eggs, she bade Mary farewell and watched as she started down the lane. Part of the way down, the buggy stopped and she leaned out of the window, pointing to the field. Shana looked in that direction, but seeing nothing, started to approach the buggy.

"Looks like she's in trouble," Mary was calling out.

When Shana looked again, she noticed the cow, down on her side and breathing heavily. "Dear God," Shana whispered and, thanking Mary, ran to the house to put Noah in his crib. Then, her heart pounding, Shana raced back outside and across the gravel driveway to the pasture. She quickly jumped over the wire fence, cutting her leg in the process. Ignoring the pain, she ran through the mud, her bare feet slipping as she approached the cow's side.

Only three other cows had given birth on the farm since she had been there and, except for one, she hadn't witnessed the process. The one time, Emanuel had called out for her help, to hold the lantern while he rolled back his sleeves and assisted the cow with turning the calf. And, as Shana quickly assessed the situation, the small hooves that had projected out of the cow spoke of a similar situation.

She dropped to her knees and, uncertain what to do, she tried to imitate what she remembered Emanuel had done. Gently, she helped guide the calf as it made its backwards descent into the world. The legs poked out and she reached for its front legs, carefully steering it in a way to cause the cow the least amount of pain.

Shana prayed out loud as the cow bellowed softly, weakly pushing with what strength she had left. And, fifteen minutes later, the new calf stood wobbly on its feet. The mother made no move to get up and clean the calf so Shana grabbed the calf and, half racing and half tripping, carried it to the stables. With a warm sponge, she washed the confused, newborn calf, praying even harder that Emanuel would soon return.

Almost an hour later, Shana sat on the fresh hay she had spread on the ground, her back to the cold cement foundation as she stared at the now sleeping calf. She had finished cleaning the newborn and managed to fill a bottle with fresh milk to feed it. Now, exhausted, she stared at it, feeling a sense of accomplishment for saving its life and a sense of doom for the mother that still lay in the pasture.

"Shana?" Emanuel called out as he walked through the empty barn. The sun was setting and, without any lights, the barn grew increasingly dark. When he came around the corner, Noah in his arms, he stopped short and quickly took in the situation. Her hair was in disarray and her clothes caked with mud and blood. He stared at the calf, nestled into the soft, fresh hay. "The cow?" he asked as he looked back at Shana.

Shana shrugged. "I don't know, Emanuel."

He shifted the baby in his arms before kneeling down beside her. "You alright?" With his free hand, he brushed her hair off of her forehead. "You saved the calf, Shana. If you hadn't, neither would have survived."

She lifted her eyes to meet his concerned gaze. Against her will, a few tears trickled down her cheeks. "I was so scared," she whispered tearfully. "I didn't know what to do."

Emanuel stood up. Holding Noah tight against his shoulder, he reached down to help her up. "I need to tend to the cow and you need to clean up." He smiled at her, his eyes glancing over her shoulder at the sleeping calf. "The Lord was smiling on that calf today," he said.

Inside the house, Shana allowed herself a long shower, washing the dried mud off her legs and blood from her arms. When she finally turned off the water, she heard Noah crying. She quickly dried off and dressed, leaving her hair wet and hanging down her back as she hurried into the bedroom to lift Noah from his crib. His cries didn't cease and, realizing how late it was, she sat on the edge of the bed to let Noah nurse while she fought the images of the day from her mind.

After feeding Noah, Shana carried him downstairs. The grandfather clock chimed from the living room, reminding Shana that she needed to start preparing the evening meal. To her relief, Noah slept while she quickly cooked some corn and heated up left over chicken from the previous night's supper. When Emanuel finally came in from the barn, Shana had the table set and was waiting for him, the supper left warming in the oven.

She heard Emanuel washing his hands in the washroom

and, after shutting off the faucet, he walked into the kitchen rubbing his face in a clean kitchen towel. His clothes were covered in mud and his face looked long and tired. But he spared her a smile and affectionately placed his hand on her shoulder. "Jacob was kind enough to help with the cow."

Shana frowned. "Did you fetch him?"

"No, he stopped by the Beiler farm to bid them farewell." He sat down at the table, the damp towel draped over his shoulder. "Mary Beiler mentioned she had stopped by and we had a downed cow. He stopped in to see what had happened."

"Well?"

Emanuel shook his head but did not continue the conversation. Instead, he took the towel off his shoulder and handed it to her. She understood that he probably didn't want to talk about it. Losing even one cow was upsetting. The cows were not only their livelihood, but indirectly, an extension of their family. Yet, as Shana took the towel from him, she sensed that his silence stemmed from another place. "Soon we'll need to bale the second alfalfa cutting. Jacob has offered his older son to help us."

"That was kind of him," Shana replied as she served him his meal. She was confused by his lack of emotion over the cow.

"He's a good neighbor."

"What did you do with the cow?" she managed to ask. "What will happen to the calf?"

He frowned as he looked up at her. "The cow will be butchered and the calf raised for sale. No different than any other calf."

Noah began to cry as she set the plate before Emanuel. She hurried over to his crib and picked him up. She felt her own tears surfacing as she thought of that poor calf, born only to live in a dark box for several months before it was sold to be slaughtered. She tried to forget about it as she comforted Noah.

"Aren't you joining me?" Emanuel asked after he bowed his head in prayer.

Shana carried the baby over to the table and sat down. "I'm not very hungry tonight, Emanuel," she said softly. She rubbed Noah's back until he quieted down. "He's been fussing a lot today," she commented. His head bent down, Emanuel continued to eat, his own thoughts somewhere else. Shana sighed, wondering what she had done to provoke his silence. "How are things at your parents?" she finally asked, breaking the deafening quiet.

"Lillian asked for you," he replied solemnly. "We've been invited for visiting the Sunday after next."

Shana nodded, even though he was not looking to see. "Our last instructional is that following Sunday, isn't it?" For the past four months, they had been meeting with the ministers for *die Gemee nooch geh*, the instructional prior to taking the Amish baptism. Usually the meetings were at the same time as the Sunday service, although they had missed one week due to the birth of Noah.

Emanuel set his fork down and leaned back in his chair. He wiped his mouth with the napkin he had laid across his lap and stared at her with his piercing blue eyes. He looked older with his mustache-less beard. Yet, the smooth china complexion, so deeply tanned from working in the fields, spoke of his youth. "Shana, you must learn to accept death on the farm as well as the life it brings forth. This is part of being a farmer's wife as well as an Amish woman."

"Am I being chastised?" she asked, shocked at Emanuel's words.

"Reminded," he said, his tone short and words direct.

"I see," Shana replied, her own anger suddenly rising at him. "So, let me understand, Emanuel. Are you reminding me that, once I take the vow and become a baptized member of the church, I can no longer get upset when we have to kill a chicken or sell a calf to the butcher? And, of course, getting upset when a cow dies in birth right in front of me, I should spring back to all happiness and not pause to mourn?" She stood up, hurt at his coldness. "Is that a prerequisite to becoming a baptized member or just a prerequisite to being your wife? I'm sorry if I feel for the loss of any life, Emanuel, or if it inconveniences you. I feel, Emanuel. And death makes me sad," she finished abruptly.

She waited for him to admonish her words. But he remained silent, refusing to engage in an argument. Instead, he quietly finished his meal before he left the table and disappeared upstairs. She stood there, listening as he moved around. The floorboards creaked in their bedroom and she heard him walk into the bathroom. Several minutes later, as she was clearing the dishes off the table, she realized he was not coming back downstairs. By the time she finished cleaning the kitchen, it was almost nine o'clock and, knowing Emanuel would be rising early to work in the fields, she took Noah and retired upstairs herself.

In the darkness of the bedroom, Shana put Noah to bed and, as quietly as possible, she striped her clothes and hung them on a peg in the wall. She put on her nightdress and crawled into bed next to Emanuel. His back faced her and her anger subsided as she feared his silence.

Putting her hand on his arm, she gently shook him. "Emanuel? Are you sleeping yet? I don't want you to go to bed angry," she whispered. When he did not respond, she lay back on her pillow and stared at the ceiling, trying to sleep as she listened to the gentle breathing of Noah from his crib and Emanuel from her side.

Chapter Twenty-Two

Shana hadn't heard Emanuel get up but, as she listened to the rooster crow at the sun, peeking over the horizon in its daily fight to break through the gray overcast, she knew that he must have just gotten up for the morning milking. She hadn't slept well and her body felt drained. Noah had woken up several times throughout the night and, knowing Emanuel would not rise to console his son, Shana had continually crawled out of bed and sat with Noah in the rocking chair by the window to let him nurse.

She forced herself out of bed and hurried over to Noah's crib. "Good morning, my beauty," she said softly as she picked up Noah and placed a gentle kiss on his forehead. "You kept Mommy up all night, didn't you?" She quickly changed his cloth diaper and dressed him for the day in a miniature version of Emanuel's Sunday dress. "We have a busy day, don't we, Noah? Gardening and cleaning. Maybe we can beat the rain and go visiting. Or ask your daed to ride to that market for apples and we'll make more applesauce."

She laid Noah on the freshly made bed as she got dressed. She chose a plain sky blue dress that Sylvia had helped her make during her stay on the farm. Then, she took down the dark Halsduch, her black bodice cape, and put it over the one-piece dress. She pinned it at the waist with a straight pin and smoothed the front of the cape over the dress. Brushing her hair off her forehead, she followed the instructions Sylvia had given and rolled it back and twisted it at the nape of her neck. Finally, she reached for the white organdy prayer cap and, hesitating for only a minute, she placed it on her head and tied it under her chin.

She took a step back and stared at her reflection. Her face

looked fiercely plain, yet her cheekbones were too high and her mouth too pouted. She didn't feel Amish and, she realized, she certainly didn't look it. She wondered what Emanuel would think, especially after their argument the evening before. While she had been slowly conforming to the Amish way, she had not gotten into the habit of fully dressing Amish. But she knew, with her baptism only a month away, she needed to get used to it. With her parents' visit over, she felt the time to start was now.

Downstairs, Shana spent the first hour and a half of her morning washing Noah and Emanuel's clothes. She liked to get it out of the way since it was the chore she disliked the most. By the time she hung all of the wet clothes on the line outside, it was time to feed the baby and start preparing Emanuel's breakfast.

That morning, she forced a smile into her heart as she fried his bacon and scrambled his eggs. She felt uneasy from the previous night's argument. They rarely argued but she hated it when their words grew strong. She knew that Amish husbands and wives shouldn't argue but she was having difficulties in dealing with Emanuel's impatience with her. His silence was even more hurtful than if he snapped back at her.

When the morning milking was over and Emanuel came into the house, his breakfast was ready and Shana greeted him with a warm smile. She noticed his slight hesitation when he saw her typical Amish garb. But it was the organdy head covering that caused him to raise an eyebrow. Yet, he said nothing as he dried his hands on a crisp, white towel before he sat at the table and waited for Shana to serve him.

"How is the calf?" she asked, sitting next to him with her own small plate of scramble eggs.

"Fine," he replied solemnly. He kept his head bent over as

he ate. "I'll be needing your help with the milking from now on, Shana. It's just too much for me to handle alone," he said.

Shana cringed inside but kept her thoughts to herself. With caring for the baby, house, garden, and chickens, she barely had enough time to cook, wash, and sew. But she knew that more of the cows were giving milk now and he had enough work in the fields to justify his request.

"Of course, Emanuel." She listened to the gentle breeze that fluttered through the kitchen window. The stiff green shade brushed back and forth against the glass. The rooster crowed from the chicken yard and she heard the horses neigh. "I thought maybe we could make applesauce this afternoon, with it looking like rain and all," she said in order to break the silence.

"It won't rain and I have business over at the Beiler's farm."

"Business with the Beiler's?" she asked, knowing that he had his own reasons for not telling her about purchasing most of their farm. "Perhaps Noah and I could ride along to visit."

"Perhaps," he said. Then, he finished his meal in silence.

Shana spent the rest of the morning in the garden. With Sylvia's help, Shana had learned to love working in the garden. She prided herself on keeping it free from weeds and bugs. All of her vegetables thrived on the love and care she showered on them. Most days, she'd pick weeds from the narrow aisles between her plants while Noah slept on the porch, close enough for Shana to hear his cries.

By noon, she had plucked her fresh tomatoes and cut any ripe heads of lettuce. She carried these in her apron and took them into the house. She set the tomatoes on the windowsill by the kitchen pump. Emanuel had promised to put in regular plumbing later that month, although Shana found she didn't necessarily miss it, especially with the faucet in the washroom.

It was shortly after twelve-thirty when Emanuel came in from the barn and hung his hat by the door. His shirt was dirty and his face sweaty. Following his routine, he washed his hands, face and neck before entering the kitchen. He forced a smile at Shana as he walked over to Noah's crib. While he waited for his supper, Emanuel sat on the old sofa and held his son. Shana listened to him talking gently to Noah in Pennsylvania Dutch and felt a twinge of jealousy that she did not know what he said. However, she understood the significance of Noah understanding the language of his ancestors.

"Dinner's ready," she said as she set his plate down on the table, trying to sound cheerful.

He waited for her to sit next to him before he bowed his head in prayer. Then, as he picked up his fork, he said, "Tobacco's almost ready to cut. Another two weeks, I think. And shortly after, we'll fill silo."

"We'll?"

"Daniel and Steve are coming to help. They'll stay for a day or two."

Shana nodded, wondering if that meant he would reciprocate and lend a hand at his father's farm but she did not ask. She was simply relieved that his silence had lifted. "It'll be nice to have the company," she replied.

"I ran over to Beiler's this morning," he announced. "So, if you want to make applesauce this afternoon..." He left his sentence unfinished, an unspoken apology for his unusually demanding conduct from the day before.

"That would be nice, Emanuel," she said softly, pleased with the sacrifice he had made.

After supper, Emanuel hitched Lady Priscilla to the buggy while Shana cleaned up the dishes. Then, picking up Noah, she hurried outside to the driveway. The sky still hung gray but the clouds looked as though they were breaking. "I believe you're right, Emanuel. About it not raining today."

He held Noah while she climbed into the buggy then lifted the baby to her awaiting arms. "Could use the rain, though," he said softly.

The drive to the market, almost four miles away, soothed Shana. She hadn't left the farm in so long that the rhythmic plodding of the horse's hooves against the road was a welcome escape. She held the baby tightly, a soft breeze blowing in through the cracked windows, and shut her eyes as she listened. "I'll always love that sound," she murmured, more to herself than to Emanuel.

"What sound?" he asked.

"It's so gentle and calming. Peaceful," she continued, opening her eyes to look at Emanuel. He nodded his head, understanding of what she spoke.

There were two other buggies waiting outside of the market. Also, parked alongside, were three cars, one with out of state license plates. Shana handed Noah to Emanuel before she lifted her skirt and climbed down. She noticed his eyes glancing over her attire quickly as he waited for her to smooth down her skirt and follow him into the store.

It was a different market than the one they usually visited in town. But, this Amish market helped them with their day-to-day needs. Shana hurried down the aisles, picking a few essentials that would tie them over until their next big shopping trip. The wide planked wood floors creaked under her weight. She liked this store better than the one in town. Since this market was off a dirt road in the middle of some farms, the tourists didn't know about it. Occasionally an out-of-state car might happen upon the store but they tended to behave better than the rude and pushy tourists that so often stared and tried to steal their pictures when they shopped in town.

Shana smiled as she passed another Amish woman who greeted her with a simple, "Good day, Shana."

She loved knowing the people of the community and feeling their love and friendship. The uneasy mood from that morning slowly lifted from her shoulders as she made her way to the large barrels of freshly picked apples. She glanced over her shoulder, her eyes seeking Emanuel. She spotted him by the door, Noah fussing in his arms, as he spoke with an older Amish man. For a moment, Shana watched him, her heart warming as she saw him laugh, his eyes crinkling into those familiar half-moons. The baby reached up and brushed his fist against the bottom of Emanuel's beard as though vying for his attention. Emanuel shifted him in his arms, continuing his conversation with his neighbor.

"Two bags of apples," Shana told the young clerk who came over to assist her. "That should be enough for applesauce?"

"Depends how much you aiming to make."

"Enough for the winter," she replied.

"Better make it three, then," the clerk said. "You can never have too much, ja?"

Emanuel saw her at the counter and, saying good-bye to the Amish man, came over to help carry the bags out to the buggy. Shana took Noah from him and made some quick small talk with the young Mennonite girl behind the register. Then, glancing out the store windows, she saw Emanuel waiting for her so she grabbed the last small plastic bag, bid the young girl good-bye, and hurried out to meet Emanuel.

He stood by the buggy, his face long and taut. Impatiently, he motioned for her to hand the last bag to him. "Let's go, Shana," he said in a low voice.

"What's wrong, Emanuel?"

"Get in."

She started to hand him Noah and follow his order, trusting his stern command, when she noticed the three boys sitting on the back of a beat-up blue Chevy pickup. They were large boys, the oldest at least nineteen. He tilted his straw hat back on his forehead and grinned. "Ain't that cute? Little Englische girl pretending she's Amish," he said loudly. It took Shana a minute to realize he was talking about her.

"Hey, Amish! Didn't have any cousins left to marry?" the other boy shouted at Emanuel.

Shana's mouth fell open and she whirled around to Emanuel. "What did they just say?"

"Get in the buggy, Shana," Emanuel ordered again, this time taking Noah from her arms and gently pushing her toward the open door.

"How do they know I'm not Amish?" she demanded, her face getting red with rage.

"Just get in, Shana. Don't be bothered by the likes of them."

This time, she listened to him and climbed into the buggy. She forced the rage out of her heart and shut her ears to their taunts as Emanuel urged the horse to back up. Shana bent over, covering Noah as they passed the pickup truck, the boys still shouting out insults and laughing. Silently, Shana prayed until they had traveled far enough down the lane where the boys' taunts could not be heard except as a distant echo in her ears.

She glanced at Emanuel but followed his example by not commenting. She shut her eyes and said a silent prayer that Noah would never face such humiliating persecution in his life. Before she could stop herself, tears started streaming down her cheeks. How could those boys be so cruel, she wondered in bewilderment. She wiped the tears from her face and was thankful for the reassuring squeeze Emanuel spared her as he touched her leg.

They had almost made it home when a car crept up behind them. Shana turned around to glance out the back window and caught her breath. "It's them, Emanuel," she said, her voice hoarse and her heart pounding inside her chest.

"They won't do anything," he said stiffly.

But as the words slipped out of his mouth, the pickup sped up and began to pass them. The pickup slowed down enough so that they rode parallel to the buggy. One of the boys in the back tossed an empty bottle at the horse before the truck passed and drove down the lane. The horse shied up, rearing as the bottle hit him. The buggy lurched forward and started to tilt sideways. Shana clutched Noah with one hand and steadied herself against the door with another. She opened her mouth as though to scream but nothing came out. Emanuel tightened the reins, shouting for Lady Priscilla to calm down. Then, the truck vanished in the distance and the buggy steadied, he turned to Shana, his face white and his hands shaking.

"Are you alright?"

"Alright?" she spat out. "They tried to kill us!"

"Noah?"

"He's fine, Emanuel."

"Thank God," he whispered.

"We should go to the police!" She leaned back in the seat, her own hands shaking. "How can they be so cruel? So unfeeling?" The words slipped out without any thought before them. "Those boys should be horse whipped! Taught to respect other people, not taunt them!"

"Shana!"

"We're talking about respect for our lives! Our child!"

"Going to the Englische authorities will not change anything," Emanuel said softly.

"Perhaps it will stop them from doing it again!"

"Our ancestors faced worse persecution than that. And, I suspect, that will not be the last time. Whether their words and actions are right or wrong, we are not to judge them, Shana," he reminded her.

"Judge them? What's to judge?" she snapped back. "We could have been killed!"

"And we weren't." He reached over and touched Noah's cheek. "Going to the police is not our way, Shana." He met her gaze. "And neither is reacting to violent actions with violent words. With one month to baptism, you should realize that there is more to our faith than just dressing Amish, Shana."

The blank look in his eyes frightened her. It wasn't anger. No, she didn't think Emanuel could get angry. Perhaps it was disappointment and frustration. Or perhaps it was fear that she would fail him as an Amish wife. "Just get us home," she whispered miserably. How could he reprimand her for reacting to the accident that could have just happened?

She felt ill, her stomach queasy and threatening to unsettle. She had been hearing more and more of the modern-day persecution of her neighbors. From Emanuel's uncle whose barn had been burned, to a neighbor several towns over who found his herd of cows shot, the violent torment was specifically directed at the Amish. Now, those boys had not only directed their verbal abuse at the Amish, but at Emanuel and Shana in particular.

It frightened her that strangers knew about her upbringing and who she was. It was as if they had singled them out from among others. But, even worse was the realization that Emanuel expected her to forget about the incident as though the incident had never happened. As she held Noah, she wondered if she'd ever be able to forgive as easily as Emanuel had just forgiven those horrid Englische boys.

Chapter Twenty-Three

Shana felt the deacon's wife untie the ribbons holding her black prayer cap and remove it from her head. The bishop laid his hand upon her head. "Upon your faith, which you confessed before God and the many witnesses of our Church, you are baptized in the name of the Father, the Son, and the Holy Spirit," he said. The deacon poured water in the bishop's cupped hands that dripped it over the top of her head.

The bishop pulled her hands from her face. His German words sounded harsh and forbidding. While she didn't understand every word that he spoke, she had been well trained on the deep meaning behind the ceremony. She also understood that she had taken the final step over the line that separated her past from her future. The line that she crossed as the bishop laid his hands on her shoulders, helping her to stand as a new member of their community, was the last remnant of the present.

"In the name of the Lord and the Church, we extend to you the hand of fellowship, rise up."

She raised her eyes and greeted her new family. There were tearful nods of approval from some of the members, although most of them kept straight faces as they recognized the seriousness of Shana's new commitment to not only their way of life but to the community as a whole. As she stood before her neighbors, Shana realized that she had just turned the key to the trunk where she had locked away her never-to-be worn again wedding ring and other material reminders of her non-Amish past. And she would try, she silently vowed, to keep locked in that trunk her non-Amish memories, as well.

The baptismal ceremony, which followed the regular two

sermons, had focused on walking the straight and narrow before the bishop had offered one more opportunity to turn away from the Amish commitment to life. Kneeling before the congregation alongside Emanuel and three other young adults, Shana had declared her desire and promise to renounce the outside world and practice obedience to God and His church. She had promised to be faithful for life to Christ before confessing that she believed that Jesus was the Son of God.

No one verbally acknowledged her commitment after the baptism. Instead, Shana joined the women in the kitchen, her new home away from home, as they prepared the midday meal. Shana helped set out the breads, cold salads, and pies that the women had prepared. Occasionally, someone would lay their hand on her arm or smile at her as their eyes met, but no words passed beyond the regular course of conversation.

When Noah cried from the downstairs bedroom, Shana wiped her hands on a towel and smiled at Sarah Yoder as she escaped the kitchen to fetch her son. She sat on the sofa on the far side of the kitchen, Noah nursing hungrily at her breast. Shana rubbed his back, oblivious to the people that moved around her. No one paid attention to her feeding the baby. To them, breast-feeding was natural, a part of life. Shana fought her own modest shame and patiently let Noah finish. She wiped his mouth with a rag and smothered his face with kisses. He gurgled happily and Shana took the opportunity to quickly change his diaper.

"How quickly they grow, ja?"

Shana glanced over her shoulder and smiled at Lillian. Emanuel's family had come to their church for the baptismal ceremony. "Perhaps I'll think that when he starts walking", she replied.

Lillian laid Jacob on the bed next to Noah and quickly followed Shana's example. With expert hands, she had Jacob changed before Shana had finished with Noah. "It amazes me when I see Linda every day. She's so big. Soon she'll be going to school and Jacob will be helping Jonas with the milking and plowing."

Shana laughed. "He hasn't even stopped nursing yet, Lillian."

Lillian laughed with her. "Perhaps it seems like he's already grown since I know he'll have another brother or sister in seven months."

"Oh Lillian!" For a quick moment, Shana didn't know whether to be happy for her or sad. Little Linda wasn't even three yet. So many children in such a short amount of time. But, as Shana saw the radiant glow in Lillian's eyes, she remembered the wonderful feeling she had the day Noah was born and every day since, and she knew that there could never be too many children. "That's wonderful!"

"Just as wonderful as your baptism today, ja?"

Shana met Lillian's joyous gaze and nodded. "Today has been wonderful. And I owe a lot of it to you. *Danke* for your help and love, Lillian."

Even though Lillian fought it, a blush covered her cheeks. "We introduced you to God, Shana, but it was Him who showed you the light." But Shana could tell that she was pleased with the compliment.

They rejoined the other women in the kitchen and sitting room. Shana held Noah in her arms and sat down on the sofa. Tenderly, she laid the baby on his back on her lap and let him cling to her fingers. Carefully, she pulled him upward, smiling as he began to laugh. "You're almost ready to sit up by yourself, aren't you?" she asked him. Then, clutching him gently to her shoulder, she gave him a loving hug. "Don't grow up too fast on me," she whispered into his ear.

While the rest of the women scurried around the kitchen, some joined Shana as did Lillian and a few young mothers. Shana watched as Katie worked with the other women, expertly finding her place in the line of duties. Even Sylvia fit in. Shana smiled to herself as she rubbed Noah's back. Was it only a year ago that she had felt so awkward and out of place among the Amish women when they worked in the kitchen? Now she felt confident and secure in her place as mother, wife, and worshipper.

"We'll be quilting soon, Shana," Linda Yoder said, sitting down next to Shana. She leaned over and brushed a wrinkled finger across Noah's cheek. "Sister Sarah is hosting a party next week. Now that the silo is filled and the plow's away until spring. You should join us."

"I'll speak with Emanuel," Shana replied.

Linda Yoder responded with a smile. "Winter months will soon be upon us."

"Soon," Shana said, rubbing Noah's back. "Not looking forward to the cold."

"Ja," Linda agreed. "But the summer harvest is done."

"We still have to hang the tobacco," Shana pointed out.

"Josef doesn't crop tobacco." Linda quickly added, "But there's always work around the farm."

Lillian quickly agreed. "And when it finally ends, it gets warm and begins all over again."

The other women laughed good-naturedly and even Shana had to smile. With the end of the autumn came the hanging of tobacco and once that was finished and it was too cold to work in the fields, Emanuel would spend most of his days working in the barn, painting or fixing things but there would be very little work until late March when everything began again with the advent of the warm weather. Spring, she realized, was truly the season of rebirth.

The men started passing through the kitchen, each filling his plate full of freshly prepared food. The children lingered near the doorway, waiting for their turn. But they would have to wait for a while longer. After the married men were finished with their food, it was time for the women to eat. Only then would it be time for the children to fill their plates. Shana watched one young boy, no older than eight, leaning against the doorframe, his hands thrust into his pockets, and his black hat tilted back on his forehead. He watched with envy, his eyes large and round, as the men crowded around the table.

Shana watched the men, her eyes resting on the familiar back of her husband. She studied his every movement, the way he politely handed the serving spoon to the next fellow in line or nodded at an older man who joined them. At one point, as he stood up to leave the table, he caught Shana's eye. A trace of a smile crossed his lips, lighting up his face. But no words passed from his lips. For Shana, his expression said the words that they were both feeling.

Katie came over and took baby Noah from her. She held him in her arms and cooed over her youngest grandchild. "What a big boy you are becoming," she said.

"Oh Mamm, please," Shana begged quietly. "I want him to stay a baby forever," she added with a smile.

Katie laughed. "Don't we all? But one day, perhaps sooner than you'd like, you'll be at another baptism and welcoming him into your church."

"That will be a proud day for both Emanuel and me," Shana replied.

"As it is for Jonas and me." She handed the baby back to Shana. "We live our lives obeying God, Shana, and hopefully our children learn from our example. People can look at us and know that we are Christians, that we live holy before God. Our lives are like an empty field and religion provides the seeds. But we still need to cultivate those seeds for them to grow into a good, bountiful crop."

"Then Emanuel is my sunshine and my community is the soil," Shana said.

"What about the rain?" Lillian teased.

"The rain?" Shana repeated. She thought for a moment before she smiled. "God's words. The Bible is the rain." The rest of the women smiled their pleasure with her answer and even Shana felt moved by the advice that Katie had bestowed on her. Indeed, if a year ago she had felt as though she didn't belong, Shana never felt closer to the people before her.

Chapter Twenty-Four

The winter months passed slowly. The mornings were brutally cold and Shana hated getting out of her warm bed. But every day, she arose at five o'clock with Emanuel to help with the milking. Afterward, she'd hurry back to the house to cook him breakfast. Shortly after cleaning up the dishes, she'd dress and feed Noah while Emanuel bathed. Some days, they'd go visiting, fighting the brutal cold to share the midday meal with Katie or Lillian. Other days, Shana would help Emanuel shred the corn stalks or, later in December, strip the dried tobacco. All the while, she'd hurry back to the house to check on Noah who, for the most part, slept through the mornings.

In the afternoons, she'd tend to her household chores while Emanuel hauled manure from the barn to the fields, taking advantage of the hard, frozen ground to spread the natural fertilizer. From the kitchen windows, Shana would often see him driving the mules from behind the barn into the fields. She knew that he felt the bitter cold winds that blew across the farm nestled in the crutch of the valley. Sympathetically, she'd watch him until he disappeared as she kneaded dough to make fresh bread or a piecrust. It didn't take long for her kitchen to warm with the inviting and delicious aroma of the baking bread.

By suppertime, she'd have the table ready with thick slices of bread, homemade jam, and steaming chicken soup. Emanuel would hang up his hat and wash before coming into the kitchen. "Smells like you've been busy," he'd greet her. After the meal, when the dishes were washed and put away, Shana would sit at the table, nursing Noah while Emanuel read aloud from the Bible. By eight o'clock, on most nights, the kerosene lantern had been shut off and the Lapp farm settled in for the night, the noise only broken by the occasional bellow from a cow.

It was early-February when Shana realized that she was pregnant again. For a couple of weeks, she kept the secret to herself, enjoying the pleasures of savoring the young life that grew within her womb. She found herself caressing her stomach, humming to herself as she hung laundry or cooked supper. She tried to imagine what the new baby would look like but she could only picture Noah's sweet face with his vibrant blue eyes that so resembled Emanuel's.

When she washed Noah or played with him in the afternoon by the kerosene heater, she couldn't help but smile. His six-month-old curiosity and fascination with everything amazed her. She'd watch him smile when she tickled his belly or blew warm breath on his bare feet. He could sit up by himself now and she's often find him sitting up in his downstairs crib, watching her as she cooked and cleaned. When she caught the baby's eyes upon her, she'd set down her towel and hurry over to smother him with kisses, which always bought that innocent, one tooth smile to his face.

By mid-March, as Emanuel, restless from the bitter winter, waited for the weather to warm, her secret escaped. She had just finished her first trimester and had almost gotten over her morning sickness, which hadn't been as harsh as during her first pregnancy, when he confronted her about the upcoming addition to their family.

"Noah's almost eight months now," he started as he sat on the sofa, Noah asleep on his lap.

"Another week or so, I believe."

Emanuel watched as she kneaded some dough on the

counter. She had become an expert baker during the winter months with no more accidental ingredients in her creations. "Ja, a big boy."

"Bigger than yesterday," she teased.

"Soon he'll be walking, ja?"

"And then he'll be helping you with the milking and going to school. Maybe he'll get married soon, too," she teased.

"Let's start with walking," Emanuel laughed.

"He'll be a handful by summer's end, I'm certain," she added.

Emanuel rubbed his son's back gently. Shana glanced over her shoulder at him. She loved watching him with Noah. His big hands that plowed the fields and worked the mules cared for the baby so gently and lovingly that tears sometimes came to her eyes. Emanuel looked up and caught her staring at him. "Perhaps Sylvia should come visiting again this summer. She's finished with all of her schooling and, as you pointed out, Noah might prove a handful."

"Sylvia's help is always welcome, Emanuel. But I could certainly manage," Shana replied.

"Ja, you could, of course," he replied, looking disappointed for just the briefest of moments.

"But," Shana quickly added. "Perhaps Sylvia should come anyway."

"*Vell*, if you can handle the chickens, the garden, the house, helping me with the milking and planting, and caring for young Noah by yourself, her help won't be necessary. It isn't as though we have such a large family, ja?"

"Ja," she mimicked, a smile lighting up her face. "At least not yet."

"Not yet?" he asked hopefully.

"Perhaps by summer's end..."

"Ja?"

"Ja," she finally admitted.

Emanuel shifted Noah on his lap. For a long moment, he remained silent as he held his son. Shana watched him, her cheeks rosy and her eyes bright. She waited for his response. But, instead, he stared down at Noah's sleeping face. He brushed his fingers down the infant's cheek. Finally, he looked up at Shana. "I will speak to Sylvia." Yet, his somber words could not hide the pride in his face.

By April, Emanuel had plowed the section that Shana would garden with a slight expansion, at her request. Then, her days were full with gardening on top of all her other chores. Sometimes, when she hurried to the house to answer Noah's cries, she'd think back to the night Emanuel had asked her to marry him. She'd smile when she remembered her ignorance about not having any work to do during the day. Now, her days were so full, she often didn't complete all of the chores she had planned. Yet, at the end of every day, she'd go to sleep beside Emanuel knowing that what she hadn't done could be handled the next day.

Emanuel began plowing the fields at the same time. He plowed the back acreage for the corn and, when that was completed, he began disappearing toward the Beiler farm. While she knew that he was plowing the new land, she kept his secret silent, waiting for the right moment to ask about the land that he had purchased but never mentioned to her. He plowed from before sunrise to well after sunset. He was weary and tired at night, more so than she remembered from the previous year.

When he finally came in from the fields, he'd barely stay awake for supper and retired to bed immediately afterwards. She'd help with the early morning and evening milking but, beyond that, her chores kept her from assisting Emanuel in the fields.

One day, when she had seen him retreating to the new land, she brought Noah and a pitcher of fresh iced tea out to the fields. At first he didn't see her. But Noah started to cry and Emanuel quickly reined in the mules. He greeted her with a smile and took the pitcher from her hand. She soothed Noah, rubbing his back and shifting him in her arms. "You're very neighborly to plow the Beiler's old fields," she teased.

"I'm plowing the Lapp's fields," he stated before he dipped the ladle into the pitcher and drank some of her homemade iced tea.

"Have some of your relatives moved onto their farm?" she asked playfully.

He dipped the ladle again. "You know that the Meyers moved there."

"The Mennonites?"

He smiled. "Ja, the Mennonites."

"I haven't met them yet but I'll make a point to visit. They are just married, yes?"

Emanuel reached out for Noah and took him from her arms. "Ja, just married." He lifted the baby over his head, laughing as Noah smiled and gurgled in delight. He did this several times then, too tired to continue the game, he held the baby against his shoulder. "One day, Noah will need land to plow, too," Emanuel finally admitted. "With land so scarce, the opportunity to expand will only come along so often."

Shana nodded and looked around herself. The land was flat

and dipped a little closer to the Beiler's old farmhouse in the distance. "What are you planting here?"

"Wheat."

"That's a lot of work for one man," she said, returning her gaze from the field to meet Emanuel's eyes. "Perhaps it isn't Sylvia we should ask to stay with us this summer but Steve or Daniel instead."

"Hard work is from the Lord," he replied wearily.

"With corn, tobacco, alfalfa, and wheat, you'll need some assistance."

He took off his hat and wiped his brow with the back of his arm. His blue eyes danced across the horizon, staring toward the fields by the barn that were waiting for the corn to be seeded. "Perhaps with planting, ja," he finally said as he slid his hat back onto his head. "Perhaps Daniel could come and help if Daed doesn't need him."

That evening, Emanuel returned from the field early to milk the cows. After an early supper, he hitched Lucky Monday to the buggy and waited for Shana to emerge from the house. She wore her black cape and bonnet with Noah wrapped in a warm blanket. Emanuel let her into the buggy first, holding Noah while she climbed in. Then, after he settled next to her, they rode over to Katie and Jonas' farm.

The trip took over an hour and, with all of the jostling, Shana was thankful to arrive. Three and a half year old Linda ran out of the house to greet them with Lillian following closely. "What a surprise!" she exclaimed as she took Noah from Shana's arms. "We didn't expect you 'til after the autumn planting."

Katie quickly emerged from the house, her feet bare and her glasses slipping slightly off of her nose. "We're just getting ready for supper," she greeted them.

"We've eaten," Emanuel replied. "Is Daed about?"

"Ja. Doing the milking."

Emanuel quickly disappeared, leaving Shana to follow the women into the house for some iced tea. She sat quietly at the table with her glass while Lillian and Katie hurried around the kitchen for some finishing touches to the evening meal. Sylvia and Susie cooed over Noah until Katie directed them to set the table. Linda clamored around, trying to peek at the baby. Shana smiled while she watched her.

"Momma had a baby like that," Linda exclaimed, pointing to Jacob in her mother's arms. "But he's bigger."

Lillian reached over and tugged at Linda's braid. "And we're going to have another baby like that in the summer."

Shana lowered Noah so Linda could see him better. "You were a baby once, too."

"Was not," Linda argued.

"You shouldn't disagree with your elders, Lindy," Lillian gently scolded her. "Apologize to Shana."

"Hear Sylvia's going to be visiting you again this summer," Katie said to Shana, her own simple acknowledgement of the upcoming birth of her twelfth grandchild.

"August, I suppose." Shana smiled as Sylvia looked up from the table, obviously unaware that she was going anywhere. But the glow in her eyes as she met Shana's gaze told her that she was anything but disappointed. Susie nudged her in the side to finish the job at hand.

Lillian shifted Jacob in her arms. "Ja, it wouldn't do to have Susie come visiting for so long. Amos Zook might worry when he came calling and she'd be gone," she teased. Shana's eyes caught the red flush that covered Susie's cheeks. But, she didn't reply to Linda's gentle ribbing or Sylvia's hushed giggle.

"You have a beau, Susie?" Shana asked innocently, although she already knew the answer.

"He's not my boyfriend," she replied softly.

Katie dropped some freshly peeled potatoes into a pot of boiling water. "Seem to know that he's driven you home from two singings already."

"And I saw him waiting for you after church last Sunday," Sylvia quietly added. Susie's cheeks flushed again and she cast a silencing glare at her younger sister.

"He's just being neighborly," Susie said softly.

"Indeed," Lillian said before she turned to Katie. "Perhaps we should plant more carrots and celery in the garden this year." They laughed at her reference to the subtle sign of an upcoming marriage: More carrots and celery to serve at the wedding day's feast. Then, the teasing over, the subject of Amos Zook was dropped and the preparations for supper continued in silence.

While they waited for Emanuel, Lillian took Shana next door to her house to show her a new quilt she was making with Katie. It was laid out across a large wooden quilting frame and already, the beautiful floral quilting pattern could be seen amidst the white and red cloth. They were still looking at it when Shana heard Emanuel calling for her from outside. By the time Shana carried Noah outside to the waiting buggy, she noticed Daniel crouched in the back. She greeted him with an encouraging smile. He flashed her a large, shy grin back but didn't say a word.

The ride back was in silence except for Noah's gurgles and coos. Finally, the rocking of the buggy put him to sleep. Shana felt her own eyes growing heavy and fought the urge to follow Noah's example. Back at the farm, she fixed Daniel some leftovers for supper while Emanuel excused himself for bed. Shana kept Daniel company while he ate, although her seventeen year old brother-in-law was still withdrawn from any woman, even his sister-in-law.

"We're glad your daed was able to let you stay with us and help with the plowing and planting," she said as she cleared his plate.

"Ja," he replied.

"Who will help your father?"

Daniel answered slowly. "Steve and Sylvia. Maybe the two little boys, too."

"Well, there's a lot of work for everyone, isn't there?" she quickly washed his plate and set it aside. "You can sleep in the downstairs bedroom. That way Noah won't bother you if he wakes up."

Daniel nodded and got up from the table. "I imagine Emanuel will be waking me early so I'll say good-night," he said before disappearing into the back room.

Shana watched him as he left the kitchen and smiled to herself as she finished cleaning the kitchen. The rest of her chores completed, she sat down at the table with Emanuel's Bible. Yet, she couldn't concentrate as she thought over the events from that day.

She felt emotion in her heart as she realized the sacrifice that Jonas had made to let Daniel help Emanuel with his plowing and planting. There had been no questions asked or major discussions. Emanuel had requested and the family quickly readjusted. She shut the Bible and stared at the shadows that danced on the wall from the kerosene lamp. There was no spiritual guidance in the Bible for her tonight. Any lessons she needed to learn today she had learned from the love and generosity from Emanuel's family.

Chapter Twenty-Five

Shana heard the bottle smash outside the window and down the lane as she made their bed. For a second, she wasn't certain about what she had heard and bent back down to tuck in the corner of the faded blue quilt. She hummed to herself, mentally listing the chores she wanted to get done that day: Washing the clothes, cleaning the bathroom, maybe even helping Daniel and Emanuel with the planting. But, when she heard the gravel kicking up in their driveway as a car sped off, she stood up and quickly turned to the window. Squinting, she looked outside.

A young boy emerged from around the side of their barn and jumped into the back of a blue pick-up truck that had pulled up to the end of their driveway. The truck sped away, three young boys with long brown hair sitting in the flatbed, laughing. She forced the window open and, for a long moment, just leaned against the sill, confused and uncomprehending what she had seen and heard. Then, her heart suddenly lurched into her throat and she ran from the bedroom and down the stairs. It was early afternoon and the sun was high in the sky. They hadn't been fortunate enough to have rain for the past week and the air was thick with humidity.

As she hurried through the kitchen, Shana spared a concerned glance at Noah, sleeping in his crib by the kitchen table, before she tossed open the door and walked outside onto the porch. Her heart pounded inside her chest and she said a quick prayer. "Please God, not us," she whispered. But a gentle breeze broke through the hot air and, sure enough, she could smell it now. Fire.

Her first reaction was to scream for Emanuel but she knew

he wouldn't hear her from the fields. They were working the plot of land that bordered on the Yoder's farm to the north. It wouldn't help anyway. She had heard too many stories to think they could save the barn. But there was a chance of saving whatever animals were still inside the barn. Most of the cows were out in the pasture but the horses were inside.

She ran across the driveway and, the billow of smoke apparent now, she ignored her fear as she threw open the barn doors and entered. The hay must have caught first because the fire had already spread like wildfire. Through the rising smoke, she could see the two horses jumping and banging against the stalls as they tried to get out. Shana ran over to the stall doors and quickly struggled with the rusty bolts, sliding them back to unlock the stalls. Then, as carefully as she could, she flung the doors back to let the horses run toward the opening. Lady ran directly for the barn door, away from the smoke, but Lucky Monday continued to rear up, his eyes wild and frightened.

Shana slowly backed away, trying to avoid the thrashing horse. But Lucky Monday suddenly lunged forward out of the stall, the door flinging backward and knocking Shana to the ground. Her head smashed against the cement floor and she felt the horse run over her, its one hoof tripping over her crumpled body. For what seemed a long while, she laid there, dazed and winded. She could smell the burning hay and wood. She could hear the crackling of the flames and sizzling of the burning paint. And then, she felt the intense heat and the pain.

In just a matter of minutes, the barn would be engulfed in destructive fire and she knew her only chance was to get out. It was too dry and the fire was burning too fast. She struggled to her feet but everything swam before her eyes. She could hear some of the cows in the pasture just outside the barn bellowing. They could smell the fire and she could hear their fear. She needed to get to them, to open the gate for them to escape into the outer fields. But, she couldn't figure out how to get there. The smoke was thicker now, almost blinding. It had gone up so quickly and now, she was disoriented and lost inside, only feet away from safety.

"Shana!"

She could hear someone calling her name. She followed the sound, even though her vision was all but useless. She coughed and felt something warm against her legs. She reached down and grabbed the hem of her skirt to cover her mouth. She heard her name again and, to her relief, broke through the smoke as she found the open doorway. She stumbled outside, her eyes shut and her legs weak. She kept walking, away from the heat and the pain. Except, she suddenly realized, the pain didn't go away.

"Dear God!" she heard someone say.

She tried to force her eyes open but could only make out the outline of a dark shadow racing toward her. She dropped the skirt from her mouth and, feeling a pair of arms grabbing for her, she collapsed. "Shana! You're covered in blood!"

"Where's Emanuel?" she managed to ask Daniel.

She tried to open her eyes but Daniel seemed blurry. She tried to focus on his face but she could barely keep her eyes open. Had he said something about blood? She couldn't remember. Had he spoken at all? She didn't wait for his answer as she whispered, "Save the cows." Then everything went black.

It was nighttime when she woke up. Her throat was dry and her eyes stung. She tried to look around the room but it was dark. Outside the open window, she heard the night crickets chirping and an occasional moo from the cows. They seemed further away, distant. She tried to move but the searing pain in her abdomen and legs stopped any further effort. A soft whimper escaped from her throat and she wrapped her arms around her belly, curling up into a ball to fight the pain. Something didn't feel right and tears slowly welled in her eyes. The soft glow from his lantern illuminated the room. She realized that she was downstairs, not in their bedroom. Her eyes slowly adjusted. Everything seemed strange and she couldn't understand where she was.

"Emanuel?"

"I'm here," he replied softly as he set the lantern down on the nightstand. His knees cracked as he sat in the chair next to the bed. He leaned forward and touched her forehead. "Don't try to talk, Shana."

"Where are we?"

"The Meyers," he answered softly. His eyes were sunken in his face and they lacked the usual glow that came from mischievousness or hard work.

She started to sit up and cringed from the pain. "Where's Noah?"

Emanuel smiled faintly in the gentle, orange light. "He's here," he reassured, putting a hand on her shoulder and gently pushing her back down in the bed.

"Why are we here?" she asked softly.

"Don't you remember?" A puzzled look crossed his face as he explained, "There was a fire. The doctor felt it best to stay here until you were better and the house cleared out from the smoke."

"How long have we been here?"

"Two days."

"Two days?" She repeated, reaching for his arm. "What happened?" She could see Emanuel bit his lower lip and she wondered what was wrong.

"It was arson, Shana. Someone deliberately burned our barn."

"Oh, Emanuel!" she cried out as she started to sit again. She leaned back into the pillow and tried to recall what had happened. Slowly, she remembered, bits and pieces. She spoke slowly, "I saw who did it. A pick-up truck and three boys."

Emanuel sighed and smoothed her hair back. "That's not important, Shana."

"They burned our barn," she said quietly, almost a forced comprehension of what had happened. "The horse...it knocked me down," she whispered.

"Shana," he began softly.

"I couldn't find my way out of the barn. It was so smoky." She looked up at him. "It burned so fast. It was hot and it hurt me, my eyes, my nose, my body. It was Daniel's voice that guided me out of the barn, Emanuel." He ran his finger down her cheek.

"Shana..." he started to say, his voice sad and pained.

"I would have died without Daniel," she realized with a hint of panic edging into her voice. She could sense that he was holding something back, hiding something from her. Dear God, she quickly prayed, don't let it be Daniel. "Where is he? Is he alright?"

He shook his head that Daniel was fine.

"The house? The herd? What happened?" she demanded, her voice shrill.

"You've been very sick and we've been very worried about you." Shana felt her ears start to ring and she realized that whatever had happened had happened to her.

"Emanuel? What happened?" she asked, her voice barely a

whisper as she reached out to grab his arm. "You must tell me what happened!"

"The baby..." he started, his voice low and his words hesitant.

"The baby?" she asked, confused. Then, those two words sunk in and she realized. The pain she felt was not from the horse having knocked her down and trampled over her. It was from a miscarriage. She had miscarried in her sixth month. There would be no baby in August. "Where is my baby?" she asked, her voice shallow with disbelief.

"The baby is with the Lord," he finally said. "We buried her this morning."

"Buried?" she repeated in a whisper.

"I'm so sorry, Shana," he forced out as he reached for her hand. His eyes began to well with tears but he held them back as he began to sense the anger behind Shana's realization. She clutched her empty belly and let out a low, deep wail. He had said that they buried "her". The unborn child had been a daughter, a little girl that hadn't been given the chance. It had been robbed of the life that Shana had breathed into her. Shana moved away from his touch, holding her sorrow within and sharing it with no one.

"They killed my baby," she cried. And Emanuel hadn't even waited for her to bury the unborn. "They killed my daughter!"

She cried out loud, her sobs echoing in the silence of the house. She ignored the second light shining into the bedroom from the doorway. She barely heard the female voice speaking in Dutch and Emanuel's response. She sensed that he got up and left the room but she saw nothing. She could only feel the pain in her heart, the swelling emptiness as she grieved for the death of the child she would never know.

Chapter Twenty-Six

"Shana? People are arriving," Emanuel called from the washroom. He poked his head into the kitchen. "Shana?" he asked, wiping his hands on a small towel. He set it on the counter and walked over to the sofa where she sat with Noah in her arms. She stared down into the baby's sweet face as he nursed from her breast. Her face was pale and her expression long. Emanuel knelt in front of her and stroked Noah's cheek as he peered into her face. "Are you feeling well?"

Her eyes flickered from Noah to Emanuel. For a moment, he thought he saw anger in her gaze. "It's hardly been two weeks, Emanuel. Do you think I'm feeling well?"

The bitterness in her tone startled him. She hadn't spoken much since he had brought her back to the farm. She had stayed at the Meyers for two more days, enough time for Emanuel and several neighbors to clear away what remained of the barn. When Emanuel brought her and Noah back from the neighbors' farm, Shana had cried when she saw the emptiness. The cows stayed in the fields with the mules and two horses. There wasn't the large, friendly barn to welcome her and to house them. Only a burnt foundation was left to remind her of what once had been there.

Now, the fresh lumber was stacked neatly in the yard and the buggies were pulling into the driveway. Neighbors and family had donated most of it. For the past two days, Emanuel, Daniel, and two neighbors had worked at preparing the new foundation and getting the rest of the necessary supplies ready. The air was filled with laughter, friendship, and good faith for today their neighbors and family would join together to build a new barn.

Trying to ease her sorrow, Emanuel touched her knee. "The

Lord gave us life to live and rejoice in what we have, Shana. Not to mourn for what is lost."

"The Lord also gave us the intelligence to make laws for protecting ourselves against the injustice of evil, Emanuel."

Abruptly, he withdrew his touch and stood up. "Who are we to judge evil? We have spoken about this, Shana." He glanced over his shoulder. Outside the kitchen window, he could see the buggies in the driveway. In spite of the miscarriage, Shana would be expected to be hostess to these people. Enough time had elapsed where her mourning should have passed. "It is not our way."

"It's my way!" she hissed.

"Not anymore," he said harshly. "Need I remind you of your commitment? Not only to me but to your community? To the people that are just now outside, offering their assistance and love in a time of need? What has happened was God's will, Shana. Stop feeling sorry for yourself and dwelling on your loss. Reap in the benefit of what we have gained, the love and support of our neighbors." He could hear the people talking outside as the buggies continued to roll up the driveway. They were laughing and singing, happy to be able to come to Emanuel and Shana Lapp's assistance. Emanuel lowered his voice. "Let us pray for stronger backs, not lighter burdens."

Shana frowned as his words rang in her ears. "That's what your parents said when we announced our marriage. Are you comparing the death of our child to our marriage?"

His patience at an end, Emanuel took a deep breath and said, "I won't hear any more of this talk, Shana. It is not up to us to judge those boys. And, even if you found those boys, it would not bring back what we have lost. It is best to move on." At the door, he reached for his hat and slid it onto his head. His back to her, he hesitated before going outside to greet his family and neighbors. "I'd advise you to forget the Englische laws, Shana, and mention your ideas to no one." Then he was gone.

For the rest of the morning, her kitchen was flooded with women and young children. The women cooked and laughed, enjoying the day and time spent together. There were so many people helping with the raising that not one person had to work too hard. There was time for visiting and joking amidst the work at hand. Younger children helped on the ground, carrying smaller lumber or picking up nails while the men worked together to raise the barn's frame and the women worked at making a hearty midday meal.

Shana tried to forget the bitterness in her heart. She tried to chat with the women and listened to their friendly gossip. No one mentioned the increase in persecution against their community in the past several months. Nor did anyone ask her about the fire or what could have happened if she hadn't gotten out of the barn when she did. To them, she had lived and there was nothing to mourn. To them, it was forgotten. But Shana couldn't forget the three young boys laughing as they drove away. Nor could she forget that her unborn daughter was laying in the cold ground not far from their farm.

"Shana, you look so weak," Lillian said, laying her hand on her arm. "Perhaps you should lie down, ja?"

But Shana shook her head adamantly. "When I lay down, I think. When I think, I remember. And then I get angry," she confided. The confused look on Lillian's face told Shana that her sister-in-law didn't understand the anger she was feeling over the loss of her child. "Lillian, perhaps if someone had stopped those boys before, we wouldn't have lost our barn or, more importantly, our child."

Lillian glanced around the kitchen, making certain that no one was listening. "Will stopping them bring back the things you have lost?" Her expression remained pleasant and friendly but her tone was reprimanding.

"Perhaps not, but it may prevent your barn from burning and you from losing a child!"

"Shana!" Lillian clutched Jacob closer to her chest, her eyes widened and her voice sounded fearful. "You must remember that the Lord giveth and that He taketh. It is His way and His way is the law."

Shana felt her pain rising in her throat. She fought the urge to cry again. She had cried too much already, mostly from the emptiness but partially from her frustration. "I just can't believe that those boys are sleeping every night and they don't even know that their cruel prank murdered my daughter."

"Would that bring her back? What is it you want from them now that truly matters?"

Shana was about to respond but she felt a hand on her arm. Looking up, she saw Katie's concerned eyes meeting hers. "Whatever you are thinking, child, speak wisely; for the choices you make can turn against you and affect the people you care about."

"Mamm," she started.

But Katie silenced her again. "Who are we to judge, Shana? The Lord reserves the right to judge others but He offers us the right to forgive sins against us. To forgive shows our commitment to the Lord's way and to His will. There is no alternative for you, Shana. Forgive the boys and show the loyalty you have chosen or risk the possibility of being shunned," she whispered. "Now, no more of this talk. The men are building the barn and we must prepare their meal," she said, her voice suddenly fresh and cheerful.

For the rest of the day, Shana worked alongside the women as they made pitchers of iced tea and served it to the men. At noon, the men sat at the picnic tables that neighbors had brought over for this day. On the ground behind the benches, the men laid their straw hats, lining them up in neat rows. The women stood behind the men, their heads bowed, while everyone silently prayed over the midday meal. Then, for the next half an hour, the women silently served the men their food. Shana helped by refilling the baskets of bread and dishes of chutney and relishes. Afterwards, there were dishes to wash and food to be put away.

Throughout the day, she would pause to glance out the window to the spot where the skeleton barn slowly emerged. It was near the same spot as the old barn, although it seemed further from the house. At first, she saw the musical harmony as the men lifted the frames onto the new foundation, all in unison. Later, she watched as the men climbed onto the frame, lifting and hammering the inner beams into place. Finally, after all of the dishes had been cleared and the last pitcher of iced tea had been made, Shana sat on the porch steps, Noah cradled in her arms, as she watched the remaining boards being nailed into place.

"Your garden looks wonderful, Shana," Sarah Yoder said as she sat in the shade while embroidering a hand towel.

"It's grown well this year," Shana modestly replied.

"And your chickens?" Katie asked.

Shana smiled. "They're hardly any work but every couple of weeks, I keep finding new additions. I don't know where they hide their eggs from me." Some of the women laughed. "But they're welcome. We had a visitor in April who kept helping himself to my pullets," she added referring to the fox that had carried off at least three young hens before a neighbor's dog killed it.

"God is wonderful, ja?" one of the older women sighed. "In the face of sorrow, He finds the time to bring new life."

Her words were spoken innocently, unaware of Shana's miscarriage. Shana fought the urge to cry. She had tried all afternoon, hoping to forget, at least temporarily. But even in the beauty of the symbolic life the community had restored to their farm, she couldn't forget the ugliness of death that still lingered in her heart.

By the time the sun lowered in the sky and the last buggy had rolled out of their driveway, their new barn blocked the rising moon, needing only a fresh coat of paint. In just one day, a new barn had replaced the old and was expected to wash away the memories that had so quickly burned in the fire. Shana recognized the effort of the people and genuinely thanked them as they finished the raising and began to gather their families together to return home for their own evening chores.

Shana couldn't help but wonder if the same time and money the community had pooled together to assist them would be directed at another family the following week or the week after that. What kind of faith is this, she wondered, that allows us to be so blindly led by controllable circumstances? Who is next, she asked herself as she watched the last buggy pull out of the driveway. Which one of them is about to feel the pain and agony of such senseless persecution?

Chapter Twenty-Seven

The police car pulled up the driveway, stopping in the shade of the new barn. It had been a while since she had seen a car pull into their driveway. The police car looked foreign and unreal mixed with the tranquility of the farm. Curious, Shana finished hanging up the laundry and wiped her hands on the black apron that covered her plain, faded purple dress. She ducked underneath the clothesline and greeted the two uniformed officers. They smiled at her pleasantly as they crossed over the green grass to meet her.

Shana stood apart from them, her heart pounding inside her chest. The last Englische people to stop at the farm had been her parents, almost a year ago. Even during her visits to town, she rarely had to confront the Englische, the people of her past. Now, standing barefoot in the typical Amish dress that she saved for laundry and grass cutting days, a blue bandana covering her head for she didn't wear her prayer cap while cleaning, she felt awkward and shy. Certainly they knew she had left their ways to marry an Amish man, the town was too small for them not to have heard about it. She wondered what they thought of her.

"Good morning," she finally said, breaking the silence.

"Mrs. Lapp," the taller officer started, absentmindedly twirling his hat on his finger.

"Shana," she prodded politely.

He nodded once then continued. "Last night, four teenage boys were picked up on the other side of town. They had started a fire on an Amish farm. A neighbor saw them and identified them."

Shana lifted her chin. "Was anyone hurt?"

The other officer shook his head. "The fire destroyed the

barn but there were no injuries. However, we have a feeling that these youths may have some connection with the fire that took place here."

"That is a shame about the barn," she concurred slowly. She felt her pulse quicken and she tried to ignore the throbbing in her temple. Forgive them, she told herself. Just forgive them. "But it doesn't concern me anymore," she heard herself say. It had been over a month and she wanted to forget.

"They were driving in a beat up blue pick-up," the first officer finished. "They aren't first time offenders, Mrs. Lapp. We want you to come to the station and identify them."

"I see," she said softly but offered nothing more.

"Will you?" the younger officer said as he stepped forward. It was clear that he was frustrated and wanted nothing more than to stop the arson. "These kids have been destroying Amish farms for the past year. They have no respect for your property, your religion, or even your lives. They slipped through the cracks in our system the first time. If you can identify them, we can stop them from doing this again."

"If I identify them," she asked, "the law will send them to prison to pay for the crime, ja?"

The officer tried to explain what she already knew. "The law will protect you, your family, and your community from this happening again."

"As I'm sure you are aware, I am familiar with the laws of the Englische, Officers. Your law will put the boys into a youth shelter or, perhaps, just slap them on the wrist. That won't bring back my baby and, you can see, that our barn is already replaced. Your law may prevent those particular boys from setting more fires, but it won't prevent others. I am also familiar with the laws of the Amish. God's laws," she said. She could see the two men shifting their weight as she explained her position on the matter. She didn't care if they felt uncomfortable with her words. "And it is not up to us to judge or to choose their punishment."

"If someone had identified them before, Mrs. Lapp, you might not have lost your baby," the officer snapped. "You can prevent others from similar suffering as someone else could have prevented yours."

Shana winced at his words, feeling as though he had flung a knife at her. Had she not come from his world, she would have taken offense at his harsh treatment. "Don't think I haven't thought of that, Officer. Every night as I lie in bed, praying for the soul of my unborn daughter, I pray for my own and those of my community who would not let me testify."

It was true. Many nights as she stared at the ceiling, listening to Emanuel sleep beside her, she had thought about how someone else could have saved her baby. Sleep didn't come easily for her, though. Instead, she remembered the boys who threw the bottle at the horse and knew that, if Emanuel had let her tell the authorities, those boys would have been arrested then and there and her baby might have lived.

She shut her eyes and took a deep breath, lowering her voice. "Those boys...the one who started the fire, his face will forever be engraved in my memory. In my heart, I wish nothing more than justice for what they did to our farm and to my child. But, I have chosen a way that will not allow me to follow my heart. Not this time."

"Mrs. Lapp, if you've seen the boys, you must come and identify them. Our laws can force you."

"I'll remind you again that I left your ways and your laws.

Whether it is right or wrong, I am not able to come to the station and identify those boys. I'm sorry you made the trip out here for naught," she whispered and started to walk away from them. "Good day," she retorted with stiff, even words.

Later in the afternoon, after she had finished her chores and taken a fresh shower, Shana sat in the freshly cut grass near the fields of growing corn and played with Noah. She held him up as he tried to steady himself on his weak legs. A toothless smile lit up his face whenever he wobbled and Shana caught him from falling. In his miniature suspendered pants, which were still a size too big, and his bright blue shirt, he was the vision of a baby Amish man. He was the image of Emanuel, from the tiny brown ringlets that crowned his head to his big, blue eyes that beamed up at her in crescent moons.

"That's Mommy's boy. You can stand!" she encouraged. But this time, when he fell, he toppled forward into her arms. She laughed as he nuzzled against her chest. "You did that on purpose, didn't you?" she said, lifting him into the air and over her head. He gurgled and smiled as she brought him back down to the ground and tried to get him to stand one more time.

"Is he walking yet?" Emanuel teased as he walked up the hill in time to see her laughing with Noah.

Shana looked up and smiled. She cradled Noah in her lap, his small fingers wrapped around her thumbs. "Running the marathon," she teased back.

Emanuel took off his hat and wiped his forehead with the back of his hand. Then, sliding his hat back onto this head, he stretched out on the cool grass next to her and leaned his head on his hand, staring up at her. "No doubt from your coaching, then." Noah struggled out of Shana's arms and crawled over to his father.

Steadying himself, he tried to stand, his one small fist entwined in Emanuel's curls. But his legs wouldn't quite support him and he fell backward.

Emanuel caught him and pulled him against his chest. "Keep that up and you'll never be able to work the fields with me, Noah," he teased. He looked over at Shana, pleased to see a smile playing upon her lips. "It has been a while since I heard you laugh."

"It has been a while since I had a reason," she whispered, a soft reminder that the past few weeks had been anything but happy ones at the Lapp farm; especially when she had missed the last church Sunday, a fierce headache keeping her at home with Noah. But she wanted to try, to return to life in order to mend her fences with Emanuel. "How are the new crops?" Shana asked, hoping to change the subject.

"Ears are sprouting."

"Already?"

"Ja," he nodded. "The alfalfa is doing well, too. It's just a matter of enough sun and rain now. And the Lord's blessing, of course."

"Daniel was a big help."

"Without him, we couldn't have done it. With the new field and so much plowing, it was too much for one man and even two. We'll need an army of children to help us after Daniel starts working his own farm, ja?" Emanuel teased, reaching over to tug at Shana's prayer cap string hanging over her shoulder.

The smile rapidly faded from her face and she stiffened at the mention of more children. Noticing the quick shift in her mood, Emanuel directed his attention to Noah. But Shana quickly broke through his wall of silence. "The police were here today."

"What did they want?" he asked suspiciously.

"They caught some boys two towns over. They wanted me to come identify them." She hesitated, noticing the darkening in his eyes. "Of course, I said no," she quickly added and looked away.

"Of course you said no," he repeated.

"Of course," she confirmed softly.

Emanuel stood up and bent over to pick up Noah. He stared down at Shana. "I know what you're thinking, Shana. You don't need to identify them now. If they've been caught, someone else will identify them. The Lord will pass His judgment on them. It's time to open your heart and forgive those boys."

Quickly, Shana jumped to her feet and faced him. "How can you stand before me, holding our son in your arms, and tell me to forgive them for killing our daughter?"

"They burnt the barn, Shana. They did not intend to cause your miscarriage."

"But they did."

Emanuel bowed his head from the blow of her words. Although she could not see his eyes, she could feel the power of his frustration. He rubbed Noah's back and shifted the baby in his arms. Finally, taking a deep breath, he said, "If you go to the police, the community will shun you. There has been talk already of bringing you before the elders. They are meeting on it tomorrow night."

"What?"

He raised his eyes. She could sense the pain he felt at the awkward position her sorrow had placed them in. "They are saying that you may have taken the vow without truly believing, Shana. That you haven't adapted to our ways and they were too hasty in letting you take your baptism." Emanuel turned away from her, averting his eyes from the shocked expression on her face. His voice was soft as he added, "If they excommunicate you, they will have to excommunicate me as well." Then, he walked away, carrying Noah on his hip.

Shana stared after him, her heart pounding inside her chest. That explained his distance from her. He had been keeping to himself, waiting for her decision. People must've talked to him, told him about their concerns. Katie had warned her. Emanuel had broken his own values by fighting with her about going to the police. Now, reality was facing her. Was identifying and testifying against those youths worth losing her family and the community she had fought so hard to become a part of? Was the loss of her unborn child worth the destruction of her marriage?

It was her turn to lower her head. She stared at her bare feet in the grass. It felt cool under her feet and, while she usually felt free from not being confined to wearing shoes all summer, her heart suddenly felt imprisoned. Her ears were still ringing from his words. She knew what that meant. Once excommunicated, they would no longer be a part of the community. All of their friends and even Emanuel's family would not be a part of their lives. There would be no Daniel to help with the crops when Emanuel was short-handed or Sylvia when Shana had her next child. They would be alone, an island in the midst of a sea of a loving community whose waves would never touch their shore.

Chapter Twenty-Eight

It hadn't surprised her when, after the Sunday service, Bishop Studer had dismissed the children and non-members of the church while the congregation discussed a particular matter that had been plaguing the community. Her heart had practically stopped as the bishop, waiting for those dismissed to disappear outside, finally turned his gaze upon her. She sat on the hard bench, her hands folded in her lap. But when his eyes met hers, she knew that Emanuel's prophecy was about to come true.

They called her to the front of the room. She stood up and, slowly, forced her way up the narrow aisle on the side of the large, opened kitchen into the living room where the men had sat during the sermon. She felt the heat from the hundred and fifty pairs of eyes on her back as she stood before the five older men, dressed severely in their Sunday black slacks with a black vest over their starched white shirts, who represented their church districts. These were the men, she realized, who had already decided her fate.

Like the other women, she wore her Sunday's best outfit, a black dress with a black apron over it, completed with her white prayer cap, the freshly iron strings hanging over her shoulders and down her back. But even with her prayer cap, she expressed her own Englische ways: The strings should have been tied under her chin. She kept her head bowed, her eyes wide and frightened.

She hadn't slept for the past several nights and, most mornings, after she had cleared away the breakfast dishes and Emanuel was in the fields, she had allowed herself to cry. But then, after the tears had been wiped away and her face freshly washed, she had sat down in the living room. She stared at the grandfather clock for twenty minutes, enough time to listen to the beauty of the chimes twice. Then, overcoming her fright, she had sought comfort from the very Scriptures the people who had taught her to seek solace from the Bible and allowed her into their lives would base their decision upon, when voting to ask her to leave.

"Shana," the bishop began solemnly. "You know why we have asked you here, ja?"

She nodded her head. "Yes."

He placed his hands together and nodded his head with her. Shana, her shame too great, fought the urge to raise her eyes and look at him, The bishop continued with a stern tone in his voice. "You have failed the community and our church."

The house remained silent as Shana could hear her heart pounding inside her chest. She wondered where Emanuel was and whether or not he could feel the intensity of her horror and humiliation. He had warned her but it was too late. The Zooks had spoken with Emanuel several days earlier that someone had seen the police at their farm and reported back to the deacon that Shana had spoken to them. No one asked what she had said. At Emanuel's urging, she had not volunteered this information. "Wait until asked, Shana," he had coached. Now, she realized, no one was going to ask.

The bishop stepped forward and stood in front of Shana. "Your loss is the loss of the community, Shana. But it is over and nothing, except the will of God, can change it. You are still a newcomer to our ways. All of our instruction and teaching could not prepare you for the pain you felt so recently. But God willed the loss of your unborn. Our Ordnung does not permit dwelling on such losses. To dwell upon it means you are questioning God's Will. To question His will means you are straying from the teachings of the Bible. In your straying, you are denouncing the very vow that you so solemnly took last year. Last summer, you had approached me, taking me aside to tell me that you wanted to raise your children Amish, to feel God's love and live within the Ordnung. Yet, now we are faced with the realization that your children cannot possibly be raised Amish since you have not fully accepted the Amish faith and way of life yourself!"

He placed his hand on her shoulder, waiting until she forced her eyes upward to meet his gaze. She was surprised to see concern and tenderness in his dark gray eyes, especially since his tone had been so harsh. "The leaders of our district have spent many hours discussing what to do about this obvious rebellion against the church and the Ordnung." His hesitation added to the weight of his next words. "Do you understand what it means to disobey your vow to the Ordnung?"

"Yes," she whispered.

"Did you learn of the consequences of such rebellion prior to taking your vows of faith?"

"Yes," she repeated softly.

"Do you realize you face the *Meidung*? Being shunned from the community until you have confessed your sins and reconfirmed your vow of loyalty to God and His word? Not being able to socialize with your friends and family? Including your husband? That he cannot take food from your hand and eat at the same table?"

"I do." She fought the urge to cry.

"Ja, we have spent many hours discussing and debating your sin, Shana. And, as a community, we have decided that, should we impose *Meidung* upon you, we should have to impose it on ourselves." Out of the corner of her eye she saw a wave of nodding from the congregation behind her. She lifted her head and stared at the bishop.

He continued. "In many ways, Shana, we have failed you as well. We accepted you into our community and our church, based upon your willingness to accept our faith as your own. We had acknowledged the difficulties involved with an Englische taking our vow. We had promised to work with you, assist you in learning the life and beliefs behind the vow. But in your time of loss, we turned our backs on you before you were ready to let go. So, it is I, as representative of our district, that stands before you in asking your forgiveness as we confess our sins."

The bishop sank to his knees and bowed his head before her.

Confused, Shana glanced over her shoulder, scanning the room for Emanuel. She saw him as he, too, stood up and approached her. For a moment, she met his gaze and questioned him with her eyes. But, his expression remained solemn and he bowed his head as he stood up in front of the rest of the congregation.

"And I, as your husband, must confess my impatience with helping you, Shana," Emanuel said softly, walking toward her. "When you needed me in your time of adjustment, I did not offer you guidance or assistance. I, too, turned my back on you when I had promised I would never depart from you in any circumstance for which a good Christian husband is responsible. I did not guide you spiritually when you required it. I ask for your forgiveness." To her increasing dismay, Emanuel knelt beside the bishop.

She stared at the two men kneeling before her. Then she realized that these two men symbolized all in her new life that she had been fighting against for the past two years: First in her courtship, then in her marriage. She had fought the religion and then her husband. Yet, when she had broken her vow, they asked for her forgiveness?

She looked over the downcast eyes of the congregation behind her. These were the same faces, the same people, who had been there when the barn burned down to help rebuild, supplying the lumber, the food, and the labor. These were the people who had opened their arms to her, a stranger to their beliefs and labors, teaching her how to garden and can the foods she grew.

Who had turned their backs on whom, she wanted to cry out. She had been the one who, after all of their goodness, had questioned everything about them. She had been so close to fighting her way out in order to seek what the Englische called justice and throw her rebellion in their face. After they had offered an outstretched hand of hope and love, she had almost tossed it aside for her own self-gratification.

She swallowed and, not knowing what to say or do, reached down and helped both of them to their feet. She smiled at Emanuel through her tears and whispered, "There is nothing to forgive." She turned her eyes on the bishop and nodded her head. "If I ever questioned God's Will in the tragedy that struck our farm and family, it is due to my own ignorance. If I was lost, I see now that I am found. God never left me. He has been surrounding me in my community and my church. If I forgot that in the wake of the tragedy, I have been shown the light and will remember forever the gift you have just given me. And I will never question His Will again."

She felt enlightened, the burden of her grief finally lifted from her shoulders. She finally understood that, for the past two years, she had been fighting against the invisible shield of goodwill from her community. Where else had she ever felt the love and care that she had felt here, today? From her courtship to her marriage to the birth of her child, she had felt the power of the Amish behind her at all times. Whether the decisions that Emanuel and Shana had made, both separately and together, pleased everyone, was irrelevant. Instead, once the decision had been made, the family and the community had accepted it and moved on, not praying for lighter burdens but for stronger backs to carry God's Will, never questioning it, never trying to escape it.

"Oh Emanuel," she whispered, grabbing his arm as the bishop having resolved the issue of Shana's 'disobedience' dismissed the congregation for fellowship. "I understand it all now."

He reached out as a neighbor handed him Noah. Cradling their son in his arms, Emanuel stared down into his face. "It is amazing, ja? How God can create such a wondrous being and give it the capacity to think, feel, live, and love!" He looked up and smiled at Shana. "I only pray that Noah will one day experience the same wondrous being in his wife as I have in you." Then, without another word, Emanuel slipped into the crowd of men that were filing out of the room to the sunshine outside.

Shana stared after him, her heart swelling with love. She fought the urge to smile, to laugh aloud in her glorious happiness. She watched as Emanuel stood on the porch, Noah snuggled against his hip while he spoke with several men under the shade of an old oak tree. She saw him laugh, his eyes crinkling into half-moons, his face radiant from his own happiness and, perhaps, a touch of relief.

Virtue may have a high price, she thought as she took a final look at Emanuel and Noah before she had to return to the kitchen to help the women prepare the after-sermon meal. But, she realized, every sacrifice she had made was worth that moment.

Indeed, she was blessed but the realization was worth more than the blessing. She was blessed to be able to stand there at the window and look outside at the two men she loved while surrounded by the community that had offered to teach her about their traditional values and adopt her into their way of life. At last, she realized that she had found the faith in God to provide and, with that, came the feelings of belonging and identity that she had sought. At last, she realized, she had finally become the Amish woman she had desired to be.

ABOUT THE AUTHOR

The Preiss family emigrated from Europe in 1705, settling in Pennsylvania as the area's first wave of Mennonite families. Sarah Price has always respected and honored her ancestors through exploration and research about her family's history and their religion. At nineteen, she befriended an Amish family and lived on their farm throughout the years. Twenty-five years later, Sarah Price splits her time between her home outside of New York City and an Amish farm in Lancaster County, PA where she retreats to reflect, write, and reconnect with her Amish friends and Mennonite family.

Find Sarah Price on Facebook and Goodreads!
Learn about upcoming books, sequels, series, and contests!

Made in the USA
Lexington, KY
24 October 2012